Karen- Thanks for reading!

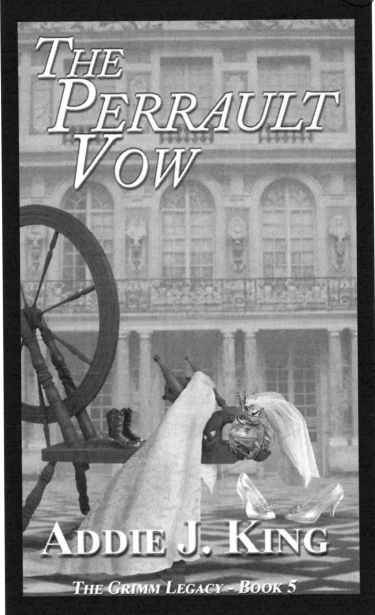

THE PERRAULT VOW

ADDIE J. KING

THE GRIMM LEGACY - BOOK 5

Loconeal Publishing

Amherst, OH

D1561481

THE PERRAULT VOW

This book is a work of fiction. The names, characters, places, and events in this novel are either fictitious or are used fictitiously. Any resemblance to actual events or persons is entirely coincidental.

Loconeal books may be ordered through booksellers or by contacting:
www.loconeal.com
216-772-8380

Loconeal Publishing can bring authors to your live event.
Contact Loconeal Publishing at 216-772-8380.

Published by Loconeal Publishing, LLC
Printed in the United States of America

First Loconeal Publishing edition: September 2016

Visit our website: www.loconeal.com

ISBN 978-1-940466-56-9 (Trade Paperback)

ALSO BY ADDIE J. KING

DEDICATION

To Mary Jane Woodruff, Grandma extraordinaire, and one of the earliest and most supportive fans of Bert. It's only fitting that his story be dedicated to you.

Hope it all works out in the end the way you wanted it . . .

CHAPTER ONE

*T*hunk. *Thunk. Thunk. Ribbit.*
It took a few minutes for the knocking to penetrate my sleepy brain. It had been a late night, studying for the upcoming bar exam, which was less than a week away. I sat up, yawning, as the knocking noise sounded again.

Thunk. Thunk. Thunk. Ribbit.

That was when I realized two things.

First, my fiancé, Aiden Ferguson, was still sound asleep next to me in the bed, snoring, one arm thrown over his eyes. As jealous as I was at his ability to sleep through the racket, I was more concerned about the second thing. The knocking and the ribbit were coming from the other side of the door from a location no higher than my ankles.

It had to be Bert, the former prince turned frog, and not one of my roommates. He was living with me in the big house that had belonged to my evil faerie queen stepmother. The house had been given to me by her court when I'd helped knock her off her throne. And if Bert was knocking on my bedroom door this early in the morning after the massive study session last night, something was up.

I had a bad feeling about this.

I eased out of bed, and opened the door, and sure enough, Bert was sitting in front of my bedroom door, reaching out to knock again.

"What could you possibly want this early in the morning, Bert? And how are you this awake?" I grumbled.

He pointed to my Vote Yoda coffee mug sitting on the floor next to him, steam rising from the coffee within. Slightly mollified by the appearance of caffeine-laden life juice, I grabbed the mug and sipped, willing the stuff to work quickly while trying not to gulp and burn my mouth. Bert wasn't stupid, though; he waited until I'd gotten a decent amount of coffee inside me before announcing, "We have visitors."

Nothing good started with early morning visitors. And from the tone of his voice, it wasn't likely to be a meter reader, a door to door salesman, or the Avon lady. It was more likely to be something magical. And the fact that he'd had coffee at my door told me it was an emergency.

"There's a pair of glass slippers on the front steps," he started.

I raised my eyebrows. Glass anything wasn't unusual, given that Aiden and I were getting married in a week. Relatives and co-workers, F.A.B.L.E.S. members, and faerie realm contacts had been sending wedding presents for weeks. I honestly hadn't realized that we knew as many people as we did, and no matter what I tried to do to keep the whole thing small, understated, and affordable, it kept feeling like others were trying to make it into the Wedding That Ate Dayton. I'd said no to doves, butterflies, pixies, for-real faerie lights, portals to a magically decorated space, artifacts, and even offers of personal slaves. Aiden kept throwing up his hands and hiding in the basement with his research and computers; he wasn't much help, and was just as overwhelmed as I was.

"It's not another wedding present, is it, Bert?"

"No box, no wrapping paper, no ribbon, no streamers, no balloons, no magic, no card," he said. "No idea where it came from."

It did sound more like magical mayhem than matrimonial celebration. In my experience, it wasn't unusual for things (a frog, galoshes, a tinderbox, a bottle with a label saying, 'drink me') to show up and touch off a magical emergency.

"Is it magical? Can you tell?" I asked. Some of us had figured out how to smell magic; others could sense it, like Bert, who didn't exactly have a nose anymore.

"I'm not sensing anything," he said. "I think Aiden should get out his gizmos and gadgets and scan it before we bring it in the house, though, just to be on the safe side."

At the mention of his name, Aiden sat bolt upright in bed, his red hair sticking up in a mad cacophony of horns and spikes, mashed flat on one side and in angry disarray on the other. "Wazzat," he muttered, looking around through sleep-matted eyes for whoever had said his name. Bert explained, and Aiden stumbled out of bed. He tripped on his slippers, landing in a heap on the floor with a thud, then bumped his hip against the footboard of the bed as he stood up and grunted with the impact.

Yeah, my future husband was a klutz; and it had nothing to do with the barely awake problem. Aiden's father was high court faerie, but his mom was one hundred percent American, born and bred human. His mixed heritage contributed to a severe lack of coordination. I was used to it, but Aiden hated it, and he hated the attention that came with others trying to either help him up, or treat him differently. As long as he wasn't stuck in a situation he couldn't get out of, violently ill, gushing blood, or breaking bones, I'd learned to let him deal with it; though I still struggled with letting him be.

He picked himself up, looking more awake, and came around the bed to where I stood with the mug of coffee in hand. He took a sip out, then handed the mug back, and kissed my cheek before heading to the stairs. I heard a thump from the bottom of the stairway and winced. I just hoped he could keep from bruising any part of him that would show in the wedding pictures next week.

Bert grinned. "You sure you don't want in on the betting pool?"

Several friends and family members had laid bets on Aiden tripping on the wedding day. I'd refused to participate, but Aiden himself had tossed five bucks in, saying he thought it likely he'd end up bruised, bleeding, or otherwise hurting before the end of the day. I thought it was macabre; Aiden told me it was likely to happen anyway, so he might as well profit from it. It was hard to argue. We didn't make a lot of money, and we did want a little bit of a honeymoon after our wedding. If the magical emergency took up all our time and money, we'd be lucky if we got anything more extravagant than a tent in our own backyard.

Another of my roommates, Mia Andersen, my comrade-at-arm at law school, my best friend, and my soon-to-be maid of honor, came up to my door, yawning.

"I see you're up earlier than expected," I said.

She nodded. Normally a fairly talkative person, she'd been less outgoing since her father was killed last Thanksgiving by Bigfoot. The funeral had been difficult, but she'd clammed up completely when people asked for details, not only because it was traumatic; it was also hard to explain. Say too much and people would ask questions we couldn't answer without sounding completely loony; say too little and it would seem like we were ignoring Tobias's bravery and the truth about his death. He'd saved all of our lives. I'd agreed to a bigger wedding than I would have otherwise because it got her to engage and be her old self for large portions of time. I'd do a lot for those glimpses of my friend.

Mia shook her head. "Bert knocked on our door, too, but he didn't bring us coffee."

Her boyfriend, Jonah, came up behind her. "Because you won't kill him if he forgets coffee. You'll grumble, but Janie here? With a magical emergency? Needs coffee to function."

Was I really that bad? Maybe I needed to rethink my coffee consumption.

Or maybe I needed to stop stalling and go see what those glass slippers really were.

CHAPTER TWO

We all headed down the steps toward the front door. Aiden was already there, holding some kind of magical detecting mechanical gizmo of his own invention, one I hadn't seen before. Not surprising; he was constantly experimenting with gadgets and devices meant to detect magic before humans could be drawn in by otherwise nondescript items. It must be a new one.

The device was silent.

As I got to the door, Aiden picked up the slippers, and sure enough, when he touched the glass, his magical whoziwhatzit went crazy.

"Put it down, Aiden," I said. "No reason to tempt any kind of fate. I wonder, though, does it only react to someone's touch?"

"Or to someone's *magical* touch?" he asked.

Good question. If it reacted to humans or faerie court members, it could react to Aiden for either reason; since his father was of the faerie court and his mother was human. He gently set the shoes down on the ground.

Bert was right, though. There was nothing attached to the shoes to tell us where they might have come from, or what they might be about, or who they might be from. There was nothing to mark them as a gift. So how had whoever it was managed to leave it without someone in the neighborhood making off with something that actually looked fairly valuable; or without some neighborhood animal breaking, chewing, or peeing on it? We lived in a pretty nice neighborhood in Oakwood, a suburb of Dayton, Ohio; but that didn't mean there weren't rambunctious teenagers, stray cats, or dogs who'd slipped their leashes. Of course, it was still early. The neighborhood was still fairly quiet. At seven in the morning, most of those who might cause trouble were still sleeping off their midnight jaunts, but there were also some nosy neighbors, and a neighborhood watch group that took itself way too seriously at times.

Aiden couldn't be the one to test the shoes. His touch had set them off; but what did that mean? Then something occurred to me. "Aiden, your dad, is he coming over today for another fitting?"

Aiden's father was the head tailor for the faerie court my stepmother had once headed; he'd insisted on being the one to outfit Aiden for the wedding. He'd tried to insist on making my wedding dress, but I didn't want to take the risk of having a gown that might - even accidentally - be subject to magical problems at wedding catastrophe level. I was determined to have a simple, non-magical wedding. Aiden, however, couldn't bring himself to tell his father no. They'd been working carefully towards a closer relationship for the better part of a year after a falling out they'd had when Aiden was a teenager. I'd been pushing him to find ways to involve his father in his life. I guess I'd unwittingly set myself up to have Geoffrey involved in the wedding and the planning, and, truth be told, he'd actually been a big help in navigating all the minor details I'd never have thought of on my own.

"Yes, he's coming over in about an hour. He says he's going to have to double check my measurements because he thinks he wrote them down wrong. My hope is that he's remembering that I just need one suit, and I don't need anything too crazy. I'm afraid he'll overdo it trying so hard to be helpful."

"You could have told him no," I reminded him.

He smirked. "Yeah. Right. He was so concerned about being able to contribute that Jonah even agreed to let him make a suit for him to wear as best man. That way he leaves you alone."

I had to give him that one. I did appreciate that. I grinned at him. "Yeah, not changing my mind on that one. You and Jonah are on your own. Mia, Allie, and I have our dresses. The alterations are done; they're hanging up, pressed and ready for the day, so we don't have to worry about them between now and then. My thought was that your dad might have some idea about where those slippers came from. Anything we can do to prevent a magical explosion in the next couple of weeks would be amazing. I figure we have enough people wanting to help that the price for information should be lower than normal."

Yeah, everything with magic had a price; which was part of why I'd drawn a hard line about magical anything related to the wedding.

Mia was standing behind me. "Janie, we've got to get some studying done today. There's only a day or so left and I'm not sure I'm ready for the multi-state questions on the bar."

I nodded at her.

The bar exam started the day after tomorrow. Today was Sunday. At this point, I was pretty sure we were both prepared. There wasn't much that we were going to learn or retain in the last couple of days, but we kept cramming anyway. If we weren't studying like maniacs, we were working on last minute wedding details. There had been some insanely long days, but all of it was almost over. I was going to be glad when there were no more envelopes to stuff, birdseed to wrap up in squares of netting for the guests to throw at us, menus to print and roll with ribbon to place at each place setting, and little paper boxes to fill with Hershey kisses for favors for each guest.

Aiden agreed to ask his dad about the slippers, then grabbed a couple of towels from the kitchen to avoid touching the shoes with his bare hands. Jonah had to leave for the theater; even though he'd turned down a bit role for the week due to the upcoming wedding, he still had a job organizing and maintaining sets and props at the Schuster Center for the Performing Arts, which was downtown. Mia and I headed for coffee refills and our books, which were still piled all over the kitchen table from our study session last night. The highlighters came out and we got ready to start in with the flash cards and outlines, drilling each other on elements of a crime and legislative intent.

"Do you wish we'd decided to stay in Columbus?" she asked, before we'd even gotten started. "The drive is going to make it a few long days."

"You want to sleep in a hotel? I don't know about you, but I'd feel better sleeping behind a threshold every night during the one week of our careers that we cannot afford to lose sleep due to magical craziness. I want to see Aiden at night, and know that we're still okay. And I'm afraid of what might come up if we're gone."

I just didn't like the idea of being out of the house that long. Our cross country trip last fall hadn't resulted in magical emergencies at home, but the amount of magical crazy we'd had on that trip had me a little worried. How was I going to enjoy a honeymoon if I couldn't bring myself to stay in a hotel only an hour away?

I didn't have a good answer.

Luckily, Mia agreed with me. "I'd feel better seeing Jonah before we go to bed at night, myself. I get it. There's just so much going on this week, maybe it's better that we can check in. And sleeping in my own bed is always a good thing; seeing Jonah every night is an added bonus. Besides, I don't want to spend the money on the hotel room, but it's a lot of driving with tired minds."

"Well, our minds will be less tired if we're completely prepared. Let's start with Torts," I said. "Intentional Torts are the beginning of personal injury law . . ." and we were off into a quick review of concepts we'd learned our first year of law school.

Two hours of review later, Aiden finally appeared in the kitchen, his father, Geoffrey, standing behind him, a more immaculate echo of Aiden's own disheveled good looks. I glanced up from reviewing bilateral and unilateral contracts in my notes from the first semester of law school, just in time to see looks of concern on their faces. I'd seen looks like that before. I had a bad feeling about this.

I put down the pencil in my hand, and removed the highlighter from between my teeth before sighing. "What did you guys find out?"

I kinda didn't want to know the answer. I mean, anytime that I asked for an answer to a magical question, it never ever turned out as something that could be fun, or good timing to deal with it. Aiden must have seen something on my face, because I saw a smirk lurking around the corners of his mouth.

Geoffrey didn't even bother trying to hide it; he laughed out loud. "Janie, the look on your face is priceless. I know it's your wedding. I know you've got the bar exam. I know this is just about the worst timing you could ever have had, but you were right to ask the questions you were asking. The items on your doorstep this morning? Magical. And it looks like we've got a magical mystery on our hands."

You know, my life just happens like that. I sighed. There was no real way to fight it; the only way to deal with it was to put my head down and barrel through it. At least I'd be too busy to get nervous about the bar exam or the wedding.

Hey, I had to find a positive way to look at this, or I was going to lose my mind before it was all said and done.

CHAPTER THREE

"So what's the magical sitch?" Mia asked, the tone in her voice as resigned to the situation as the voice in my own head seemed to be.

Geoffrey had a plastic grocery bag in his hands, and when I got up from the table, I realized that the glass shoes we'd found were inside the bag. Made sense, I thought, to be able to carry them without touching them. Plastic was completely man-made, an artificial means of carrying those items, so it was less likely to react to magic the way something made out of plant fibers might react to a spell or a latent magical ability. We'd learned that as Jonah had been coming into his magic over the last year or so. As the long lost descendant of Johnny Appleseed, he'd discovered that the embarrassing tendency to magically encourage plants could actually put him in touch with his many times great-grandmother, and that he could use it for good. He'd been hiding it and covering it up with plastic and latex and claiming massive pollen allergies for most of his life. On the other hand, we now had some pretty bodacious rose bushes in the backyard that he'd been practicing with. And they were providing many of the flowers we were using for the wedding . . . so I guess I couldn't complain about magic and organic matter reacting together.

"Well, I'm pretty sure I know whose shoes these are," Geoffrey started to explain. "If I'm right, though, that means something may have become horribly unstuck from previous arrangements. And that could mean some seriously weird things going on this week."

"Cut the suspense. Whose shoes are they, and what do we have to do to give them back to their owner?" I asked, going to refill my coffee cup again.

"I don't think you understand," Aiden said. "There's a serious question about who really owns the shoes. If you give them back to the person who created them, there are those who will claim you're ignoring the person who bought them at auction. If you give them back to the person they were stolen from, there will be claims there was no theft, but a false claim against family members. If you give them to those who stole them, the person who bought them will feel cheated. The magical courts haven't been able to determine who owns the shoes, so they've remained in deep storage for centuries. If they're in storage, it's almost like the parties involved have forgotten about them, and can function as normal rational beings."

So the magical folks would be affected by this as well as us lowly humans, huh? I guess I better keep that in mind. "So then how did they end up on my front door, as if being presented as a wedding gift?" I asked.

I'd learned to ask the question that seemed most relevant first, and to dig into background later. I didn't care yet about the legal status of ownership; that might be important later, but right now, the more important question was why I was currently involved in the chain of possession of those shoes. It was starting to sound like I didn't want anything to do with them, and that brought to mind the next question.

"How dangerous are they? Is anyone going to be hurt?" Glass slippers were see through. I didn't see anything that made me concerned for anyone's safety, but magic wasn't always something that screamed danger unless it was active, and wouldn't be inside that plastic bag.

Bert hopped into the kitchen, but he didn't say anything. One look at his face, however, told me he had plenty to say. I started out watching him while the others started to explain.

Geoffrey cleared his throat. "I'm not sure you want to get involved in this, Janie. Especially with the wedding. This has catastrophe written all over it, and you've already got enough diplomatic headaches with the wedding. Did you have anyone from the courts look over the seating charts?"

What seating charts? I wasn't assigning seats to anyone, like a kindergarten hall monitor or a strict third grade teacher. I was having a buffet, and I thought they could decide on their own between chicken and fish without too much fuss. Doris and her friends were doing the catering, and had promised to prepare as much as possible of both; so people could actually have both if they wanted. Beyond that, well, I'd turned over the rest of the food decisions to her, figuring she had the knowledge and contacts, as well as the cooking and catering experience, to make it great.

She was also making our cake, a multi-layered confection of cake, fruit fillings, butter cream, and sugar that I was sure would be enough to feed a few battalions of Marines for a month. I didn't care about the food; I just wanted to be married to Aiden. I didn't care if the folks from the faerie court sat with Wonderland refugees, or whether my friends from law school sat with the F.A.B.L.E.S. crowd. I didn't care if we had leftover cake. I didn't care if someone was a vegetarian, there would be plenty of options for everyone if I knew Doris. They were all adults; it was on them if they couldn't behave. If they were unhappy with the reception, well, it was my wedding, after all. I shrugged. I'd never seen the importance of a seating chart.

Geoffrey let out a long suffering sigh. "You really have no idea how big a deal this wedding could be diplomatically, do you?" It was a question I'd heard from him repeatedly since we'd announced our engagement.

"Look, regardless of whether I've violated the Treaty of Versailles or not, I'm getting married. That's the biggest thing. If someone doesn't like where they're sitting, it's not my fault if they think they're seated next to the wrong person. It's theirs, and if they don't like where they're sitting, they should move. Right now, the bigger concern is whether some magical badass is going to show up and eat the wedding party rather than whether there's something I should be serving other than chicken or fish, or whether the right people are sitting together."

"She's right, Dad. That stuff just isn't important to us, but keeping everyone alive and safe is." I was grateful for Aiden's support

Geoffrey placed the plastic bag of glass shoes carefully on the counter. They clinked together softly as he let go of the bag, and he moved them slightly to keep them safe from being knocked over, probably a smart thing with Aiden standing so close to him. I handed Geoffrey a mug of coffee, already sugared and creamed to his liking. He sipped before gently admonishing me about my lack of social graces.

"This wedding could be a major boost to you down the road. You're talking about opening your own law office when you get your bar results, right? Isn't that what's paying your bills right now? That's business. Cultivating good relationships with magical dignitaries can only help your bottom line. Making your guests feel important makes them likely to call you down the road when they need help."

"And I've said before, that I've already built good relationships with people and beings in multiple realms, and am already getting my name recognized for what I've actually done in my field, rather than about who got the biggest piece of cake at my wedding reception. I've invited only those who are positive contacts, and everyone on the invite list is mature enough to realize that being a grown-up is a good thing, and keeping the relationship we already have is a positive."

He looked sheepish.

"What aren't you telling me?" I asked.

Geoffrey blushed a bit.

Oh, shit. I thought. *Who the hell has he added to the guest list?* I worried about how to ask, then I came right out and asked. He might care about etiquette, but at this point, it was about safety.

He didn't answer right away, instead shifting the conversation back to the glass slippers.

"These shoes haven't been seen in a few hundred years. They're part of a larger collection of items that have all been under the radar for a long time. I thought they were lost, and we'd never see them again. I don't have a clue who's had them all this time, or where they've been hidden, but I do know a number of people - and yes, I do mean people - as opposed to magical folk, or those from other realms, who were involved in the plan to secure some of those items. The concern is that someone is getting into that stash of magical items when they shouldn't. Some of those items are very dangerous, more than the shoes. And if they're into those items, then why give anything away? Why show your hand, that you have access to the stash, and to the items involved, by giving them to someone who's been unraveling magical secrets for the last three years?"

Had to admit, he was making awfully good points. I didn't think of Geoffrey as a strategic thinker. He normally had an agenda and it was pretty straightforward about protecting Aiden or Doris, and to a lesser extent, now that we were getting married, me. This didn't seem to impact either of them, and I wasn't sure yet how it affected me. In fact, I wasn't sure I was the actual target, since I wasn't the only one living in the house; and there hadn't been any kind of tag or label on the shoes when they'd shown up, according to Bert. I wasn't all that sure I wanted the answer to the questions he was asking at the moment. But why was he focusing so much on the items instead of . . . failing to answer the question I had just asked?

I had a bad feeling about why he was hesitating to answer my question about uninvited guests.

"Geoffrey," I said, quietly. "If I haven't invited someone to the wedding, then they aren't welcome, are they? If we tried to escort an unwanted guest away without an invite, how much trouble would that cause?"

"Lots."

My stomach sank into my toes. "So who did you invite?"

"The Queen of Hearts asked a boon, to invite a guest as her plus one. I was there to negotiate for some items our court needed to complete some magical tasks, unrelated to the wedding, and she asked if I was involved in planning. I told her I was, and she made the request. I could hardly say no when I was there to obtain a favor for my own sovereign. I'm sorry, Janie. I should have told you."

"Who did you say yes to?" My voice was getting quieter, masking the fear and rage hurtling down through my stomach and into my bones. I had a good idea who he was talking about and there was a reason why she wasn't on the guest list.

"In my own defense, I must say that she just asked to bring a guest. I didn't know who she was asking for until she returned the RSVP." He had put down the coffee cup and was backing away slowly.

"When did you find out who it was? How long have you known? And you must have known that I wouldn't like whoever it is. Why hide it for so long?" And I thought I'd had the master RSVP list; he must have hidden it the minute he'd seen the name.

Aiden also turned on his father. "You didn't even say anything to me. Why is that?"

Geoffrey looked defeated. I had a pretty good idea who he'd invited. And I was pretty sure they had neatly boxed him in, giving him little opportunity to say no.

"He invited Evangeline, my evil faerie queen stepmother." Also known as Queen Eva, the one who'd had me kidnapped, tried to trap me in the faerie realm, killed my father, and broken Aiden's arm. The same one I'd trapped in her lies, stabbed with a screwdriver, and covered in iron gall ink. I momentarily wondered if that stuff had washed off; with the iron content, it was like acid to a faerie being. I hoped she wasn't scarred too badly; she'd be monumentally pissed if I'd ruined her complexion. Wait; she was supposed to still be incarcerated. Did that mean she was free?

Crap on a cracker. She was the last person I wanted showing up at my wedding. I thought people would have known she'd be *persona non grata*, since she had tried to lie to me, had kidnapped me, and tried to kill me.

Those kinds of things just don't get you invited to sit in the family section at one's wedding.

CHAPTER FOUR

A iden lost his temper, yelling at his father. I was the one to stop him. "Aiden, I know this isn't what we wanted. It isn't what *I* wanted, and it's probably the most dangerous thing that could have happened. But I've got a funny feeling your dad was manipulated into extending that invitation."

"What do you mean?" he asked, ready to keep yelling the minute I let go of the arm I'd grabbed to get his attention.

"I mean that the Queen of Hearts is Evangeline's sister. They've probably been in touch while she's been incarcerated, now that the Queen of Hearts is no longer a prisoner of the White Rabbit. They probably decided that between the two of them, Geoffrey would be the most vulnerable to obtain an invitation from."

Even incarcerated, Evangeline would still have a long reach and plenty of allies that could get Geoffrey added to a diplomatic mission to another realm, and find a way for him to be cornered by the Queen of Hearts. I bet anything that she made him feel like she'd tank their negotiations if he said no. If he had said no, then Evangeline would have found a way to have Geoffrey shamed at court, and would have offered to find a way to push that shame aside if he got her an invitation for herself. Geoffrey wasn't a bad guy, but he'd spent so many years sucking up to Evangeline, or to use her court name, Queen Eva, trying so hard to gain an advantage he could use for his half human son, Aiden, that doing her bidding became second nature. Aiden and his father had had a huge falling out right after she had tried to kill me. I'd been the one to intervene and encourage them to try to start building a better relationship, though Aiden had been very reluctant to give him another chance.

I wondered how much of a blow this would land in their still rocky relationship. I wasn't all that happy with Geoffrey myself. And now I had a bigger problem.

"We can't stay here now," I said, starting to close up my law books. "The ceremony is at the house. Even though we aren't hosting the reception, Evangeline will take it as an invitation past the threshold, and we're toast. You've given her carte blanche to the house. I can't take that chance. Geoffrey, there was a reason why you were the only magical guest invited to the ceremony itself. We didn't want to take the chance of anyone crossing the threshold while we were studying and taking the bar and getting ready for the wedding. I didn't want to worry about warding the house while I tried to figure out how to put on my gown and veil."

And tried not to cry because my own dad wouldn't be walking me down the aisle, since he'd died three and a half years ago. I knew I'd be a bit of an emotional wreck, and I just didn't really want magical shenanigans causing issues at that moment, but now I'd have to deal with them no matter what. I'd planned to ask Geoffrey to walk me down the aisle, as the father of the bride, since mine wasn't around anymore. Had Mia's father, Tobias, still been alive, I'd have asked him. I was glad, at that point, that the invitation hadn't yet been extended. I'd reserve judgment on that one for now. Maybe I'd just walk myself down the freaking aisle.

"Give me some credit," Geoffrey said. "I was very clear about the date and time and limiting the invitation to the actual wedding and reception, and was clear about the times and locations for each. I even mentioned the ceremony wasn't inside the house, but in the backyard. As long as there's no indication of any part of the ceremony taking place in the house, you should be fine. I'm sure you've got enough people you can station around the house in order to protect you and your friends for that short period of time."

Well, that much was a relief. At least we weren't going to have to scramble for a place to stay during the week leading up to the wedding. It might be smart to stay somewhere else the night before the wedding, but that was one night rather than an entire week. I probably could get a few of the Wonderland refugees to stand guard and sound an alarm or something in the house on the day of the wedding, but the ceremony itself was just supposed to be the inner circle: Aiden and I, Mia and Jonah, Allie and Bert, Doris, Harold, Stanley and his wife, and Geoffrey.

Stanley and his wife were supposed to be helping with the flowers. Mia was my maid of honor, and Bert, well, he was sort of the ring bearer, sort of the mascot, and sort of the all-around wedding guru. I guess you could call him the wedding planner as well. I had a ton of friends, and some distant cousins, who were a bit put out that the ceremony was so limited as to guests, but when they realized we were doing it as a way of keeping costs down, they were okay with it. It had helped that I had explained to them that it was less likely for Aiden to get flustered and fall down with fewer people involved. If they were close enough to be invited, they were close enough to us to understand about Aiden's lack of coordination, and didn't ask any questions.

This could have been worse. It wasn't good, but on the whole, if that was the only bad thing . . . wait a minute, what was I thinking? Evangeline would have some reason for wanting to be at the wedding. Otherwise, why would she even care? She hadn't even liked being my stepmother. And since the last time I'd seen her, I'd had her kicked off her throne, tossed ink in her face, and shoved a screwdriver in her neck when she'd attacked me. I didn't really think she was planning to come just to savor the orange blossoms. What kind of revenge could she possibly be planning?

"Geoffrey, they were going to manipulate you into giving an invitation no matter what. I get that. You still shouldn't have extended it, and we'll have to discuss that later. Best thing to do now is to come up with a plan for how to deal with it. Aiden, I think you need to talk with Harold and Stanley about organizing shifts of some of the Wonderland people, the ones best adapted to our world, the ones that can use a cell phone without looking out of place and able to sound an alarm without the neighbors calling to have us committed. I know Alfred is on that list, and I think he should be put in charge," I said, starting to get organized.

I know I was letting him off the hook, but I knew we needed Geoffrey's insight, and maybe his connections, while we tried to find our way through the other side of this. But sooner or later, he needed to grow a backbone, and maybe start doing things without concern for political expediency.

On the other hand, my dad was gone. Mia's father was now dead. Allie's father still didn't always realize that he was a father due to magical influence that had robbed much of his memories. Jonah's adoptive father was dead, and his biological father was long gone. Geoffrey was truly the only dad left around for any of us, no matter his flaws, and I was dead set that Aiden not lose that connection.

My future husband looked pissed at his father, but he nodded. "Smart, Janie. Alfred would love to do this for you, and you know it."

Alfred was also known as the Mad Hatter; he'd been an alcoholic when we'd run into him in Wonderland, and had gotten the Queen of Hearts to let him move to Ohio with us. We'd gotten him into fashion designing classes, allowing him to continue working with hats without the damaging effects of the chemicals he'd been using in Wonderland, and also helped him get sober. He'd become a loyal friend. It was why I'd thought of him; he wasn't family, but he was reliable enough to be counted on to not feel like he had to kowtow to the Queen of Hearts or her sister, my evil faerie queen stepmother. That solved, however, there was still another issue to deal with.

"Geoffrey, you said something I think is pretty important. You mentioned 'deep storage" and 'previous arrangements'. Why do I get the feeling that this is bigger than just a pair of glass slippers? I mean, I know my Disney movies. I know who the glass slippers belong to. But I don't remember that the shoes were a part of anything other than the magic of the fairy godmother and that it turned into a test of who was the real Cinderella. If nothing else, some people can try on the shoes so we know who the target is this time."

Every time some magical emergency had sprung up, there had been someone who had been a target. Me as the target of my evil stepmother because I was a descendant of the Grimm Brothers, Mia as a relative of Hans Christian Andersen, Allie as the daughter of the real Alice who had been trapped in Wonderland, and Jonah as the long lost many times great-grandson of Johnny Appleseed. I honestly was happy that we had the shoes, and was hoping we had a litmus test that could speed up the process this time. Whoever was on the hook here, we should be able to find the right person just by having them try on a pair of shoes, right?

"Bert can explain better than I can. He knows more about it," Geoffrey said.

Bert could explain? I looked down where my froggy friend sat on the floor, waiting for someone to pick him up and put him on the counter so he could contribute to the conversation better. He had a rather sheepish look on his face, and he was being uncharacteristically quiet. Something was definitely up. What in the world was going on?

Bert fidgeted like a nervous old lady betting her pension check at the racetrack. He hopped back and forth from one foot to the other, acting like he was going to explode if he didn't start talking.

"Bert, what's going on?' I asked.

"It's the Money Pit. People have been digging there for treasure for years, but no one has ever guessed the true treasure it held. Instead, they just kept allowing humans to continue on their treasure hunts, believing they'd never get close enough to find the items we'd hidden. It was a good idea. It's still a good idea that those items remain hidden for a long time, maybe forever. Some of the things we've buried down there are way too dangerous for anyone to realize they still exist. Some of them would start fights, legal wrangling, and otherwise cause issues in the magical community. Keeping those items hidden keeps the peace."

"Who decided this?" Aiden asked. "Who in the world got together and agreed to take such a measure? I just can't see anyone in the magical community setting aside their own personal stakes and agendas long enough to come up with this. So who made the list of items involved? Then how in the world did they decide where to put it all? Come on, Dad, you know what I mean. Deciding things in the faerie realms without a supreme ruler or dictator to issue orders just doesn't happen. When they talk about deciding things by committee in the faerie realm they just bicker and fuss like old canasta playing biddies who are more concerned with their cards than the life going on outside of their card game. Heck, most of them figure they've got eternity to sit on their objections; time doesn't seem to matter, and they're never in a hurry."

Aiden was right about *that*. The faerie court realms weren't exactly known to be the spirit of cooperation, even when both parties in a dispute wanted the same outcome. There was just no way enough people would agree on all of those details without, well, going to war, or at least a really bloody and prolonged battle. Or the entire project being buried under a mountain of bureaucracy and abandoned as too difficult to finish.

Bert cleared his throat. "It's been a long time since I've thought about this. Not too terribly long after I left my family's castle for the last time, I learned there was a commission in Paris to study folk tales, and to determine if there was any danger to the general populace regarding certain artifacts that were in the hands of mortal humans. I didn't ask a lot of questions before I went; but when I got there, it was your predictable bureaucratic nightmare mess. And that was just with the humans involved. They hadn't even started getting the magical realms involved; in fact, I wasn't sure they really understood the true issue when I showed up for the first meetings."

"If it was the humans, then who in the world was in charge?" Aiden asked. "I wasn't aware of there being much of an organized human presence regarding magic much before the Grimm Brothers."

"Oh, this was the start of human involvement in dealing with magics. It was the first time humans had gotten involved; in fact, it was their idea." He cleared his throat. "Janie, your ancestors took their cues from the man who spearheaded the whole thing, when it was their turn."

"Who in the world are you talking about?" I asked.

"A lawyer, by the name of Charles Perrault. He's known for collecting French fairy tales, some of which were related to the tales collected by the Grimm Brothers. He's the one that started the whole thing when it comes to humans trying to protect themselves from magic."

I had a vague memory of hearing that name before; hard not to when my father had been a professor of fables and folklore before he'd died. "Another lawyer, huh? That explains a lot."

CHAPTER FIVE

M ia agreed with me. Why so many lawyers involved? Then again, when it came to government, political sciences, diplomacy, and international relations, many, if not most of the people in those fields, held law degrees. What was one more? At least we might have a leg up on understanding the background of how it all originated, given that we'd just graduated from law school a couple of months ago. Who knows, maybe this last minute magical emergency might even help solidify some concepts in our brains before the bar exam, looming in just a few days. Our first year, I'd figured out contracts through dealing with my stepmother's broken promises. Hey, it could happen again.

That brought my stepmother to mind again. "Okay, look, here's the deal. Geoffrey, you are absolutely forbidden to invite anyone else to any wedding function this weekend. That means from Friday at noon until Sunday at noon when we leave for the honeymoon. There are no weekday wedding activities before that involving guests, and no one is invited on the honeymoon. That should help limit your exposure. Do I have your promise you will abide by that rule?"

He grinned. I was tying him up pretty tight. I knew he was bound by the cultural and social mores of the magical court; they took the breaking of a promise very seriously. While they might try to wiggle out of it on a technicality, most of them wouldn't push another to break a promise. I'd used that against Evangeline in the past, now I hoped it would give Geoffrey some cover from any court pressure to expand our guest list. It looked like he got my reasoning, given the look of comprehension and relief on his face.

I moved on to the next item on my mental agenda. "Geoffrey, is Aiden's suit ready for the wedding? Do you guys have any further fittings or work to do on it before next weekend? What about Jonah's?"

Aiden shook his head no, but his father murmured that he'd like to see his son try it on one last time today to make sure no minor adjustments were needed. My dress had the alterations completed last week, and as long as I didn't collapse into a vat of Chunky Monkey ice cream from all the stress, we were good to go. Mia's dress was also done, hanging next to mine in the spare guest room. The boys' suits were hanging in the library, where Bert usually slept, and all the rest of the wedding paraphernalia was taking over the living room, with gifts piled all over the dining room table. No one had any reason to go check out each other's wedding attire; keeping us all from inadvertently causing issues.

"Mia, you and I are going to take a quick break from studying this morning and go check in with Doris about the last minute catering details, and then we're going to go into research mode with Bert to look into Charles Perrault, and see what we need to find out about these items."

She nodded.

I realized I must sound like some kind of general, barking orders, and tried not to sound like I was ordering people around. "Aiden, once you boys have the suits figured out, I think your dad can work on last minute adjustments to your clothing. In the meantime, you and Jonah take your gadgets and go sweep the reception hall for magical booby traps, and then go talk to Alfred about setting up a watch for the house for the day of the wedding. Maybe we should have someone watching while we're in Columbus for the bar exam as well . . . I know Mia and I will be too tired to really be looking for much when we get in each night."

He nodded, and smiled, before grabbing my arm and sweeping me up for a kiss. It was exactly the right thing to do, distracting me from the massive to-do list in my head and reminding me why I was going through all of this during the most stressful week of my life. I loved him, and I didn't want to wait one minute longer before tying my life to his. His distraction worked, too, leaving me smiling and somewhat fuzzy brained when he let me go. He smiled a half-satisfied smile and swept off with his dad to start on his list of wedding tasks. I was happy to see they took the slippers with them. I wouldn't want those just lying around the house where they could cause havoc. I certainly didn't want to be around them much this week. I didn't want to take the chance that some magical craziness would torpedo the bar exam for me, much less the wedding

Mia smiled at me. The hollow look on her face from earlier was gone, and I knew she was looking forward to the wedding at the end of the week. But as I looked closer, I decided it wasn't the wedding that was making her happy: it was the concept of having something magical to solve. For the first time since her father's death last November, we had a magical mystery, and it seemed she was looking forward to getting into it. We packed up our books into less-messy piles on the kitchen table; then I poured myself another cup of coffee in a travel mug. This was going to be a multiple cup kind of day. I was pretty sure it was going to be an entire week of days like that.

Bert didn't say much to us as we headed for the Escalade I'd inherited from my stepmother when she'd been stripped of her crown. Yeah, not only had she lost everything in the magical realm, they'd stripped her of her human realm property and given it all to me as reparations for her actions against me and my father over the years. As if a house and a car could make up for the fact that she'd killed my dad. I felt a sudden surge of rage at the idea that my dad would miss my wedding, but his murderer had an invitation to watch the entire proceeding. That wasn't useful, and wasn't anything I could do anything about, so I swallowed that bitterness and kept going, choking down the tears, putting the key in the ignition and setting Bert between the front seats where he normally rode when he went somewhere with us. Mia settled into the passenger seat and buckled up.

"You okay, Janie?" she asked.

I shrugged. "Look, none of this is ideal. Maybe I shouldn't have agreed to plan the wedding so close to the bar exam. I had no idea just how stressed I'd be, and if I'd known, I'd have tried to schedule things different, but I don't want to wait to marry Aiden. I could be wearing burlap, carrying dead flowers, and under siege, and I'd still want to go ahead and marry him. The wedding's my prize to myself for getting through this week; it just got a little bit harder this morning. We'll get there, and I'll be married, and then we'll go from there."

She smiled at me, then got serious again. "Maybe we should talk again about me moving out after the wedding."

We'd gone round and round about this for months. "Look, Mia, I'm good with you staying. I'm good with Jonah staying. For right now, without an ongoing, steady income, how are you going to get an apartment of your own? Yes, you pay rent to me, but you know that if the money isn't there right away, I won't give you a hard time about it. I know where the money came from, so I won't give you a hard time about that either. Can't we table this conversation until after we have our bar results, after we know if our idea for opening a law firm ourselves will start to work, and after we're both a little more stable? Besides, why give up sleeping behind a secure threshold before you have to? And I know if you guys moved, Aiden would want to be involved in warding your new place. He doesn't have time at the moment, so giving it some time would also help him feel more secure about it."

"But you guys will be married. Aren't you going to want kids?" she asked.

I pulled the vehicle carefully out of the garage. The Escalade wasn't something I would have picked for myself; it was huge and cumbersome and it sucked gas like a vacuum on steroids, but it was paid for. Even carrying insurance for that monstrosity and keeping it filled with gas cost less than a car payment for a new, more fuel efficient vehicle. The Buick I'd been driving before had become Aiden's car. No matter how many fender benders he got into, that thing was like a tank, and was more protection for him than anything else we could have afforded. I managed to pull the Escalade out of the garage without losing a mirror (we'd gone through several), and we headed off towards Doris's house.

"Mia, look, I don't know what's in store for us. Do we want kids? Sure. Are we planning to start trying right away? No. I want to get our law practice off the ground first. I want us to be more financially secure. And even if I got pregnant on our honeymoon, there's still nine months before we start needing to use another bedroom, and there are plenty in the house. I'd like to have some time to just enjoy being married. I'd like to relax before we get our bar results. I'd like to spend some time with you, with Aiden, with Jonah, and with Allie and Bert, before we decide to close ranks and start building the Ferguson-

Grimm clan. So, are we eventually going to raise a family in this house? Sure. But we're not going to have sixty bazillion kids running through the house the day after the wedding, and we're certainly not going to kick you to the curb. This is your home as well, at the moment. We'll talk as things change, but otherwise, I'm happy to have you here. You're the sister I never had. So why would I ever push you out before either of us were ready for you to go?"

She got quiet for a minute, which was good timing for me to merge onto the highway and head for Doris' house without any distraction. On a Saturday morning traffic wasn't all that crazy, but that ramp could be a pain if other drivers weren't paying attention.

"I appreciate it, Janie," she said. "I'm not sure there's any apartment out there we could easily afford at the moment. I'm just worried about paying the rent. We're not doing internships this summer since we're both taking the bar, and we didn't take summer jobs so we could study. We've all been living off the money we earned from Paul last fall, but that's going to run out soon, especially with the wedding, and I'm just worried I won't be able to pay my share of the bills and the rent. If I had to move in with Mom, I could."

And Mia's mom didn't have a very big place these days, either. She'd given up a two-bedroom apartment when Mia went to college, to save money, and she'd ended up paying for a big chunk of Tobias's funeral last fall. Mia had also paid a big chunk for that out of her share of the fee from chasing down a big blue ox for Paul Bunyan.

It had been nice to have money to pay for things, to be able to chip in myself for Tobias' wake, and then I realized this was the real issue on Mia's mind. I mean, no question did she want to stay with me, but she didn't want to be a charity case. She had refused to take a bigger share of the proceeds from Paul's retainer (I had offered due to her father's death). She had refused to reduce her rent payments when she felt like she couldn't keep working during the school year due to stress. She wouldn't even let me pay for her bridesmaid's dress. Her extra money had gone to pay for the funeral, and I'd catered the wake with Doris and the others helping, but she hadn't let me do more because I had to pay for the wedding. Aiden's salary was also helping, but there was a limit to Doris's resources to pay for it. I had nothing left of my inheritance from my dad since that had paid my law school tuition. No matter how limited I'd wanted the wedding to be, there was still plenty to pay for, and less money to do it than any of us had really thought of.

"No, I want you living with me right now," I said. What I didn't say was that I was still worried about her after her father's death, and didn't think she was ready to move out anyway. I didn't get much of a chance to elaborate on it, though, because we were at Doris's small, ranch style house.

Neat and tidy, with rows of white daisies planted in straight lines bordering a small walkway from the street, Doris' house would never be considered opulent, but it was definitely a home. We walked into the house and into the aroma of something baking in the oven I couldn't wait to stick a fork into whatever smelled that good.

Maybe the day was looking up. Baked goods normally do put a smile of my face, and the ones out of my future mother in law's kitchen were to die for.

CHAPTER SIX

D oris was in the kitchen; as usual. She had several filled cake pans all over her kitchen, cooling. When I asked what they were for, she told me they were for my wedding cake, which she was baking and freezing ahead of time, so that in a few days, she would just have to put on the butter cream and flowers. I almost wanted to steal a pan and take it with me, but two things kept me from doing so. The alterations for my dress were already done and letting out the seams after eating an entire cake would cost more money. And I figured she had a system for knowing what layers she needed and what she had baked, and I didn't want to throw her off. That wouldn't be a nice thing to do, when she wasn't letting me pay for anything other than the ingredients for all the food for the wedding.

"Smells wonderful, Doris," I said, sniffing the air with relish.

She blushed. "Thanks. I still have to make the filling and the icing, but having the cake layers baked will save me a ton of time later; and getting the baking out of the way means the kitchen will be plenty cooled off when I go to ice the layers. It helps when the kitchen isn't hot; that icing melts easy."

It was July. And she should know; she'd worked in bakeries and in food service for years. It made sense to me. But I was here for more reasons than just sniffing the cake that I'd get to shove up Aiden's nose in front of our friends and family in a week. I wanted to know if Doris knew anything about Bert's revelations. So I asked. I wanted to see his reactions to what Doris might know.

"I remember hearing something about this. I wondered for a long time whether there was anything in that treasure trove of artifacts that would help us protect people in this area, or our families and friends, from the harmful effects of magic. I know I probably wasn't the only one to think of it, but I wouldn't even begin to know where to look to find it. I've been around F.A.B.L.E.S. since right after Geoffrey left, just before Aiden was born, and not a single one of the members ever really talked about it except for Harold. He told me about it one night, but we've not talked about it since. To be honest, I thought it was a tall tale, someone he was telling me to try to entertain me."

She wiped the flour off her hands by rubbing them on her apron before opening the refrigerator.

I was thrilled when she brought out some cupcakes, handing them out to Mia and I like we were schoolchildren enjoying an after school snack. It made me smile, and I couldn't help but think that whoever my future children might be, they would have a wonderful grandmother, ready with baked goods and a kind smile. I couldn't think of anything better, but it made me wonder if I'd be allowed to come in with them after school every day for cookies and milk. Wasn't that a crazy thought for a grown woman?

Doris bit into her own cupcake, leaving a slight smear of chocolate at the corner of her mouth. After she swallowed, she said, "Well, I had heard about the Cinderella shoes, those glass slippers you mentioned. I know there's supposed to be a set of boots made for a cat, a set of bloody keys, a spinning wheel, and other items, but I don't know why they were all secreted away. I do know that this collection was the first time humans had amassed such a collection, and there was significant negotiation regarding whether humans would keep the items, how they would keep them safe, and who would have access to them. And that's just within the various human governmental organizations, much less negotiations with magical factions."

Bert spoke up, chocolate smeared across his face from where he'd been eating his cupcake. Of course, he didn't really have hands, so he'd just put his face straight into the swirls of chocolate frosting.

"Charles Perrault is the one who got everyone to agree. That man could sell ice to Eskimos. I've never seen anything like it. If Perrault wanted to get a compromise on something, people practically fell all over themselves to work something out. He got the humans to agree that France should make the security arrangements for the items, that England would provide the ships for transportation, and that the Scandinavian countries would provide the technical details to France for the location of where the items were to be secured. No one country had complete information on where the final hiding place would be, so that no one human would be able to appropriate the items and use them against another of the countries involved in the agreement. It was amazing, almost like Perrault had known ahead of time which county would have volunteered for which duty. Of course, it's always possible he had worked it all out ahead of time, but it just seemed like his nominations took the diplomatic world by surprise at how easily everyone accepted their assignments."

I wondered if Perrault had been like some of the arrogant assholes I'd gone to law school with; good looking and popular, but expecting things to always go their way, or whether he would have been genuinely interested in getting people to work together and thinking about the bigger picture. It seemed to me the first kind of charismatic leader generally ended up being in charge, and while the second kind of person was probably better qualified, it would be rare that such a person would actually be allowed to be in charge of an organization that would actually benefit others. I'd been on plenty of committees that had proven that over the years. The people with the best ideas were never the ones actually in charge of implementing them. Those implementing them had the ability to torpedo the best laid plans anywhere, *and* make themselves come out smelling like a rose; looking like they'd actually accomplished something monumental, instead of tanking it, and then taking credit for progress made.

Bert was probably completely unaware of my inner monologue, but he knew me pretty well. He could probably guess what I was thinking. He kept talking, telling me more about Perrault.

"Perrault made sure the items got to their hiding place in a way that was nearly impossible for humans to access, and out of the way enough that magical folks wouldn't even think to look for it there. Everyone knew it wasn't a permanent arrangement, but no one had an idea for a permanent fix, so the years went by and no one ever changed it. The temporary solution became the permanent answer because no one ever came up with a better idea. There were only a handful of folks who knew the actual location, and none of them are talking."

"How do you know that?" I asked. "When more than one person tries to keep a secret, it's that many times more likely that the secret gets out, and quickly."

Bert gave me a hard look. "I know that none of them are talking, because I'm the only one still alive. If they talked, they did it well before they died, which has been a few hundred years ago. I'd have heard by now if someone had blabbed. I keep my ear pretty close to the ground on this issue."

Bert knew the secret of where the items were hidden? That meant we weren't going to have to do any amateur detective work in order to figure it all out. Hallelujah, maybe I would get through the week with something resembling sanity. Wait a minute.

"How many might know that you were part of the inner circle, one of the keepers of that secret?" I asked.

If that was the case, then *Bert* was the target of whatever magical badness was heading our way.

And it was up to us to protect him. He'd protected us plenty, helping out as much as he could, endangering himself and basically being as loyal a friend as one could ask for. He'd made mistakes, sure, but we all had. This time, it was our turn to protect him.

I'd be damned if I let him down.

CHAPTER SEVEN

I must have given Bert a truly strange look, because he got defensive. "Janie, I know what you must be thinking. You're thinking I'm stupid for getting involved in something like this when I don't have any personal magic to protect myself, but that was why I left Europe right after that issue was settled. I came to the New World, and started working with the individuals that became F.A.B.L.E.S. many years ago. None of them knew what I'd been up to in Europe. I only mention it now because it seems to be relevant. I haven't spoken about this whole affair in centuries. I can't believe that anything about that could be all that relevant now."

"Bert, we've been here before. How many times do we have to have a magical whoziwhatzit show up at just the worst timing, to tell us that someone is in danger, or there's something from their background or their past that might be causing them some kind of danger? It's just that it's your turn this time." And in some ways, I was going to enjoy the shoe being on the other foot. He'd been there to drive home the impact when it had been my life on the line, and even though he'd been incredibly supportive, it still had stung those few times when he had laughed at my naïve reactions to the situation. Not that I was planning on laughing at what could be a truly dangerous situation, but it was definitely nice for the shoe to be on the other foot.

"But I can't tell you where the stuff is hidden. I took an oath. If someone showed up and tortured me, I can't tell them," he said.

"Bert," Mia said, quietly. "You think they would torture you for the information? Anyone who has done any research on any of us wouldn't torture the person they wanted information out of. They'd pick another one of our group. They'd pick the person that means the most to you. That's Allie, or if they can't get to her, it would be Janie or me. They'd torture us until you cracked."

His eyes widened. There was no way he'd thought that far ahead to think about the danger this could pose to the rest of us. There was no way that we were going to get through this with all of us in one piece if we didn't start thinking further ahead. I'd found that out the hard way when my stepbrother had knocked out all of my friends in order to kidnap me, and when my stepmother had broken Aiden's arm to try to cow me into doing her bidding. Both had been tests of my mental fortitude, and I'd been glad I hadn't had to really choose in the end. Who was to say what any of us would choose if forced into it? Maybe it was better to just never get to that point.

And just how bad was this stuff that he'd taken such a vow? Or that someone would look for it so desperately. On the other hand, did I want to know his secrets? Or would I be in more danger, and put Aiden and the others in more danger, if I did know? Or would whoever it was assume we all already knew because of how close we were to Bert, i.e., knowledge by association? Okay, enough mental speculation. It was time to get some real answers.

"Okay, look, let's take this one step at a time," Doris said. "Bert, the good news here is that you have plenty of friends who aren't going to let you run off like Allie did, and we're not going to let you go down without a fight. If they capture you, we'll come get you, and if they get one of us, we'll trust in you to do the right thing. Fair enough?"

"Fair enough," he said, turning back to his cupcake. "But if they torture you and you tell me not to tell, I'll remind you of that for the rest of your life. No matter how long or short it is."

Deal, I thought. I was counting on long.

We spent the next few hours helping Doris chop up fruit for the filling she planned to make for the cake. Strawberries piled up, raspberries were macerated in sugar, and pineapple was sliced and chopped and made into a jam for filling the different cake layers. We mixed up butter cream and baked macaroons to place on the table with the cake. We chopped nuts for the decorative parts, and she tried to show us how to make icing roses she would store in the refrigerator until it was time to put them on the cake. Mia and I tried to help, but I'm sure we made more of a mess than we helped. Bert ate more icing than he should have, and ended up with an upset stomach, although that was better than the hangovers he used to get. Maybe I should keep icing around in the fridge to give him when he was upset with something, rather than the beer Jonah and Aiden sometimes got for him, even though he hadn't gotten drunk in a long time.

I hadn't cleaned up frog vomit in a while. I took away the icing roses before he puked red and pink and blue all over Doris's clean tile floor. Instead, he fell asleep, snoring on the table with his head pillowed on an icing bag.

We left him snoring and took a break, heading into the living room, where Doris had a number of wedding crafts lying around in various stages of completion. Doris picked up a wreath that was halfway wrapped with blue ribbon and began winding the ribbon around the grapevine, following the pattern she'd already started. She inserted small fake white flowers as she went, and I was amazed to see that she could continue to carry on the work as she talked without a break in the action. I wondered how many of these she'd done over the years, supporting her kids and taking on side jobs, making cakes and general craft work. I had no question she'd done this kind of thing before. I just couldn't remember exactly what the wreath was for.

I must have had a puzzled look on my face, because she answered my unasked question. "I didn't talk to you about this, but I figured that a wreath to put on your front door on the day of the wedding would be a nice touch. I already had all the materials, so I just needed to put it together. Isn't this the same color blue as Mia's dress?"

I was touched by the thought, and said so. "Doris, my bigger question, before we wake up the amphibian glutton in the kitchen, though, is how dangerous is all of this? Shouldn't Bert be warning people of this kind of danger before he spends too much time around people?"

"And would you kick him out for not telling you, Janie?" she asked, a bit on the sharper side. "Does it really matter? You know he would have kept it quiet to protect people, especially you. The poor dear has probably been worrying about his safety and everyone else's for most of his life, and that's an absurdly long time to play what ifs in your head. He's not someone who does well alone. He picks up friends. You've seen that, and you count yourself as one of them, I know. But how much agony does he go through every day, worrying that his need for human friendship will mean their endangerment and death?"

She was right, and I hadn't meant it quite that sharply. Maybe the number of magical emergencies was wearing on me. We'd had five, including this one, in less than three years. That was a lot of magical craziness for anyone, much less to have it come up this week. I'd spoken sharper than I should, and when I saw Mia's face, that clinched it. I muttered an apology. "Yeah, and I've wondered in the past myself if I should be walking away from everyone to protect them and I couldn't do it, either. I certainly can't blame him for not doing what I couldn't do myself. I hope he didn't hear that, and if he did, I'll apologize."

"Look, Janie, I know that you've got a lot on your plate this week," Doris said. "I'm happy to do whatever I can to help. The boys are already going to stay here the night before the wedding to keep them from seeing you before the ceremony. Why don't you have them stay all week? Mia, your mother is coming by later tonight after she gets off work. I'm sure she'd be happy to have you girls, and Allie, come stay with her this week."

I turned her down, based on the conversation Mia and I'd had earlier. Mia's mother didn't have room, and if we weren't going to sleep behind our own threshold, we might as well have gotten the hotel rooms that all of our contemporaries were getting in Columbus to take the bar exam.

"Janie, why haven't you flat out asked Bert more about what's going on?" Mia wanted to know, changing the subject as she cleaned up ribbon bits from the carpet.

She was right. I hadn't. I hadn't even realized that I'd let him off the hook so far. Was I so stressed out that I was that distracted? Apparently, I was.

CHAPTER EIGHT

I left Mia and Doris to the crafts in the living room and went to wake up the sleeping "beauty" . . . the frog in a sugar coma in the kitchen.

"Bert?" I asked, calling his name softly. "We need to talk."

"Urgh," I heard. Maybe letting him have that much icing wasn't a good idea. *Please let there not be frog puke in kitchen.* I wouldn't have it in me to leave it for Doris, and I'd cleaned up enough frog vomit to last multiple lifetimes.

"Bert?"

"I'm awake. Don't ever let me eat that much icing again. It's awesome, but . . . Too. Much. Sugar." He was holding his stomach.

I hoped we didn't have a medical emergency. What would that much sugar do to him as a frog? "Bert, we need to talk. About the slippers, about all of it."

He sighed. "I saw that coming. I'd hoped you wouldn't ask, but I know you've gotta. I'll tell you what I can, but there's some I can't tell you."

"Can't or won't?" I asked.

"Both," he said. "There's a magical geas that was cast against revealing the final piece of the puzzle, but at the same time, I don't want you to be in danger."

A magical geas? No wonder he said he'd know if someone blabbed! "What happens if you tell? Where you in on the casting to protect the secret?" I asked, pulling up a chair next to where he was sprawled out on the kitchen table, still holding his distended belly.

"Yes, I was in on it. If someone tells, then a magical signal appears in the sky above each of our locations. The shape of the signal depends on who told."

"How do you know if people found a way to tell after they were dead?"

He laughed. "How would they do that? The minute they wrote it down, or otherwise tried to preserve the information, the rest of us would have been signaled."

"Are they all dead?" I asked. "How do you know that?"

Bert pulled himself into a bit more dignified position. "You know, there weren't that many of us involved, it was four hundred plus years ago, and most involved were humans. About a hundred years ago, I hired a genealogist to research whether all of them had actually died; they had. They only ones left were the ones who were magical, or altered by magic, like me. The last one died a month ago. I keep tabs on them."

I guess I would, too, if I was in his situation. I'd want to know if the others were still around. I'd want to know if I was the last one with the secret. So what would happen if Bert told, if he was the last one left? Did I want to know the answer to that one? I chickened out.

"So what can you tell me?" I wasn't sure I wanted to know if he'd spontaneously combust, or if he'd die of horrible oozing sores. Better to steer clear of that for just a bit.

"I can tell you that Perrault was the one who organized the geas. He was the one who thought it was a good idea to continue to provide magical protection for as long as possible. He was the one who came up with the idea of how to magically protect the secret."

"Wait a minute. I thought you said Perrault was human," I said. "How'd he get the magical know-how, or the magical ability to do it?"

Bert chuckled. "I didn't say he cast the spell himself. And I didn't say he didn't do a ton of research before he came up with the idea. Your own ancestors, the Grimm Brothers, were completely human, but still figured out how to bind your stepmother's abilities. They had help casting it, and they had help coming up with how to do it. Perrault wasn't any different, and that's where the Grimms got the idea for using magic. Eva never expected it from humans, and that was her mistake."

He had a point. I was assuming Perrault had done the work; but who knew how many different conversations he'd had before he'd gotten to the point of being ready to pull the plug and ask for specific help in casting a specific spell. The first step would be to find out what kinds of things could be done, and then how to pull it off. It wasn't any different than the approach I'd taken in the past to figuring out the magical emergencies I'd faced in the last couple of years: who was in danger, then how to protect them, a two-step process breaking things down to get to a solution.

Come to think of it, it was a logical, analytical approach. A *lawyer's approach.* It made more and more sense the more I thought of it.

"Okay, so Perrault did some research, came up with the idea of a geas, and then got someone to help him cast it the way he wanted it done. So, who helped him?" I asked.

Bert shrugged. "I don't know. That person wasn't there when it was cast; only the people who were involved in the actual securing of the items were present."

That didn't quite add up. My brain spun and spun, looking at the possibilities.

"Bert, you said that you were the only one left," I stated.

"Yup."

"Were there other magical beings involved in the secret?"

"Yup. But they're gone as well."

Another click into place. "Okay, so I think we have two possibilities. Either someone involved with this secret faked their death, or hid magical abilities so you wouldn't know that they helped cast the spell itself . . ."

"Or?" he prompted, sitting upright, his upset stomach seemingly forgotten.

"Or someone helped cast the spell that wasn't even in the room, and there's a deeper conspiracy here than you know of." I sighed. "Not completely unheard of when we've been dealing with magic."

"Or humans," Bert said, rolling his eyes. "Humans are just as bad about hiding things as the magical folk; sometimes they're even worse."

He had a point; and maybe I was counting on such a thing. After all, I was planning to practice law in a few months, if I passed the bar exam. I was counting on people hiding things, having secrets, and wanting to handle their affairs discretely to pay my bills down the road. It would keep me afloat, even if the magical folks stopped paying. And so far, we'd had just one magical client who paid, but he had paid handsomely, in cash, with a large up front retainer. I couldn't throw stones at just the magical set for deceit; no matter how jaded I was after my encounter with my stepmother.

"So where do we start, Bert? We don't have a lot of free time this week. How do we find out even where to start? How do we find out whether the person, or being, involved, is alive or dead? How do we start to protect whatever is in that stash of artifacts? Is there anything in that pile of stuff that could cause a reaction if we do the wrong thing to protect it? And how do we find who might still be around who could have been involved, or at least would have knowledge of who might have been strong enough at the time to cast from afar if that was the case?"

Bert was quiet for a bit before he answered. "Those are all good questions. I'm not sure I know where to start. But I think I know someone who might."

I thought about it for a minute. "You can't be serious."

"Well, I know two people who might. Why don't we start with the second one and see what he knows before we ask the other one?"

"Who is the second one?" I asked. I was pretty sure who he was going to name, and I so did not want to be in her debt.

"Well, Geoffrey knows a lot of people. He knows who was around, and he knows who to talk to. Although he wasn't an actual court member yet, he was certainly sniffing around the edges."

"What do you mean?" I asked.

"He was a teenager. His father was the court tailor, and Geoffrey was in training. He was sometimes there, sometimes he wasn't, but he's got a pretty good memory for names and faces. His father was constantly trying to get him to court more often, but he was having too much fun partying in the human realms."

I snorted. "Are you kidding? Apparently he didn't get it out of his system, he still comes around."

"Yeah, but have you ever seen him drink anything other than water or coffee? He doesn't drink alcohol anymore in the human realm, and only drinks wine when social mores in the magical realm require it."

Wow. "Any idea why?" He was right, though. I didn't remember seeing Geoffrey drink anything other than coffee at my house, although he seemed to be addicted to it, constantly filling his coffee mug to the point where a human would have been jittering right out of their chair and stroking out from the caffeine long ago. "Was he that big of a party animal?"

Bert chuckled. "I didn't know him that well. I was an adult even if I was a frog, and he was a sixteen-year-old kid who didn't want to fall in line with Daddy's desires, if you listened to the court gossip. Funny how the branch doesn't fall far from the tree, does it? Well, Aiden's rebellion against his daddy wasn't the first in that family. It's interesting to remember it, but he was a wild one."

"How wild could one be back then?" I wondered out loud. I guess I never heard of wild partying that many years ago, but I wasn't a history student. I guess human nature was human nature though, and Bert seemed to back that up.

"Well, an unlimited magical purse of money to spend in the human realm, with good looks, a charismatic personality, and a chip on one's shoulder, as well as an attitude towards Daddy's position in the courts? He bounced from brothel to brothel, from party to party. He used drugs, many were legal at that time, and alcohol, and he was constantly getting into fights. Still, though, he always did have a good mind for names and faces. I didn't exactly run with him, but I know he was around. If he was in the magical realm that weekend, and if he was remotely sober, he'd remember who he saw."

"You don't remember seeing him?"

"Give me a break. That was four hundred years ago, and it wasn't like I wasn't otherwise occupied at the time. His father wasn't involved in what we were doing with Perrault, so he wouldn't have been forced to stick around."

"And if he doesn't know anything?"

"Then our best bet is going to be to talk to Queen Eva."

Shit. Shit. Double shit. With crap sprinkles on top. The absolute last person in the world that I'd want to ask for any kind of favor. And she was going to be right there, under my nose, at the wedding that I hadn't wanted her to attend.

This was definitely shaping up to be an interesting kind of week. And not in a good way.

CHAPTER NINE

It wasn't hard to get Bert to agree that Evangeline, aka Queen Eva, was a true last resort. If we got so far as to need her help, we were so screwed in so many monumental ways, that asking for her help, and the price that would come with that help, would be pretty minimal. We would do a lot of work to try to overcome any favor she might ask of me, and we might try harder than normal to stay out of her reach while she was here.

And she'd be in the front row (who was I kidding, there weren't enough people to have a second row coming to the ceremony), watching me get married, and waiting for the other shoe to drop. And speaking of shoes . . .

I seemed to recall something pretty darn violent about those shoes. The Grimm Brothers' version indicated the stepsisters hacked parts of their feet off in order to fit them into the too small shoes. I knew I didn't want to take the chance of sticking my feet in there and waiting to see if someone or something would hack off my perfectly sound, if ordinary and non-magical feet. Needless to say, it hadn't worked for the sisters.

People tended to forget that part of the fairy tale. Disney didn't exactly include it in their version, so most little girls just think of the evil stepsisters as shoving their feet comically into a too-tight shoe. Like most of the tales I'd run across, though, there was a much darker truth to the story, sometimes even darker than my ancestors had documented. I didn't trust those shoes not to have hidden razor blades inside them, even though one could see completely through them.

"Okay, Bert, so what can you tell me about the items that might be secreted away?"

He started to shake his head.

"Bert, I need to know more about why someone would want to steal those items than about what they actually are, but it's kinda hard to know what's important if I don't know what's there. I guess the question is, is there the magical equivalent of a nuclear bomb down there, and if so, what do I need to know about what's there? Do we need to worry about moving it? What if someone else has already moved it? And it's hard to know if there's a reason why it's being targeted if we don't know what it is. How many times has 'what' turned into 'why' which has helped us figure something out?"

He considered for a minute. I watched his mouth open once or twice, but no sound came out. He looked frustrated.

And then I got it. It wasn't just a spell to alert others to the secret being spilled; it was also a magical prohibition, an act of prevention. The spell kept those in the know from purposely telling, and was designed to alert all the others involved if someone found a way around the spell. Pretty darn smart, if you ask me.

Mia came into the kitchen. "So who do we have to kill?" she asked, with a half-smile on her face.

I laughed. The idea of either of us as stone killers was about the funniest thing I'd heard so far today, and it certainly had been an interesting kind of day. And I had needed that.

"Bert, you might not be able to tell us anything that would spill that secret, but I think I'm figuring some stuff out between the lines. And I'm pretty sure they are coming for you. Whoever it is wants you to give up the information you have. They probably want you to find your own way out of the geas, so that you'll be able to share that information. So we've got to figure out a few things. First, we have to figure out why they want it. We have to figure out what they want to do with those items. And then, we have to figure out how to stop them," I said.

Bert shook his head. "If something happens to me, there will be no one else who can give them the location. So maybe we should be looking into memory modification spells. If I can't remember it, then we shut down their whole plan."

"See previous problem, Bert. You're assuming they'll just give up when you say you can't remember. They'll snatch one of us. They will torture one of us. The only thing you'll have stopped is your ability to rescue whoever it is they take. Don't you dare mess with that kind of magic. I'm still recovering from the mental stumbling blocks

Evangeline put on me while Dad was alive. I'm still recovering those memories. I don't think you really want to go there, but I certainly understand why you keep thinking of taking yourself out of the equation. If you're not a player, though, that doesn't keep us safe. It makes it harder to protect us, because we don't have another way of getting any information," I stressed.

He got quiet. "Look, the items on their own are all pretty innocuous, but all of them carry a bit of a magical punch. And it's probably something that makes sense when you hear it, but wouldn't be immediately apparent by an educated guess. When the shoes showed up, I wasn't sure at first that they were the same shoes. I thought it was someone playing a sick joke, or sending some kind of wedding thing. And then I realized it could be related to this. I didn't know what to do."

That pissed me off. "Bert, like we'd ever let you face something like this alone! You've been there for me, for Mia, for Allie, for Jonah Why would you ever think we wouldn't return that friendship?"

He hung his head. Mia looked pissed at him, too.

Doris burst in, showing off the wreath that she'd finished, and wanting me to look at the centerpieces. I grimaced. I really didn't care, but she definitely did. And Geoffrey did. And Mia did. So, therefore I did. She had wrapped burlap strips around Mason jars, with blue and white ribbon and a tag with Aiden's name and my own, filled the inside of the jars a third of the way up with white sand, and a tea light sat in the sand. She showed me white paper doilies she'd made to place under the jars, and said she was planning to put out an assortment of chocolates on the doilies for the guests to enjoy before dinner was served. It was a simple decoration, but I did like it; it was understated but pretty, thoughtful without being fussy. And it showed that she knew a thing or two about throwing a party, because every party I'd been to like that had had some limitation or complication that came up with the catering or the bridal party or the facility had some issue at the last minute. Keeping the guests' blood sugar from dropping too low while fixing the problem was a wonderful thing.

I thanked her for her work, and then told her we had to get going. She agreed to finish the decorations and assured me there was no issue with the preparations or the wedding details. I think she was trying to set my mind at ease about the wedding, but truthfully, I'd have preferred to have a wedding detail nightmare than dealing with the magical nightmare.

It was time to go see what Jonah and Aiden had figured out. Or if they were still mired in fittings with Geoffrey. Of course, that could be the same thing . . . if Geoffrey had information he was coughing up voluntarily. But if the boys didn't know that Geoffrey was around when the geas was cast, then were they even asking the right questions? Did Geoffrey even know he had the information to give us?

Somehow, I figured that the answer to those questions was no. To all of them.

CHAPTER TEN

We headed back to my house silently. There wasn't much chit chat in the Escalade, other than stopping to hit a drive through and getting lunch for everyone before heading back. Hamburgers and fries might not have been the healthiest choice, but hey, I got a small and didn't get a milkshake to go with it. I should be fine. I'd just have to eat a salad for dinner.

We walked back into the house with a bag of burgers and not a lot of new answers. Allie met us at the kitchen door. "Wondered where everyone had taken off too."

Allie had been working nights at a women's shelter, monitoring a hotline and keeping watch for battered women who were running from their abusers. She'd been asleep when we'd had the commotion this morning, and none of us had thought to wake her. We'd all gotten used to letting her sleep in the mornings and so we'd done it. I gave her the quick and dirty five-minute synopsis of what we'd been dealing with that morning.

She was instantly pissed that we hadn't woken her up; more so when I flat out said Bert was the one on the hook this time. He tried to talk her down; she was having none of it. I was glad to see it.

"How dare you three keep me in the dark! You came running after me with no notice and no idea what you were facing and you decided to keep me out when it concerns the man I love? How dare you!" Allie yelled.

She was right, but I hadn't done it on purpose. Bert might have, but Mia and I hadn't.

Bert was willing to throw himself on the sword, though. "Honey, I wasn't sure what we were facing when I first saw the shoes, and you had barely been home an hour when I saw them. You were dead on your feet when you came in the door. I decided to let you sleep, here, behind our threshold, until we could figure out for sure it was a risk."

"Bullshit," she said. "But you're sure now?"

She always was incredibly practical, and was definitely showing it here.

"Allie, I'm sorry. We're so used to letting you sleep during the day we didn't even think to wake you up. That's my fault. Was it a bad night?"

She sighed. "Yes. We had a family with six kids show up at the shelter. Mom had stayed as long as she could, and Dad decided this time that beating Mom wasn't enough; he started hitting the kids. The neighbors called the cops, and the police took him to jail, and Mom finally felt like she could leave. She bundled up the kids, who, by the way, range in age from nine years old down to nine days old, and headed our way. Our shelter was almost full, but we couldn't turn them away It took all night to get them all settled. The baby went out right away, but the older kids wouldn't sleep. They wouldn't sleep in separate beds, and they all ended up in the same big pile on the bed we'd given to Mom. All of them were dirty, and two of the kids had fleas.

"We also had to call the animal shelter to take in their dog and two cats while they were with us. And it turned out Dad had refused to pay for flea treatments for their animals unless Mom did what he said for the last six months. We had kids needing baths, a stressed out mom who had just given birth nine days ago, a breastfeeding baby who wasn't getting enough to eat, and all of them exhausted. Three of the kids had bruises where we could see them, and all of them had bruises once we got them to change their clothes. Even with the crazy childhood I had, I just can't understand why someone would do this to their own children."

Yikes. It sounded like she'd had an extraordinarily bad night. And yet, her eyes sparkled and her face looked determined. She was excited to go to work at night; she liked helping people get out of bad situations. She talked about trying to go to school to get a degree in social work or in psychology, but at the moment, she was earning a small paycheck and feeling useful and fulfilled. Quite a long way from where she'd been even a year ago, recovering from the trauma of her past as a victim both in Wonderland and in the human realm.

"Everyone settled and safe?" I asked. It was the question I asked her every time we talked about her work.

"For now," she said. "And for today, that's enough. We did, however, have to warn the mom that if she left the shelter and went back to him with the kids that we would report her to children's services for child endangering. She broke down crying, but she's been to the shelter before. And gone back several times. And now the kids are getting hurt."

Ouch. "It's good that you're helping," I said. There really wasn't anything good one could say, other than to be sympathetic. I'd learned there was no way anyone could understand exactly the mentality of someone fleeing for one's life, unless they had done so themselves. Allie had done so more than once, and both times she had left behind a life and family or friends who she was trying to protect as she ran. I was smart enough to know it was hard, and to sympathize, but I still didn't completely understand all the emotional ramifications of how it felt.

"I probably did need the sleep, but Janie, I'm not fragile. I'm better emotionally than I used to be, and I'm not going to sit idly by while any of you are in danger. Especially Bert."

I got it. She started up the coffeepot again, and I was glad; I felt like I hadn't had enough caffeine myself. Bert jumped in, trying to calm her down. It didn't work.

The two of them argued, and I tuned out a lot of it, but caught enough to know that she cared for him more than he realized. And I realized her feelings were part of the issue here.

Bert had made mention in the past of not trusting that Allie could love him like she could if he was in human form. It was crap, and I'd told him so, but I think he still had a hard time believing it. He loved her with everything he had, and it scared him. But Allie had grown up in Wonderland, where many of the residents were in animal bodies, and it didn't make them lesser, or less worthy of care and friendship and affection. She was probably better poised than anyone around to accept him just as he was.

That didn't mean their lives wouldn't be uncomplicated by the fact that he was a frog; just that it wasn't the biggest impediment it could have been.

Heck, Allie and I had had many conversations into the wee hours of the night, talking about how Aiden's half magical heritage was going to affect our relationship. I think Allie had a better idea of what she was facing with Bert than I had with Aiden. Never mind the physical differences between a woman and a frog. They would figure all those things out if they were able to get a solid enough footing underneath their relationship. And we'd already seen that Bert could become a human with the use of a potion. I wondered if that potion could be made again, and how she would feel about it. I'd have to ask her one of these days without Bert hanging on my every word.

"So what are we going to do about this, Janie? How do we keep this from affecting the wedding, and keep you guys on track for the bar exam?" Allie asked.

Good question. Because I'd planned to spend all day doing a bunch of last minute cramming and hiding from wedding details. At least I had a good excuse to delegate wedding details that I didn't really care about to others in the name of dealing with a magical emergency.

Maybe this thing had a silver lining after all.

CHAPTER ELEVEN

T he doorbell rang just as I was pouring myself another cup of coffee and Allie and Bert's argument subsided for the morning.

"Is it just me, or is it suddenly cold?" Mia asked.

She was right. I was pretty sure who was at the door. It was the Snow Queen.

I answered the door. "Hello," I said, polite but friendly. I wasn't trying to play court etiquette, because if I did, I'd screw up some arcane etiquette rule. Instead, it was easier most times to just be me. I knew someday I'd have to learn all the ins and outs, but for this week, I wasn't trying to be perfect. I was glad I wasn't getting a lot of push back, but that was only going to last so long.

I was right. She swept into the house on my invitation, and I was highly cognizant of the fact that she had never done anything to put me in danger, and in fact, had helped us a time or two in the past. I wondered if she was going to ask for a favor today, because I definitely owed her one. Possibly more than one.

"Ms. Grimm, allow me to extend my congratulations and good wishes regarding your upcoming nuptials. I wish you every happiness with your husband, and wish you a good weather day for the ceremony. I understand the ceremony itself will be here at the house, in your backyard."

"That's true." I led her into the living room and invited her to have a seat. "Would you like coffee, or a cup of tea?"

She declined. "I think you're going to find, however, that you've committed a bit of a faux pas in your invitation list. I have asked around, and I think I know what happened, but I want to work with you to find a way to fix it."

Oh crap. "Where did I go wrong? I invited guests from every realm I've had dealings with in the last three years. I only invited those that I'd had actual dealings with who did not try to eat me, kill me, or eat or kill my friends. I thought that was a pretty generous definition."

"It is," she said, smiling at me. "The problem isn't your initial invitations, but rather the last minute additions that are coming to the ceremony. Everyone accepted your wish for the small private ceremony, especially given your fiancé's tendency to well, fall down and bust open his face, for lack of a better way to state that. Your guests to the reception understand why they aren't coming to the ceremony. And then I hear that you have two magical realm queens suddenly invited to the ceremony. That's probably a slap in the face of all your relatives, but it's also a slap in the face of all the other royalty in the magical realms."

I realized then she was one of the ones who would be slighted. I had no problem inviting her to keep the peace, but she had a point about the relatives. And then I had a brainstorm.

"I've not dealt with more than three actual queens. You, the queen of hearts, and my stepmother. I think I can explain to the relatives and friends, most of whom do not know about or understand magic, by the way, that I can hardly fail to invite my stepmother, and the Queen of Hearts is her sister. Are you also related to her?"

If there was some relation, I could explain it away as Evangeline being in poor health, and attribute her lack of appearances at family events and social events as related to a health issue.

"All of us royals are related in some way. I have no problem being explained away as her cousin, which I technically am." That seemed reasonable, and this was about saving face to her court, which had been my stepmother's court, rather than about being actually offended about a lack of invitation. I explained my idea about Evangeline's health being the non-magical explanation for her absence and the need for relatives to care for her during the ceremony. She nodded.

"It works. I'm not sure I would trust the Queen of Hearts to protect you from your stepmother, and I'm not sure she doesn't have a plan. It sounds like they were very organized in how they finagled the invitation. I think it's smart to make sure you have another magical ally in the audience."

She was right. It was smart. But what was the price going to be for her help? I asked.

"Count it as my wedding gift to you. You've been an ally, and I want to keep our working relationship positive."

It occurred to me that she had likely been in on sending Geoffrey to Wonderland for negotiations, but I had no proof she was in on the plot to get the wedding invitation, and there was no question she had been on our side in the past. There was no history of her targeting any one of us. "You need to know that the invitation to the wedding was limited to the date and time of the ceremony itself, and there has been no invitation to enter the house itself or cross the threshold extended. I have to give Geoffrey credit for that one."

"Indeed. He was smart. I also give him credit. You need to make sure no one extends an invitation inside during the ceremony. I would not put it past your stepmother to ask permission to come inside to use the bathroom without trying to turn it into something else."

I wondered what it would cost to rent a port o john for a couple of hours, and where I might put it in the backyard where it wouldn't be in the background of any of the pictures. Maybe behind the garage would work? I wondered if Mia could lock the doors behind us when we came out for the ceremony; that would keep anyone from trying to trick others into believing they had an active invitation to get inside the house. And, for the ten millionth time, I wondered if it would have been worth the money to rent somewhere to have the ceremony and not have to worry about anyone getting inside or tricking their way inside.

I wondered if there was something inside the house that Evangeline wanted. Was there something left behind?

"You might also see if there is something she wants of hers that was in the house. If she's finagling an invitation to get some of her own stuff back, she might be able to get it just by asking," I offered. "We'd want to make sure that anything she asked for couldn't be used against us, so we'd reserve the right to say no, but if that resolved what she was looking for, and she decided to decline the invitation, that wouldn't hurt my feelings."

The Snow Queen laughed. "If it was something that mundane, you don't think you wouldn't have heard from her a long time ago? Eva is nothing if not patient, but at the same time, trinkets from her mortal existence wouldn't mean much to her unless she felt she could use them to exact some kind of revenge. And, no offense, Janie, but if she's looking for revenge on you, it isn't going to be the kind that involves a request for a sweater or a throw blanket you've got in storage and probably aren't using anyway. Am I right?"

She was. I had put all of Evangeline's things into storage except the furniture, which I had sold most of, and a few things I had destroyed, out of concern that they might have been magical. Aiden had helped me decide what was safe to sell. I didn't think I'd destroyed any magical heirloom items, or artifacts. We only tore up a couple of things that looked like they might have had a spell placed on them, or might have been affected by a potion or something. Better to be safe than sorry, had been my mantra. I hoped she hadn't wanted something back.

"She owned everything in the house. Some of the furniture was expensive. I got rid of it, so I'd have to find a way to pay her back if she wanted reimbursed," I said.

"She's not going to go to the trouble of finagling an invite to your wedding for anything as mundane as a piece of furniture, either. She wants access, either to set some kind of trap, or to activate something already in the house. This isn't a family fight over the silver. It's deeper than that," The Snow Queen smiled at me. "So we've got to keep her out of the house."

I nodded. The idea of my stepmother free to roam the house wasn't my idea of a good time, even if all she did was the white glove test and picked on my choice in furnishings and décor. She'd had the place professionally decorated every three years, with antiques and fussy details. I had gotten rid of all of that, and used the proceeds to pay for some work on the roof, as well as property taxes and homeowners insurance for the last couple of years. I'd filled the place with secondhand, garage sale furniture that I actually thought looked more comfortable than anything she'd had. It definitely looked sturdier than most of her fussy antiques with spindly legs. And it looked more like a home than it ever had when I'd lived here with Evangeline and my dad. A home. My home. And I wasn't about to let my stepmother ruin all of that.

"I do have a plan, though, to keep her out that day." I outlined my plan for Alfred and some of his friends to patrol inside the house and to install a port a john outside for wedding guests. That reminded me; I needed to make that phone call as soon as possible to make sure that I could actually get one in a week. Who knew how far ahead one needed to call to reserve such a thing and have it delivered and installed in time? And how much was that going to cost me? Whatever it was, it was worth it to keep Evangeline from having an excuse to get inside the house.

The Snow Queen stood up from the couch where she had been sitting. "I think you've got some great ideas, but I still think it's smart for me to be there as magical backup."

"I'm sorry, I didn't actually say the words, did I?" I stood up, following her.

"No, you didn't."

"You're invited to my wedding ceremony, which will take place next Saturday afternoon, at three in the afternoon in the backyard at this address. There will also be a reception afterwards at the Marriott, where you are invited to celebrate with us at four in the afternoon. Will you join us?" I asked.

She nodded. "Sorry, I had to get the official word before I would stand on equal footing as a guest with Eva. You bested her with a technicality; she will be looking for any way to do the same thing back to you."

She was right. Evangeline had been beaten because I'd caught her publicly breaking a promise, one of the worst offenses in the faerie courts. She'd be looking for any way she could catch me up in my own words, especially if that resulted in an advantage she could exploit.

"I appreciate the thoughtfulness," I couldn't remember if I was supposed to call her Your Highness or Your Majesty, but either way, she wasn't my queen. I wasn't of her court, and I wanted to continue to deal with her as equals, not as a subject to a ruler. And saying thank you to a faerie being wasn't always smart either, as it insinuated that one was in the other's debt.

She smiled. "You're going to go far, Janie Grimm. I look forward to our dealings in the future. That reminds me, I do wish to speak to you after the festivities are over regarding some issues of trade in your realm."

"We are planning on taking a honeymoon, by the way, and will be out of touch for a week or so after the wedding," I stated.

I had thought about this one. Not only did I want an uninterrupted honeymoon with Aiden, but I figured it didn't hurt to start putting some boundaries on my availability for magical emergencies. If we ever hoped to start a family, I had to start drawing some lines with the magical set now. Visions of getting called away from school recitals and soccer matches, band concerts and spelling bees were dancing in my head. I never wanted to be that parent, the one that was always too busy with work to be there for my kids. I knew Aiden didn't want that either.

"No problem. It's waited for several hundred years. It can wait a few more days. And you're smart to ask before agreeing to take on a matter. This could get a bit involved."

Didn't it always? I wondered, as I saw her to the door. I still had a week to go until the wedding. What would tomorrow bring?

CHAPTER TWELVE

I felt a little better at the idea of the Snow Queen showing up to help keep an eye on Evangeline, but I wondered at her motives. She'd been very helpful in the past, but why? She'd said something about favors in the future, and maybe this trade matter she wanted dealt with was part of it. Or maybe it wasn't. Did she want in on the wedding to get whatever Evangeline was after for herself?

My mind spun with all kinds of possibilities as I showed her out the front door, then closed it behind her. Mia came in the room and said something about being glad the Snow Queen was going to help protect us, but I was too lost in thought to respond.

Yes, the Snow Queen had saved us from the Seawitch. And had asked for a future favor to be repaid later.

Yes, the Snow Queen had helped to save Aiden's life. And it was my understanding that Geoffrey had negotiated for that help and support on his own; it was his debt, not mine and not Aiden's.

I had freely offered the wedding invitation, hadn't even asked if it would count for that favor, because I thought she was volunteering to help us out again. What if she wanted to be at the wedding for her own ends, rather than to protect us? Was there something in the house that allowed for access to something important?

What if there was another portal in the house I wasn't aware of; a portal that would allow access to the forbidden and hidden items Bert had been involved in hiding with Charles Perrault? Did it have to do with the shoes?

I'd have to ask Bert later. Right now, I had to go see what Aiden and Jonah had found out, if anything. And I needed to ask if there were any other portals available inside the house; or why Evangeline would even want to be in the house if I didn't have anything of hers that she wanted returned.

Jonah and Aiden came walking out of the library, Geoffrey at their heels, just as I headed towards the kitchen. I turned around to face them. "So, guys, are we ready for a wedding?"

Aiden grimaced, but Geoffrey smiled. "They will look wonderful, Janie. Although you guys need to watch what you eat for the next week or so, just to be on the safe side, those suits will fit like a glove on the day of the wedding."

I hoped not too much like a glove. I mean, obviously I liked the way Aiden looked, but I didn't want to see him in the male wedding equivalent of yoga pants in front of our friends, family, and other loved ones on the day of our wedding. I could only imagine how uncomfortable such an ensemble would be for him, and I wondered if it would make him more or less klutzy.

I just wanted this to go off well. "Geoffrey, can I see the suits?" I asked. Why hadn't I asked earlier? Well, I just assumed that Aiden and Jonah would put their feet down at anything too wild. I didn't really care; my dress wasn't overly formal, though, and the wedding was in our backyard. While I didn't think it a good idea to be too formal, I was more concerned at the moment about fit from Geoffrey's statements, and I still wanted to know if Geoffrey had learned anything.

Besides, I'd rather hoped Bert would have said something if those suits were unsuitable, for lack of a better term. They were, after all, hanging in what was essentially his bedroom, and had been for the last month.

Bert was still in the kitchen, arguing with Allie. I heard their voices; they weren't done yet with their discussion. It sounded like they'd be going strong for a while yet.

Mia was sitting in the dining room, looking over her Contracts notes from first year while I had been talking with the Snow Queen in the living room, but at the mention of their suits, she put down what she had been working on and came out to join me.

"I was surprised you hadn't seen them, Janie. I'd have been in here looking at them the minute they were hung up."

I'd had a million and one other things on my mind, what with the bar exam and all. She almost made it sound like I wasn't thrilled to get married because I hadn't been jumping up and down at every minute detail.

Geoffrey looked shocked. "I thought it was some kind of mortal wedding ritual; like how Aiden's not allowed to see your dress, Janie. I just kind of assumed it went both ways. You mean you can see his clothing, but he can't see yours?"

Yeah, I thought that was kinda stupid myself, but it was what it was. I explained to Geoffrey and he took me inside to look at the suits.

They were lovely; black suits with fitted vests underneath, which was what Geoffrey meant when he'd said something about fitting like a glove. The boys had silver and white vests under their double breasted jackets, with silver and white ties. The suits were pinstriped, and I could picture Aiden wearing this as I tied my life to his. My breath caught.

It was wonderful, and better than anything I could have picked out for them myself. It was really happening. For some reason it hadn't all become real to me until that very moment. How had I not felt that way when I'd found and tried on my own dress? A mystery for the ages, I'm sure. Then again, I'd picked out the dress and gone for fittings months ago. We were down to the last details, and it was becoming very real.

The doorbell rang again, and Aiden went to answer it. As he did, I laid out Bert's information to Geoffrey. "You see, I didn't want to bring this up and embarrass you in front of your son, but there's a real chance to figure out who might be trying to derail the wedding and come after Bert. I wanted to give you a chance to let this soak in and think about it."

"How would you explain this information to Aiden if I didn't want him to know how much of a wild child I was in those days?" he asked, after a moment.

"Look, he doesn't have to hear about your extracurricular activities to know that you were around then, does he?" I asked. "Unless it's directly related to what you know, I'm not going to tell tales on you, and I doubt if Bert will say much of anything regarding your past if he hasn't already. You've got to think, though, about what you know, because if you do have information that could keep us safe, then is it worth protecting your son from your past if it means he doesn't have much of a future? Besides which, can you honestly believe that he hasn't heard rumors about your past when he was at the court as a teenager?"

I don't think he'd ever thought about that possibility, but if he knew Aiden better, it would have been the first thing he'd have thought of. Aiden had grown up not knowing his father, and not knowing about his magical heritage until he hit puberty and started to find that his arms and legs didn't work quite as well as other peoples did, and they certainly didn't work together like other people's limbs did. It was after that when he went to live with his father and learn about the rest of his heritage. He hadn't had an easy time of it in the magical realm, with other magical teenagers, including a bully named Greechuk we'd run into a couple of years ago. Aiden, of anyone, would understand a teenager who looked elsewhere for acceptance when they grew up in the magical courts. I'm sure he probably didn't want all of the details on just how wild and crazy Geoffrey had gotten, but if he had been as wild as Bert had alluded to, I was pretty sure a teenaged boy would have been asking around for information about the father he didn't know, from whatever source he could find it, and he would have gotten it. If I knew Aiden, he'd have been listening at doorways and keyholes as well.

He nodded. "Let me think about it. It's been a while."

I guess I couldn't ask for much more than that. I nodded, and headed back to the kitchen, where all of my books and notes were still on the kitchen table. Without much more information, or even more of a plan, the only thing I could do at the moment was to look over more of my notes for the bar exam. If the emergency wasn't here yet, nothing was attacking at the moment, and everyone was safe behind the threshold at the house, I was going to work on the next most pressing thing; remembering the elements of intentional torts, something we'd learned in the first year of law school.

Of course, that didn't last all that long.

CHAPTER THIRTEEN

Thunder boomed and lightning cracked as I sat down in the kitchen. A late summer storm was kicking up. My first thought was that I hoped the electricity didn't go out; we were in an older house and it wasn't unheard of for us to lose power in a bad storm. My second thought was that we had about thirty-six hours for the weather to blow itself out before Mia and I would be commuting to Columbus to take the bar exam, and I didn't really relish the idea of an hour long commute each morning and evening in crappy weather after being stressed out all day and likely not sleeping as well as we should each night. The bar would take us three days to complete. We'd have six hours in a car with a steel frame during that time, but not behind a threshold when something or someone was out to get a friend of ours.

Another flash of lightning caught my eye, and I thought I heard a voice outside in the yard, saying something about allowing her access to the house. It was a female voice, angry, but the words weren't clear due to the storm. I put down my notes and walked over to the sliding glass doors that looked out on the patio and the backyard.

We didn't have any lights in the backyard that were on; everyone was home for the night and no one was outside. There was a light from the neighbor's security lights next door, but it wasn't enough to illuminate the backyard. Even so, in the low light, it looked like something was moving in the yard. A lot of something was moving in the yard.

After a lot of internal debate over whether it was a good idea, I hit the light switch beside the door. The patio light came one, and I couldn't see the patio floor.

It was covered completely, and whatever covered it was writhing and moving and green and brown. And alive.

There were snakes and frogs everywhere, hissing and hopping and moving, so thick I couldn't see the ground. One of them tapped against the glass, and I jumped, before double checking the lock to make sure the glass door couldn't be pushed open from the outside. I tried not to think too hard about the idea that enough snakes and frogs piled up against that glass could actually break the glass, sending them all sliding right into my kitchen.

I hate snakes.

I left the outside light on, but turned and ran for the others. I rounded them all up, but turned off the inside lights coming back into the kitchen. No reason for any enemy outside to know just how many people we had in the house, or who was there.

There was a woman standing in the back yard. I still couldn't make out everything she was saying, but I knew I wasn't opening the sliding glass doors to invite her in for tea.

"What the hell?" Mia exclaimed, upon seeing the writhing carpet of snake and frog on the patio.

I shrugged. I hoped she was okay. I kept thinking about the Seawitch attacking the house a couple of years ago. The Seawitch had been trying to get to Mia and her father in retaliation for actions taken by Hans Christian Andersen a few hundred years before; faerie and magical beings really knew how to hold a grudge. It wasn't hard to see on Mia's face that she was thinking about the same thing. Tobias had been alive then, and had been instrumental in helping us hold our own long enough to get help from the Snow Queen in holding her off. Bert had also been instrumental in protecting Mia, giving up his recently found humanity in order to save her life when the Seawitch attacked. And here we were again, facing a magical bad guy, only this time with Bert as the target.

It was hard for me not to think of Tobias; it couldn't have been an easy thing for Mia, either, but she had her game face on. She also had an iron fireplace poker in her hands. She must have grabbed it out of the library, where she and Jonah had been talking about the suits.

It made me smile that she'd armed herself before heading into the kitchen at my shout, and it made me a little sad that she'd felt she had to.

Bert's face, however, was priceless. He and Allie had been shouting at each other just outside the kitchen door, and when she'd grabbed him and ran into the kitchen, he'd gone speechless. Of course, what other reaction was there to a sea of reptile and amphibian just outside of one's house?

"What the hell?" Aiden summed it up nicely for everyone.

I shrugged. "The storm started and I turned on the light when I heard her voice and that's what was there. I don't know how long she was there, and I don't know what she's saying."

We looked back out the sliding glass doors and I saw the woman was still talking, but the snakes and frogs were dripping from her lips as she spoke.

"If ever someone offers me magical powers," I said. "That's not the one I want."

Jonah snorted. As the only one of us with actual magic, I guess he really felt my meaning. He'd hated his powers to affect growing plants and trees, but he'd been learning to channel it, to make it useful, and training with his many times great-grandmother out West once a month.

"Anyone got any ideas?" Allie asked, quietly. "I've got nothing."

I wasn't far behind her. Thankfully, I wasn't the only one thinking about the next step.

Geoffrey had also come into the kitchen when I'd shouted. I hadn't realized he was still in the house. "Well, you have two problems. First of all, those snakes and frogs aren't magical constructs. They're real animals. Magic is causing them to appear as that woman talks, but it's not creating them. Second of all, isn't this going to tear up your lawn for the wedding?"

He was right. There was no way the yard would recover from this much traffic in a week without our spending some major cash to have a landscaper come in, and we might have to lay new sod to have a green lawn in time. Even if we did that, there was no guarantee that it would be ready for that many people to walk on by Saturday. And that assumed that we could get rid of the Wild Kingdom that covered it first.

"Aren't you missing a third problem?" I asked. "Namely, who in the hell is that woman, and what in the hell does she want?"

Bert piped up. "I can answer that."

All heads turned his way.

"I know who it is. Her sister was the guardian of the Perrault stash."

No one budged, waiting for more explanation.

"No one has heard about the Fairies?" he asked.

Silence.

"A widow had two daughters. One met a fairy in the woods and showed her a kindness and was gifted with the magic to make diamonds and pearls come out of her mouth as she spoke. When her mother saw the gift, she sent her other daughter into the woods with the express purpose to obtain that gift for the daughter she liked better. The second daughter, however, was rude and condescending to the fairy, not realizing it was the one who had gifted her sister. The fairy gifted the second daughter with the magic to have frogs and snake drip from her lips as she spoke. The first daughter was blamed for this curse, and she narrowly escaped the wrath of her mother and sister, escaping into the woods where she met a prince who saved her and married her," Bert said.

I wondered how much he was leaving out.

He kept talking. "The story Perrault recorded leaves out the fact that the first daughter was still alive when he was acting to protect the magical artifacts we've been talking about. He was concerned that someone might try to kidnap her and use her for their own gain."

"How could they . . ." Aiden started to ask, but Bert cut him off.

"Think about what Hitler would have done with unlimited resources. Think about Pol Pot in Asia. Think about what the drug kingpins in Central and Southern America would have done with unlimited money for corruption and bribes and guns and mercenaries. Think about what politics in this county would be like; there's a ton of money pouring into politics these days anyway, but what if one candidate had access to the riches she could produce? What kind of election would that be? What would our government in this country be like if a candidate could buy influence, could buy electors, could basically buy the election with unlimited means and unlimited power?"

That was terrifying.

Worse, however, was the idea of crossover between the realms.

What if my stepmother, or one of her contemporaries got a hold of that woman, then entered the mortal realm with the intention of taking over? She had been deposed from her own throne. She was without the power she believed she was entitled to, and she'd been locked up for her actions just before losing her power.

That didn't explain why she wanted to come to the wedding, but it did explain why she was coming back around, and why she might be so interested in what was going on magically with us. That was one hell of a carrot for someone looking to get back on top.

So what did that have to do with coming to the wedding? No answer to that one, and my shared speculation with the others didn't unearth any other insights.

Wait a minute. Didn't Bert say something about Geoffrey's wild years being financed by an unlimited purse? I hadn't heard of any other magical equivalent to that. Now, how to ask him about it without revealing the stuff I'd promised to try to keep from Aiden?

That wasn't going to be easy.

CHAPTER FOURTEEN

"Geoffrey, I'd heard something about you knowing about an unlimited purse in the past. Is that related to this?" I asked. I couldn't think of any other way to say it, without explanation, and this was still risky.

Aiden had a confused look on his face, but he didn't say anything.

Geoffrey, on the other hand, gave me a grateful look when I didn't say anything else. "You're right, Janie. I did have access to something like that once upon a time."

I grimaced at the cliché, but didn't say anything else. I wanted him to keep talking.

He did. "I once dated a girl that fits the description you've given, Bert."

Bert gave him a sideways look. "I'd always heard that she married the prince in the woods that saved her from her mother and sister."

"Well, not really. You see, I was the man in the woods, but my dad wasn't a king. He did, however, have enough influence to keep her safe from them, and I was tasked with checking on her. The magic bestowed on her by the fairy in the woods made her immortal, and I assume that it did the same to her sister, but Gabriella was still in hiding. She was terrified of her mother and sister, and so we hid her in Paris for a while, instead of the French countryside. She was in Paris when Perrault was organizing his spell, and she was the one who brought the idea of magical danger to his attention."

"Why would she do that?" Jonah asked. "She could have become a target herself. Mortals haven't been consistently obsessed with the idea of magic over the years. In fact, they've been pretty consistent about trying to kill it with fire for years. And I mean by burning people they've suspected of using magic at the stake. Even if one is immortal, I would assume that being burned alive would still hurt like the dickens."

He had a point.

Geoffrey nodded. "She still felt like she was a human, and so she felt like she needed to protect them. Look, we can stay here and keep talking about old times, which could be fun, but it's not going to protect us from *that*." He pointed to the growing pile of slither in the backyard.

"So what do we do about that?" I said. "I wouldn't mind burning that at the stake. I hate snakes."

Jonah snorted. "I've got a plan." He didn't elaborate, though; instead, he ran upstairs. We followed him.

He ran into the room I shared with Aiden, and threw open the window. The window in my room overlooked the backyard without a pile of snakes and toads up against it, so he could lean out and we could hear what the woman was saying.

"You have been hiding my sister from me. It's her fault I'm cursed. She needs to pay for doing this to me. You need to take me to her." More snakes and toads fell from her lips as she talked.

Jonah reached out the window and grabbed the branch of the tree outside, the one I'd climbed and hidden in as a child. He sent his magic into the tree, and I saw shoots of green popping out in a progression down the tree. He managed to get the magic to go all the way to the ground, and at first, I didn't see much of anything happening, but then I saw it.

There was green creeping up the woman's legs. I didn't even think she saw it at first, but it crept up her body to her waist and then her torso, before covering her mouth and muffling her words. The stream of toads and snakes stopped pouring out of her mouth.

"I don't know how long I can hold it, Janie," Jonah said, some strain in his voice. "But it gives you a few moments to figure out your next step."

Mia ran to the phone. "I'm calling the police and animal control. Someone's got to corral the snakes. I don't know if they're poisonous or not, but we have neighbors with pets who will need to go out and tinkle. We don't want to be the cause of the entire neighborhood losing their pets to a snake infestation at our house."

She was right. But how were we going to explain where they had all come from? It was summer. I couldn't even blame it on a fraternity prank, because the local colleges weren't in session in July. "We won't explain. We'll just indicate that someone is playing a prank on us and we don't know who it is."

"How do we explain her, then, and how do we keep her from opening her mouth when they get here?" Allie asked.

Mia put down the phone. "Oh."

"Geoffrey," I called.

He hadn't followed us up the stairs, but instead was pacing in the living room. I saw him pacing when I went to the head of the stairs after he didn't answer the first time. "Geoffrey, do you know how to contact the Snow Queen without leaving the house?"

He nodded. "Got a mirror I can use?"

"Sure. We've got plenty. What kind do you need?"

"One big enough that I can see her and see where she's at." was the answer.

I hadn't known she'd be able to communicate via mirror, but if it meant not having to trip over the foot-high pile of snakes in the backyard, I'd give him whatever mirror he wanted, and I said so.

"Janie, once I open a mirror to be used in this way, she can use it to see you and whatever you are doing at any time. You might not want to use one in a bedroom that anyone is using."

Good tip, I thought. I pointed him in the direction of the guest room where my dress was hanging, the one no one was using for sleep. There was an old dresser there with a mirror on top, one big enough that I had used it from time to time to step backwards in the room and see myself from the chest down to make sure I looked okay before stepping out of the house for the day. There was also a full length mirror on its own stand that he could use, one that I'd bought at a garage sale a couple of months ago, to use on my wedding day, to see my dress in full length before going outside. I looked forward to a couple of pictures of me in my wedding dress standing in front of it. "Pick what works. No one sleeps in the room unless we have guests. And we can always cover the mirror, or move it to the attic once you've figured out which one works for you."

He nodded, turning towards the full length mirror. I cringed, but at this moment, I was more concerned about getting help than I was about what mirror I took wedding pictures in front of.

Geoffrey placed his hands on the mirror's smooth glass and said a few words in a language I didn't recognize. The mirror clouded for a few moments, and the Snow Queen appeared in the reflection.

"You rang?" she said.

It made me feel better to see that she was less formal than she could have been. We were about to ask a pretty big favor, so being friendly and casual helped the little knot in my stomach that always resulted when I was negotiating with magical leaders.

I deferred to Geoffrey. I really didn't want to be the one negotiating because I didn't want to be the one taking on debts to a magical leader. I already owed her for the save from the Seawitch. Geoffrey owed her for saving Aiden's life a year ago. He took the lead without a question.

"Your Majesty, we have a bit of a problem. Madeline has appeared in the backyard and is spewing toads and snakes and demanding help in locating her sister."

"Madeline?" she exclaimed, acting thoroughly surprised. "I thought we had her tied up with our magical security detail."

"Magical security?" I asked, before I could help myself. "Security from what?"

She laughed. "You think you're the only one who might have a problem with securing their own backyard? We know we can't stop anyone and everyone who wants to come to our realm and finds a portal, but we are trying to prevent those who might be trying to harm us."

"Have you had a rash of invaders or burglars that I haven't heard about?" I asked.

She smiled. "No, we haven't. But we have had some uninvited visitors a few times. I'm not just talking about when you and your cohorts came to see us. You have at least negotiated in good faith. More and more people are learning about our existence these days, looking for us, not realizing we aren't looking to take in humans."

Wait a minute.

Some of the members of her court did like to entrap humans.

Some of them liked to eat humans. Others of them liked toying with them, keeping them in the magical realm until they went crazy and stopped eating or sleeping or just lost touch with reality when they got to the other realm. Magic would make a human insane if they stayed in the magical realm too long. Most humans who went to a magical realm for an hour or a day, or even a week, would be fine by the time they came back, if they had been smart about going. By smart, I mean, taking their own food and water and not accepting anything to eat or drink from a magical being. Such an action might be seen as an obligation that needed to be repaid, putting the mortal who accepted it in the debt of the one who accepted it.

"What was Madeline doing to help you with security?" I asked.

Geoffrey turned to me. "She doesn't have to answer that for you. I can. She was speaking at the edge of the court's holdings to fill a moat with snakes. It's a security measure that she can perform easily, so she was asked to be useful."

Useful. That was one way to put it. So what did they do with her when she wasn't being useful?

CHAPTER FIFTEEN

"What does Madeline do when she isn't helping to fill your moat?" I asked.

Geoffrey spoke up again. "The court has ordered her into silence to prevent the overwhelming of our space with her gift."

Made sense. And no question in my mind that Madeline was using the brief respite given from that order to come looking for anyone who might know the whereabouts of her sister. So who had given her the information that any of us might have about her sister, Gabriella? Who pointed her at us? That was a good question for the Snow Queen, and I asked it.

"Well, I'd love to take credit for the answer, Janie Grimm, but the truth is I don't know for sure. I can guess, but I don't want to claim a boon from you for a guess you could come up with yourself."

My stepmother would have pointed her my way. But why? It didn't take much for me to figure that Evangeline was trying to scare me out of the house. She had her invitation for the wedding. If she could force me to move the ceremony, even better. I'm sure she was trying to force it inside the house, where she might be able to slip away and do something I didn't want her to do. What if I moved it elsewhere? She could claim she didn't know it had been moved and come into the house, claiming she had an invitation that had not been revoked. Any of those scenarios got her what she wanted; inside my house.

"Is it possible she's left something magical in the house we haven't detected? We closed the portal in the basement. Is it possible there's a portal that we don't know about?" I asked.

"Better questions. I'm sure your friends have ways of detecting magic we don't. If they haven't swept the house for magical traps, you're not as smart as I thought."

Okay, we had swept individual items we were giving away or selling. I don't think we'd specifically swept each room. I guess I'd kinda assumed that we'd covered the house by sweeping all the things, but apparently we hadn't. I tried to keep a poker face as I panicked inside at what we might have missed.

"Look, we've got a bigger problem. I need to get Madeline back under wraps and get the wildlife out of the back yard before the neighbors freak, the cops show up, or before they kill the lawn so bad that I've got to move the wedding," I said.

I heard Jonah yelling from the other room that he couldn't hold it much longer. "Can you help us?" I asked.

She nodded in the mirror, and waved a hand at a junior court member standing behind her. "I'll have my people remove the snakes from your backyard and Madeline will be removed to our court. She has stepped outside the bounds of my permission, and will be punished for it. Our court member has caused you this grief, so we will do that much to remedy it. I'm sorry that it does not fix your lawn."

It occurred to me that Jonah may be able to do something about the lawn before the wedding, if we didn't burn him out before then. "Sooner would be better," I commented.

She smiled. "My aides are on their way. It should be cleared up within the hour."

She didn't know about Jonah or his abilities, or what he was currently doing. She couldn't honestly believe we'd stopped it; she'd believe that the snakes and toads were still pouring out of Madeline's mouth. I nodded at the Snow Queen and Geoffrey and ran out of the room, followed closely by Allie.

Jonah was sweating when I burst into the room where he was still holding Madeline hostage using the grass at her feet.

"You can let her go, Jonah. The Snow Queen is sending someone to retrieve her. Luckily, we don't seem to owe her anything for the assist. She's taking responsibility as the woman out there is a member of her court, acting outside of the permission she had to use her powers. They're going to clear out the snakes and toads and take the woman. No need to hold her unless she does something stupid."

"Not sure I can recast this if I need to, Janie, if I let it go." He said, faintly strained.

"It's okay, Jonah," I said. "Let it go."

He dropped what power he was using, and Madeline began talking again, screaming her demands loud enough for the neighbors to complain. I didn't say anything to her, or to Jonah, but turned to Allie, and told her to head downstairs and shut off the outside lights. Not only to prevent the neighbors from seeing Madeline, or her snakes and toads, but also from seeing the Snow Queen's minions, when they came to clean up the joint. It wouldn't do to expose magic while trying to cover up the magic we didn't want exposed. He collapsed on the bed, which made me wish I'd actually made it this morning. I felt like a slob with everyone in my room, and the bed unmade.

While Geoffrey spoke with the Snow Queen, the rest of us watched Madeline piling up the snakes and toads in the yard. I heard a faint crack, and wondered if the sliding glass doors in the kitchen were still holding. I really hadn't budgeted to replace them, and wondered how much that might cost. We had to have secure doors on the back of the house. Regardless of cost, we would have to find a way to get those fixed, and sooner, rather than later.

The Snow Queen was as good as her word. Less than twenty minutes after Geoffrey had touched the mirror, three men appeared in my backyard. I didn't see where they had come from, but I hadn't seen a portal and hadn't smelled magic. I just hadn't seen them walk up. They waded through the piles of snakes as if they weren't afraid of being bitten. Two of them grabbed Madeline's arms and the third said something and waved his hand in front of her mouth. The backyard was suddenly silent, other than slithering and croaking; she stopped talking. I blinked, and the snakes and toads were gone. I liked that kind of clean up method. Wonder if it was a magic I could learn for doing dishes? Or laundry?

They escorted Madeline off the property, and though she looked decidedly uncomfortable and unhappy, she was still silent. I'd take it. I didn't really want to take the risk that her escorts wouldn't fix my yard a second time.

Except that the yard wasn't completely fixed. The grass was flattened and there were deep furrows in the yard where the larger snakes had lain with the weight of other snakes and toads on top of them. Anyone walking through that yard in high heels was likely to trip, fall, and break an ankle, if not more. Aiden would likely break his neck if he tried to walk through the yard without getting it fixed.

I sighed. Madeline had accomplished her goal. I was going to have to move the wedding; I wasn't going to be home to even try to get the yard rolled and seeded, and even if I did, there wouldn't be time for it all to grow in. I couldn't help it, a single frustrated tear rolled down my face.

Aiden saw it, and took me in his arms. "What's wrong, honey?" he asked.

I told him my concerns about someone trying to torpedo our backyard wedding ceremony, and getting us to make our house vulnerable to someone who might try to exploit our wedding invitation as a way to get into the house. I told him about Evangeline being free to come to the wedding, and no longer in lock down like I'd thought. I ended by telling him how concerned I was I couldn't afford to fix the sliding doors with all the wedding costs, and wasn't sure the backyard could be brought up to snuff in six days.

"Janie, you're not the only one that can work on this," he said.

I gave him a confused look.

"Jonah and I are here this week while you're taking the bar exam. You guys will be taking the exam during the day and studying during the night, I know, but Jonah and I can spend some of that time working on the yard. I know Harold has a heavy roller we can use to level it out and I know he'll let us borrow it, especially this week, to prepare for the wedding." He rubbed my back as he talked, and I calmed down some. I was still getting used to having someone else I could count on, even though we'd been together for nearly three years. Our breakup a year or so ago had gotten into my head more than I'd thought. I still kept trying to do everything on my own and not relying on him to be there. I knew that was my own issue; he'd always been there for me, even when we'd been apart.

Even if he got the yard rolled, smoothing out the furrows and divots left behind, the grass wasn't fixed. The flowerbeds I'd planted earlier in the year to give them time to fill in and bloom for the wedding were likely crushed or dead. Who knew what other damage there might be to the garage or the back fence. I mentioned my concern, and thanked him for trying.

"Janie, you're forgetting something if you're worrying about the yard or the plants," Jonah said.

Holy shit, he was right. "Can you do anything with them, after the amount of magic you just used today? Or is that going to be too much?" I asked.

He smiled. "A year ago, I'd have said I couldn't do it. I didn't know how much I could do and I was always afraid I'd lose control of it and things would get out of hand. Now, after working with that ability for a year, and knowing I've got just shy of a week to get it done? I'm pretty sure I can get it all back to where it was, if not better, before Friday night, for the rehearsal. If Aiden can get that roller, and we can fix the doors and do any painting, I can do a little at a time through the week and not completely knock myself out."

"We need to know how bad it is, first, before you make that promise," Mia said, clearly trying to protect him.

Jonah looked out the window, pointing as he spoke. "Look, the grass isn't that bad. It would probably fix itself within a few weeks. I know, you don't have that kind of time, but that's just boosting and hurrying the process that would already happen. That won't take a lot of effort, and I'd probably do it as soon as we were done leveling the yard. The flowerbeds, if you look straight down, yeah, they're crushed, but I can bring back some, if not all of them. If I can bring back more than half of them, we can thin them out, maybe see if there are any plants still in the stores to fill in the difference. You didn't buy expensive plants. I'm sure we wouldn't need more than a flat or two, maybe forty bucks, to get them back to where you had them. I see some scrapes on the side of the garage. At worst, we'd need to repaint that side, but that can't take more than two buckets of paint, call it maybe fifty bucks. So, assuming the sliding glass doors aren't bad, the fix isn't expensive, we can do all of it, except the flowerbeds, in an afternoon; the rest over the course of the week. Aiden and I can take care of it. Let us."

He was right. I needed to let go. I didn't have to be in charge of all of it, and I didn't have to micromanage anything. I had to start letting them do it, especially Aiden. I had to stop expecting that something else would come up to torpedo the wedding, and our relationship.

Damn, I hadn't realized I was still holding my breath quite that much. But I was. It was why I'd refused to move the wedding back, why I'd wanted to get married almost as soon as I felt like I could. I was worried that I could still lose him, but looking up at Aiden in that moment, I knew it was going to take more than I'd given him credit for.

I knew I loved that man for a reason.

CHAPTER SIXTEEN

We came downstairs, slowly, almost expecting something else to go wrong before we could get to the kitchen, but nothing happened. Mia checked the front yard, and it looked completely untouched, as if the snakes and toads had never gone past the driveway; weird if I thought about how high they'd been stacked in the backyard.

The sliding glass door had a small crack towards the bottom, but it didn't go all the way through the glass and it didn't go all the way from one side to another. Allie brought up the idea of calling one of the glass places that repaired car windshields, to see if they could seal it to prevent a further crack rather than having to replace the entire pane of glass, and she went off to make that call.

Jonah and Aiden went outside, walking the perimeter of the yard to see how bad it was. It wasn't as bad as I'd thought, but definitely needed work before Saturday. Aiden called Harold, who offered to help as well as lend us lawn equipment, and they made a plan to start on all of it on Tuesday, when Harold was free to come over and help them. Jonah started doing what he could with the plants in the flowerbeds, and brought back two or three better than ever before saying he had to stop because he had a headache. Given the amount of magic he'd thrown around; I didn't blame him. I had a headache just from the stress of it all.

Since they'd all offered to do so much work, and it wasn't going to cost anywhere near what I thought it would, I offered to order pizza for everyone. It was the least I could do, and no one really felt like cooking dinner. It was already evening, and no one had had a square meal all day. Pizza might not be the most nutritious, but hey, it hit all the food groups with crust, cheese, tomato sauce, and pepperoni. I was even willing to add a few extra vegetables to make sure it was a decent meal, but we needed hot and filling, and likely a good night's sleep before anything else could come up.

Marco's Piazza was close by and a local favorite, and I ordered probably more than I should have. The boys went to pick it up, and also picked up some beer to go with it. Mia and I stayed away from the beer, but otherwise it was a good night. Geoffrey had never had pizza before, and he enjoyed the novelty, as well as the time with his son.

I tried to make sure everyone was caught up on everything I'd found out, relying on Bert to fill in the gaps.

"So, we still don't know exactly who is after the items Perrault stashed away?" Aiden asked.

Geoffrey stepped in. "Well, we have a list of suspects. There are some pretty powerful things hidden with that treasure trove. We know Queen Eva wants in the house, or at least wants to be here for the wedding to start something. We know Madeline thinks we know how to get to her sister. And we know the Queen of Hearts is in on Queen Eva's plan to get to the wedding, so we can't completely count her out. So what do we do?"

"I still have questions, Dad," Aiden said. "Where is Madeline's sister? Did you know her? And why is she still so obsessed with revenge?"

"Like I said before, Madeline believes it's Gabriella's fault she has snakes and frogs dripping from her mouth instead of Gabriella's gifts of diamonds and pearls. Gab had nothing to do with it. It's Maddy's fault because she's a selfish spoiled brat. Gabriella did nothing wrong. She was nice to an old lady in the woods who happened to be a fairy that gifted her with unlimited riches."

Unlimited riches. That's what Bert had mentioned that Geoffrey had when he was a teenager, about the time Gabriella had received her gift. I'd realized it earlier, but I hadn't finished asking all the questions I had. And now he was referring to them as Gab and Maddy.

"So how well did you know the sisters when you were younger, Geoffrey?" I asked. If it looked like he was hiding something important, I'd ask him again, later, in private.

He went red, as he chewed on a pizza crust. "I dated Gabriella when I was a teenager. We were pretty close for a long time, and then we decided it wasn't going to work. We were friends when we parted, but it was during the time that we were together that Perrault put together his items to hide and his spell to hide them. She financed the help with her riches; and she staked me in getting my start in the court."

I remembered hearing about nobility in England buying commissions in the army for their sons. I wondered if he was talking about something similar, but I realized he would probably have to have materials to get his start in the court as a tailor without being seen as just a clone of his father. I would have wanted to stand on my own two feet as well, and if I'd had a friend with an unlimited budget willing to stake me in such an endeavor? Well, I think I'd have had a hard time saying no to that kind of help.

"So what happened to Gabriella?" I asked. "You said she was immortal now, but where is she?"

"I don't know," Geoffrey said. "I haven't seen her in four hundred years. I do know, however, that she got herself named the guardian of the items that were hidden. She took a vow to protect those items with her life from any who would try to use them for evil. She went with them into hiding when the spell was cast. I haven't seen her since."

Aiden gave me a strange look. "Janie, you already knew that. How did you know that?"

I shook my head. "I didn't know it, not for sure, but I guessed. You didn't?"

"No. I knew, of course, that Dad had other girlfriends before he met Mom, and I'm sure he's dated since then, because I'm not stupid, and they haven't been together for a long time, or I've been completely blind and they've been hiding it, although I'm not sure why they would. I'd heard that Dad had been around the block a time or two when he was younger, but I hadn't heard any names, so I just chalked it up to Dad being pretty discreet."

I smiled. "I'd heard something about your Dad having access to an unlimited purse when he was younger, and when I asked around, there weren't any artifacts that did that. When I heard what Gabriella's gift was, I knew there had to be some kind of relationship there, even if it was just friendship. I just put it together earlier today. I'd have told you if it was something I've known for longer."

He nodded at me. He really should have known better.

Geoffrey also seemed relieved. He hadn't had to explain the wild child rumors to his son. If Aiden hadn't heard them on his own; he hadn't heard it from me, and I'd kept my promise.

I, however, was exhausted. There's only so much drama one can cram into a single day. I'd planned a quiet day of relaxing, studying, and last minute wedding detail checking. Instead, I'd gotten a magical attack, a magical emergency, family drama, and a frog who was still suffering the effects of too much icing. He'd waved off the beer the boys had brought back, and hadn't eaten much of the pizza. I heard Allie chastising him in a whisper for making himself sick, but she didn't act like she was mad; instead she acted like she was concerned. He seemed to enjoy her fussing and her attention.

It made me think that there had to be a better way to protect him, and maybe find a way to make him human again. I'd have to talk to Aiden about it. I wondered if we could replicate the potion that had made him human a few years ago, and whether he could take it again. I'd have to ask if there was a way to find that out.

By the time the pizza was eaten, the beer was consumed, and the mess cleaned up, I was almost asleep on my feet. Aiden told me I needed to crash, and I resisted until he promised to go with me.

We headed for the stairs, even though it was barely eight o'clock in the evening. Aiden sat down on the bed in our room as I pulled out my pajamas and headed for the attached bathroom to brush my teeth.

"So where had you heard about Dad and his unlimited purse?"

Crap.

"Bert was around when your dad was a teenager. He told me he'd heard about it, and then wondered if your dad had any other information that might be important." That seemed safe.

"I'll never speak to him again if he's been hiding information that could get us all killed. He's too closed up when it's important, and then he wants credit when he actually coughs up information. He's more concerned about his image than what's right or what's necessary a lot of the time." He sounded angry.

With a mouthful of toothpaste, I stuck my head back in the bedroom. "I don't think he's hiding anything important. I don't think he realized he might have information about the Perrault stuff. Bert was the one saying he might remember who was around, but he also said he wasn't around all the time, and he wasn't involved with the actual meetings or the spell. I think he just brought it up to see if there was anything he wasn't thinking of, or someone who might be a suspect that he didn't realize was involved," I explained.

He shrugged, coming over to where I stood in the doorway. He wrapped his arms around me and gave me a kiss, ignoring the toothpaste foam at the corners of my mouth. "You know about Dad's past, don't you?"

I shook my head. "What are you talking about?"

"Dad was the party animal when he was a kid. Rumor had it he was a wild child, a real off the walls kind of crazy. I asked around when I was a kid. Wasn't easy to get people to talk about him, and he wouldn't say a word, but there were enough people around who had heard the gossip and didn't care about repeating it to his kid. I even had a friend of mine ask around to those people who felt kind of weird about talking to me. There's stories about him with an unlimited purse, throwing money out of windows at street fairs. There's even a story that he's the one that started the Mardi Gras tradition of throwing beads to topless women. He was a drunk, used whatever drugs were available at the time, and was in and out of brothels and red light districts for years. I heard stories about all kinds of depraved things he did there; things I wouldn't want to even think about."

"He didn't want to admit anything like that in front of you. And I hadn't even heard the details. I think he just wants you to think good of him, especially since you've been closer lately than you've been in years. Why did you leave the courts, Aiden? I'm not complaining, because it obviously led you here to me, but what was it that made that decision for you, and kept you from talking to your dad for so long?" I turned back into the bathroom to spit out the toothpaste and rinse out my mouth.

"He was blackmailing other members of the court to allow me to rise in court standing. He tried to get me to train to be a tailor like him, but I wasn't interested in it. I was there to spend time with him, not to watch my political star rise. He makes it sound like I was going to stay there forever, but I'd never planned that. I just wanted to know my dad. He took it as a rejection of everything he stood for when I just wanted to spend time with him. The sad part is that I think part of his wildness when he was younger was exactly the same rejection of his father's pushing him, but he ended up going into the family business anyway."

That was interesting. Fathers and sons. I'd seen so many friends rebel against their well-meaning fathers and never understood it; but then again, I was a girl and my father wasn't the type to push me into his own field. He wanted me to find myself, regardless of what I ended up doing for a living, and had been so proud of me when I'd gotten accepted to law school. I'd been able to share that much with him before he died. What would life have been like if he'd pushed me relentlessly into going into academia, into teaching, into the study of linguistics and folklore? He knew our family history, and likely suspected there was more to it than just an interesting footnote in the family tree. Why hadn't he pushed me into his field? It would have been highly useful with everything that had come up in the last few years.

Because he hadn't fully believed it himself, and had spent time in a mental hospital after my mother disappeared, thinking himself crazy. He wouldn't have wanted to paint me with the same brush, so he'd been happy to encourage me as far away from all of that as he could. How much was Evangeline's influence? She'd subtly worked to cloud my memory for years. Had she also tried to push my father into pushing me away from the field that might help me to piece together the clues to stop her from ending my father's life, not realizing it wouldn't get her what she wanted?

I smiled at Aiden. "Does your father know that you didn't plan to stay in the magical realm when you came to see him as a teenager?"

"He never asked."

Sigh. How much of my life would be easier if people would speak up instead of staying silent, convinced that others knew exactly what they were thinking?

Of course, I couldn't say much. I was guilty of the exact same thing.

CHAPTER SEVENTEEN

We went to bed early that night. There had been too much drama and too much family, too much last minute wedding snafus and too much in the way of magical shenanigans. I was exhausted. Aiden must have been as well, because we were both asleep in minutes.

The next day was a whirlwind of studying, packing of lunch for Mia and I the next day for the first bar exam day, research into Charles Perrault, working on the yard, and last minute wedding details. The day was a bit of a blur by the time it was all said and done, but we were prepared for the first craziness of the week; the bar exam.

Tuesday morning dawned bright and early. Mia and I had to be on the road by six-thirty in the morning in order to beat the rush hour traffic into downtown Columbus. The bar exam was held every year in a hall in Veterans' Memorial Auditorium, just minutes from the Supreme Court Building itself. I wasn't sure how tight parking was going to be, so I had us arriving ridiculously early. We could always do some last minute cramming in the parking lot if need be. I woke up and hurried to get ready, heading downstairs to have a cup of coffee and a quick bowl of cereal to calm the nervous stomach. If I didn't eat something, and something bland, I would be sick to my stomach before noon on a day this important.

Mia apparently thought the same; she grabbed the box of cereal out of my hands the minute I finished pouring it in my bowl. We munched in silence, the boys still asleep, until Bert came into the kitchen. "I'm coming with you guys."

We looked at each other, with perfect understanding. There was no need. I said so.

"I'm coming with you guys. You will be distracted; you won't be behind a threshold, and you'll be tired on the way home." He seemed determined.

"It's a steel frame on the car. There are tons of witnesses at the bar. We have salt and nails in our pockets to protect from magic, and there are two aluminum baseball bats in the Escalade. There isn't much else we can do to protect ourselves without violating the concealed carry laws in Ohio." Mia explained. "What do you plan to do if something showed up? No offense, Bert, but you don't have magical powers and you can't swing one of the bats."

"I can make a phone call," he said. "I can sit in the car and call your cell phone if something happens outside."

"We're not allowed to have our phones in the exam. Even if we did sneak them in, and you called, we can't leave during the exam or we forfeit the test and we have to wait until February to take it again. So tell me how that helps?" I asked.

"I'm still going with you." He was being stubborn.

"What could you possibly hope to accomplish by sitting in the car all day? It's July. It'll be hot. It's probably not all that healthy for you to be in the car that long. The heat is going to be too much for you."

"I'll sit in your backpack."

"Why is it so important that you be there with me today, Bert?" I asked. "Is something going on?" I would have thought that he would find it more important to stay with Allie. I wasn't romantically involved with him, and our attacker the night before didn't ask for him; she'd asked for her sister. I asked him why he didn't want to stay with his girlfriend.

He coughed. "Well, I know Allie's staying home today. She doesn't work tonight, and she promised to stay inside the house and work on your birdseed packets and program inserts. Jonah and Aiden are working on the yard today with Harold and Stanley, and they'll be armed, as well as close enough to be within a salt line if not to dive inside if something should happen. Doris has agreed not to come to the house today, she'll be working on catering things at her own house, and Alfred is coming over to try to come up with a plan for security during the wedding. This place is covered. You two are going to be distracted. Someone needs to be looking out for you. That's my job. I'm the warning system while you two are obsessing about essay questions and multi-state multiple choice."

You know, he did have a point. I know I'd be concentrating with only half a brain, part of me worried about what might be happening over my shoulder.

He kept going, unaware of my internal monologue. "Look, Janie, you and Mia need to concentrate. I can be trying to sense magic from your backpack. If you put the bag right at your leg, I can reach out and grab your leg or your socks if I sense something, and you can concentrate on the test while I concentrate on seeing if anything is coming after you."

I considered for a moment. It wasn't a bad idea. In fact, it was a pretty darn good idea. I said yes, and allowed him into the bag I was taking. I wondered if they would check bags, and decided I probably ought to take a tea towel or something to wrap him up in just in case. I didn't know what security might say if they saw a frog in my bag, or whether they'd let me in because he didn't have answers tattooed on his back. I wondered just how crazy they'd think it was, or if they were used to people bringing in good luck charms of whatever kind for the biggest exam of most people's lives.

We got Bert situated and grabbed our packed lunches out of the refrigerator, heading out to the garage. He was quiet as I slid in the driver's seat and started the Escalade. In fact, he didn't say a word until we were outside of Dayton, heading east on Interstate 70 towards Columbus, the early morning traffic just starting to pick up for rush hour.

"Has Geoffrey said who might have been around when the spell was cast?" he asked.

"No," I answered. "He did tell us, however, that he had a relationship with Gabriella, and that was the unlimited purse that was funding his wild days."

"I'm telling you, he was in and out a lot, but I think he knows more than he's letting on."

"Bert, what else do you know? You're hinting around a lot. You're not exactly being subtle here. What else do you know that I don't?" Mia asked.

He sighed. I signaled I was going to merge to avoid going onto Interstate 270, the outer belt around Columbus that would have taken me to the airport. Instead, I was trying to get downtown, but traffic was picking up fairly quickly. Lucky we had left as early as we did; it was looking like there was a serious traffic jam up ahead. In good traffic, we probably only had about fifteen minutes to go; it was looking like it would take twice that to get off the highway.

"Janie, Mia, I think the person that's after the treasure Perrault hid away is either the witch who cursed me, or related to her. I think she's after the treasure because she wants Gabriella, but I also think she wants a few other things as well."

"Like what?" I asked. Leave it to him to drop a bombshell like that while we were driving in rush hour traffic, with other things on our brains. Only Bert would pull this. I kept my hands at ten and two on the wheel to keep from wrapping them around his throat.

"Well, she wants the cat's boots; she wants the glass slippers; she wants the spinning wheel's spindle; she wants the magic rose; she wants the bloody keys. She wants all the other paraphernalia involved in Perrault's work. She wants them all because she's going to cast a spell to harness all of the magical energy in the mortal realm in order to take over. She wants to rule the human realm. As a queen. And she won't be a benevolent ruler. She's the reason why I was turned into a frog, and she's been planning this kind of coup for a really, really long time."

"What do you mean?" I asked.

"She wasn't even magical to begin with. She's using magic to keep herself alive long enough to get revenge."

"Who is she? Who does she want revenge on?" Mia asked. "Cut to the chase, here, Bert."

"Her name is Clorinda. She was a mortal at one point, with some magical talent; but her younger stepsister bested her with magic and with love, and she vowed revenge. Clorinda was able to take on enough magics to make herself immortal and then started working on building up clout and money and power. She spent years looking for her sister's shoes and effects after she died, but we had already hidden them away a long time ago. She started by just blaming her sister, but her sister lived a full, happy life, and died peacefully in her sleep, so Clorinda started blaming those who had thwarted her revenge. That kept growing and growing, until she blamed everyone. She thinks all humans owe her servitude now, that they all owe her for slights, real or imagined, that were visited upon her by all of our own ancestors, and no one is safe."

"Wait a minute," I said. "I feel like I should know this. Did you say stepsister, and shoes?"

He nodded.

Hot damn. The person that was after Bert was one of Cinderella's step-sisters. And was also the witch who had cursed my friend, Bert. And she was back. After us, and it wasn't just Bert she was after, but anyone and everyone alive on the planet.

Talk about big goals.

CHAPTER EIGHTEEN

It was a good thing we were still early, even with the rush hour traffic, because parking at Veterans' Memorial was insane. We found a parking spot without a lot of trouble, but the line of cars behind us filled up the empty spaces quickly. I made a mental note that we needed to continue to drive over this early, and maybe even earlier, to make sure we were parking near the building, rather than having to ride a commuter bus to a secondary parking lot at the end of the day. I just didn't like the idea of being that far away from the wheels in the midst of a magical emergency. Even if the place was completely gridlocked at the end of the day, which I expected it would be, sitting inside of a steel framed vehicle was safer than standing on the sidewalk waiting for the bus with no idea how long we'd have to stand and wait.

Bert was quiet inside my bag. I'd carried a larger purse instead of a backpack, which was a little weird for me, after three years of living out of a backpack, but the security monitors were allowing women to keep their purses with them instead of in a cubby outside with the pile of backpacks. It made me wonder if there had been a security concern with the backpacks in the past. Why would someone make the bar exam a target? Then again, if someone had taken that test multiple times in the past, I could see the frustration building on someone who wasn't tightly enough wrapped to truly understand that they were likely either not able to pass the test or maybe not using the right study methods.

And law students, well, the amount of competition and type-A personalities involved? That was enough neuroses for many crazy acts. We'd seen people practically sabotage research materials in the library in the first year to prevent others from finding the correct sources. We'd seen computer lab outages in our second year, as we'd all been working in the lab on projects. There had been a sneaking suspicion that someone had purposely cut the power to put others further behind. There were plenty of tales about stolen notes, pilfered outlines, and swiped textbooks all over the school. Most of the law students wouldn't have ever considered anything like that in their pre-law school days, but there were plenty of desperate people once the stress levels got high enough, that normal societal constraints just went out the window. And the stress levels didn't get higher than the bar exam.

We went inside, and got seats near each other, setting out our pencils and erasers and ink pens and blue books to be ready for the first round. And nothing crazy happened.

The bar exam in Ohio consists of twelve essays, two hundred multiple choice questions, and one practical application that generally consisted of writing a legal brief with an argument, based on research given during the exam. That doesn't sound like a lot, but each individual essay could take nearly an hour, and the multiple-choice questions didn't always have a clear answer. It was generally finding the most correct answer out of a number of answers that were varying degrees of related to the right choice. It was easy to get yourself confused and tripped up, thinking too far outside of the box for the multiple choice questions. The essay questions weren't much easier; they involved trying to think through every angle of every legal issue and all the possible pitfalls and arguments as to why each and every concept might or might not apply.

It would last three days, with sessions in the morning and afternoon.

The head proctor got up and started in with us, pointing out the restrooms and informing us that we should try to go during breaks, or have a proctor accompany us to prevent anyone accusing us of cheating, or trying to cheat by leaving the room. There was a discussion of what to do in the event of an emergency, such as a fire or a tornado (hey, it was Ohio, after all. We did get tornados from time to time). There were instructions about medical emergencies, and I looked to my right when they talked about that. There was a woman so obviously pregnant that it looked like she could go into labor at any time sitting still and calm and about to take the test with us. It would be my luck that she would, and a magical emergency would come up at the same time. I just didn't trust that we could get through the entire three days without something completely messed up happening. That, and there were always horror stories about someone having a medical emergency and those who took the test getting up to help them and not getting extra time to finish, or failing the exam due to the distraction. I didn't know what was worse, not getting the extra time after helping someone, or ignoring an obvious problem in the sake of not failing the test. Whether those were true, or whether they were tall tales told by stressed out law school grads was up for debate, but they were stories repeated by lawyers to law students to each other for years, adding to the pressure and the stress

The head proctor had the others hand out the paperwork for the first exam question, and we waited for the official time to begin. When they started the clock and we opened the slim booklet with the prompt for the essay, I was glad to see it was contracts, and a question about unilateral and bilateral contracts, along with identifying terms of promise and performance. It was a question I felt comfortable with, given my experience in litigating such issues in front of my stepmother's court the first year of law school. I finished with ten minutes to spare, and took advantage of the extra time to turn in the booklet before making a move towards the restroom. Maybe I shouldn't have had so much coffee on the way here.

When I returned to my table, my purse was still on the floor, and Bert was napping quietly inside. Regardless of whether or not he was actually paying attention for magical threats or not, he wasn't causing a distraction and he was feeling useful. I still had time to spare, so I thought through what he'd said on the way.

According to what he'd told us, Cinderella was dead, having lived a full life and dying in her sleep as an old lady. Her stepsister had gotten the power to be immortal in order to obtain revenge, but had failed to do so before her sister died, and blamed everyone else for her failure. If Clorinda really was the one at fault, and she really was the one who was causing all of this to happen, I wondered who had had the glass slippers sent to my house. It seemed to me those would have been at the top of the list of things she would have wanted to own, to possess that which her sister had gotten ahead of her, but someone had set them on my doorstep instead.

Someone else was involved here, or someone was acting to bring us into this loop. If Clorinda was so invested in her plan of revenge, it wasn't something she'd cooked up last week, last month, or even last year. It was something she'd been on for decades, probably centuries. If that was the case, then there was no way that my friends and I could have been on her hit list, except for Bert. And if Bert was truly the target, and the means of keeping such a thing silent and protected, there was no way he'd have dragged them out of the hiding place that had worked for so long just to freak me out right before the bar exam and the wedding.

Someone else was in play. Was it my stepmother, looking for an ally? She'd been incarcerated for a long time for her actions against me. I didn't believe for one instant that she had turned a new leaf and was ready to forgive and forget. The Queen of Hearts, well, I'd liberated her from a life of solitude and incarceration, trapped in a body where the White Rabbit had drugged her into submission as part of his power grab. I had no pretensions that she and I were in any way, friends, but at the same time, I couldn't believe she'd rope all of us into a long standing revenge plot we weren't related to. I would have believed her capable of frognapping, or of trying to lure Bert away from us with horror stories of things that would be done to his friends if he didn't comply rather than an outright plot against us, which this would have to be.

Nothing happened. The first essay was over, I'd felt like I knew what I was talking about, and no magical bad guys or boogeymen were jumping out of the woodwork to come and get me. I should be happy. I should be . . . but something wasn't right.

Bert snoozed on in the purse beside me, oblivious to all but the inside of his eyelids. He wasn't much help at the moment.

We started the next round, and the next, with no further indication of magical mayhem. I thought I was concentrating the best that I could, given that I kept waiting for the other shoe to drop.

Was it just me, or was every facet of my life being ruined by the anticipation of the next magical emergency? I couldn't think about that now; the test that I'd studied for, for the past three years was at hand, and I couldn't risk worrying about it so much that I failed.

I just couldn't bring myself to face that.

I'd prefer a monster to the idea of failing the bar exam. I just hoped the monsters would hold off long enough for me to finish the multi-state section.

CHAPTER NINETEEN

Lunch came, and Mia and I headed outside, to eat our brown bagged lunches on a small spot of grass outside the building. Some people tried to head out to pick up fast food, but we didn't want to take the risk of not getting back in time and not being allowed back into the building; if we were late, we wouldn't be allowed to sit for that next session, all but guaranteeing a failure.

There were others sitting around, talking about the bar exam, obsessing over the details and trying to determine if they'd guessed right on all the issues, or whether they'd missed a detail or an argument that could mean success or failure. I thought they were nuts. After all the classes and lectures and studying and bar prep and then the exam, I figured everyone would be sick of each topic, and would be happy to move on to the next one, but I was wrong. Law students are Type A, obsessive personalities, and they don't ever seem to know how to let something go. They chew over a reason to stress out like a dog with a really meaty, marrow filled bone, and they don't let it go until well after every smidge of flavor is long gone. I'd known law students who had done this after finals, but after several rounds of this, I'd learned that obsessing over the details of a test that was over did nothing to make me feel better about how I did. All it did was make me feel like an utter loser, more than anything else I could do as a human being in that instant.

So why do that to yourself? I didn't want to, and thankfully, Mia felt the same way.

We passed the hour's break with ham and cheese sandwiches and furtive discussions with Bert about the state of things at home. Mia finally decided to go get her cell phone out of the car and call home for an update. I'd have done it myself, but she thought of it first. She spoke to Jonah, then told me that they'd rolled out the divots and grooves in the lawn, fixed three quarters of the flowerbeds, and had spoken with the glass people about fixing the doors in the kitchen on

Thursday. Harold and Stanley had made the executive decision to bring Doris and all the wedding floofiness to my house, where she and Allie could stamp, paste, stencil, tape, and be-ribbon everything to their hearts' content, where the members of F.A.B.L.E.S. could watch out for them during the day. Other members had volunteered to go ahead and paint the outside of the garage, to cover any minute imperfections, and Aiden had called the port a john people, making arrangements for a stall to be installed on Friday afternoon. They seemed to have things well in hand, and I was grateful, although I felt completely lazy for not being there to pitch in myself. It was my house after all, and others were doing all the work on it. It just seemed like I wasn't pulling my own weight, which was, of course, ridiculous. I didn't say it was rational, just that it was how I felt.

The sky seemed to get darker as we were outside, but it was Ohio in July. It's not unheard of for us to get sudden thunderstorms at that time of the year, and as I watched the sky darken, I tried to convince myself that a summer storm was all that was going on.

Rain started just as we were packing up our trash and getting ready to head inside for the afternoon session. I didn't have a good feeling about this.

And then I saw an older woman, about thirty or thirty-five years older than I, heading inside to take the next portion of the test. It looked like she had been crying, tear tracks appearing in the wrinkles I saw around her eyes and cheeks. She was dressed more like a homeless person than I would have thought for someone taking the bar exam, but then again, I was dressed in jeans and a Ramones t-shirt I'd gotten at a garage sale, my zip up gray hoodie tied around my waist so I'd be prepared for a sudden surge in air conditioning in the middle of the summer. I wore a comfortable pair of Teva sandals; cool enough for summer, but unlikely to fall off if I had to run for my life. That had been the uncomfortable truth of most of my wardrobe choices over the last year or so; what would be serviceable in case of a magical emergency.

The woman I'd seen was wearing an ankle length peasant style skirt with heavy boots and a layered sweater look; more like a person wearing all of the clothing she owned rather than dressing smart for an indoor event in July with the potential for frigid air conditioning. Something seemed off.

As I walked towards her to check on her, she reached into her knapsack and offered me a business card; it promised Ridiculous Wishes, No Returns, Cheap Rates. Buy One Get Two Free.

Yeah, that wasn't someone here for the bar exam.

Shit.

I sniffed the air as discretely as possible. Magic has a distinctive smell, taking on the odor that is most appealing to the person smelling it. To me, it still always smelled of dusty books and stale peppermints, a smell I'd always associated with my dad, a professor of folklore and linguistics and the University of Dayton. I smelled peppermint, but it was faint, which I took to mean that even if this person was magical, they weren't using magic, or if they were, it was a small amount, and probably not enough to do more than camouflage appearance, rather than cause major harm to anyone or anything. I could handle that. I reached into my front jeans pocket, touching the baggie of salt and cheap nails I always carried these days. I could always pull it out and fling it at a magical threat. It wouldn't do a lot of harm, but it would stop most magical threats long enough for me to get away, and the car wasn't very far from where we were standing.

I accepted the card, and kept myself from the automatic "thank you" that came to my lips. My stepmother had been rigid about etiquette when I was growing up, but I knew better than to thank someone who might be magical. She nodded at me, and stepped away, without saying a word.

What made a wish ridiculous? And were other non-ridiculous wishes not allowed, or maybe they were more expensive? Maybe the rates weren't as cheap, or the buy one get two free didn't apply? Okay, that was, well, ridiculous. It wasn't like I was going to take advantage of wishes from a stranger anyway, but I needed to think about more important things, like the extremely big test I was in the midst of.

The woman walked away, toward the parking lot and away from the building and the students milling around, waiting for the afternoon session of testing to start. I handed Mia the business card.

"Certainly you're not going to use this?" she asked.

I smiled at her. "No, I don't plan to. But with everything going on, it might be worth keeping the card. Remember how the tinderbox came in handy?" The tinderbox was a magical artifact that had been lent to us when the Seawitch had been after Mia. When we'd opened it, we were under siege, and an army of tin soldiers had poured out to help protect us.

She nodded. "Smart. Never underestimate help, no matter where it might come from. Don't have to take advantage, but having an ace in the hole, or a card in your pocket, so to speak, might be a good thing. Come on, let's get back inside before they lock the doors for the afternoon."

She was right. The last of the students were heading in the doors, and we needed to hurry to make sure we weren't locked out.

We made it inside and reported back to our tables, hand sharpening our pencils and lining up erasers and good luck charms (not actual magical charms of course; I felt that would be cheating, even if the proctors wouldn't have understood how they worked or how to detect them).

When the proctor told us to start, we opened the booklets for the next essay question and began scribbling in our blue books about whether a person who shoots a man who has already jumped off a building, but hasn't landed yet, could be guilty of murder, manslaughter, or any other crime, and whether the possibility of surviving the jump would impact our analysis.

And here I thought magical conundrums were complicated.

CHAPTER TWENTY

The rest of the afternoon passed quickly, with complicated essay questions in multiple topics eating up the hours. By the time we were done for the day, we were exhausted.

"My brain feels like it's been through a sausage grinder," Mia said, as we climbed into the Escalade at the end of the day.

"You're not kidding," I said. "And to think, we have two more days of this. Maybe we should have gotten a hotel room rather than driving."

"You okay to drive?" she asked, as I put the key in the ignition.

"I am at the moment, but what's it going to be like in two days if we're this tired now?"

She didn't say much. And, of course, we hit the beginning of rush hour traffic as we merged onto the highway. I had a headache. Luckily, when we got to the edge of Columbus, on Interstate 70 near the Hilliard New Rome Road exit, I knew where we could stop for a coffee to keep us going for the rest of the drive home.

We got home, exhausted, and pulled the Escalade into the garage. Aiden and Jonah were just cleaning up their yard work as we got home.

"Hi, honey," Aiden said. "How did it go the first day?"

I filled him in on the day, and about the strange lady with the Ridiculous Wishes business card. Bert piped up. "I've heard of something about that before, but it's not a danger as long as you don't use the wishes."

Aiden gave me a sideways look.

"I haven't used them," I said. "And I don't plan to, unless we need some kind of get-out-of-jail-free card. But I'd be stupid if I threw away the card and it turned out to be the one thing we need to save our own butts. Remember how we had to use the tarts to get out of Wonderland? It was a good thing we brought them with us."

He nodded. "You're right. And it turned out that you used them to save me, too, so I can't complain too much. But don't use them unless it's an emergency."

I nodded.

Bert, unhelpfully, spoke up. "Yeah, the last time I heard about them being used, a woman ended up with a sausage hanging from her nose."

"Hanging from her nose?" I asked.

"Yeah, as if it grew from her nose."

"Um, let's not put me down for that, just yet." I said. "I'm pretty sure that isn't a feature in Brides and Weddings magazine."

Mia snorted. Yeah, we'd spent many an afternoon pouring over those glossy bridal books, thick and heavy with wedding advertisements, and I'd realized just how easy it was to blow a wedding budget sky high without trying very hard.

"Okay, so we made it through the first day, without too much magical craziness, and we're still relatively sane, and home safely. So what do we need to do for tomorrow, and what needs done yet for the wedding, the house, and what have we figured out about the Perrault stuff."

Bert sighed. "I hate that we're calling it the 'Perrault stuff'. It just seems undignified."

It was. "So what do we call it?" I asked. "Does it have another name?"

"We never referred to it as stuff, or treasure, or anything like that. We never referred to the stuff. We talked about the promise to protect it, the pact we all made with each other. We called it the Perrault Vow, because we all vowed to make sure it never saw the light of day."

That made a lot of sense for people trying to hide items, to refer not to what they had, but rather what they had done. I had to give them credit. Between the geas against speaking, the vow to protect it, and anything else that was done for protection, it seemed like they had covered all of their bases. I was impressed at the lengths they had gone to in order to make sure things stayed away from those who would misuse them, or otherwise cause them to be used for evil.

I kinda wished Perrault was still around. I wished I could have met him. He sounded like a very smart man, and very thoughtful. I hoped to someday follow his example in my law practice. Of course, that wouldn't' happen unless I could make it through this week and pass the bar exam.

"Bert, why did Clorinda turn you into a frog?" I asked. It was a question I'd wondered about before, but it had been really nagging at the back of my head for the past few days.

He sighed. "I knew you were going to ask that eventually. I'm not sure I've got a good explanation, because we weren't exactly on speaking terms after she did it, but I think I can guess pretty good at what she was up to. I told you I was the youngest of four brothers, didn't I?"

I nodded, and I saw Mia doing the same out of the corner of my eye. Aiden and Jonah were standing nearby and I knew they were listening, but I didn't see their reactions.

"Well, my oldest brother, Phillipe, was the heir to the throne. Gerard was the next brother, and Henri was the third. Phillipe was a good king, and he was kind. He had a very pretty wife and two sons. Gerard was also married, and had a son and a daughter. Henri and I were very happy at the idea that we weren't getting anywhere near the throne; both of us were having way too much fun being single to ever be too overly worried about settling down any time soon. My mother and father were still alive, however, and they wanted to see us settled before anything happened to them. I think it was more about seeing whatever grandchildren they might have gotten, and enjoying them before they got too old to truly enjoy them, but Henri and I weren't interested. And then my parents threw that ball."

"What ball?" Allie asked, having joined the discussion in the garage when she came out carrying a full garbage bag.

"You said you'd stay behind the threshold today!" Bert exclaimed, getting worked up.

She put the trash in the can that would get wheeled out to the street on trash pickup day, and put her hands on her hips. "You think I'm going to stay inside behind those four walls while you go off gallivanting around with those two," she hesitated, as she pointed to Mia and I. "I've got news for you; I'm just as much a part of all of this as you are, and I can't just sit here and do nothing while everyone else is in danger! I need to help, so I did something little, by taking out the trash. I didn't do it until I saw that Janie and Mia were home. Aiden and Jonah are here, and I figured they were in the garage, and you're here. Tell me please, what risk I took in coming across the driveway to where you all were standing, in broad daylight, when there's been no magic in sight around here all day?"

Allie was pissed, and I had to say that I didn't blame her, but I was thinking that maybe the garage wasn't the place for this discussion. I wanted more information from Bert, and while Aiden had put a protective circle of salt and nails around the garage years ago to keep magic out, there was nothing stopping anyone from good, old-fashioned eavesdropping. It was time to take the discussion inside.

I said so, and added, "Plus, I'm starving. We've got to get something to eat and see what else needs to be done for the wedding."

We all trouped back inside, and I saw that Allie and Doris had been busy. Doris had dinner in the oven, a lasagna, and had garlic bread and salad and pie ready and waiting for us. They had a neat pile of ceremony programs, carefully folded and stacked on the counter, for the small number of guests at the ceremony itself. Allie, who had been taking computer classes over the last several months, had designed paper placemats with the menu and wedding information for each guest, and they had tied up little bags of birdseed to be tossed as we left at the end of the reception. A large white wicker basket held the birdseed, tied up in nylon with ribbon and tags with Aiden's and my initials. Stacks of boxes of tea lights and pillar candles in their boxes stood in the corner, next to a rolling plastic crate filled with all kinds of ribbon and nylon netting and tulle.

I hoped they hadn't gone overboard with the frilly stuff. I really wasn't a frilly kind of girl. Even my dress had very little in the way of lace, ribbon, or flounce. But they'd definitely gotten a lot done. And a hot dinner as well? I was impressed, and very happy.

The lasagna came out of the oven, piping hot, but everyone was hungry, and didn't care to wait for it to cool much. We sat down around the table, and started shoveling in food while I prompted Bert to keep telling his story.

"I mentioned the ball that my parents threw?" he asked.

We all nodded.

"Well, you've heard about that ball. The idea behind the ball was for Henri and I to choose brides. I wasn't all that interested, and Henri wasn't, at first, either, but Henri was struck by lightning, so to speak. There was a very pretty girl, beautiful even, and he fell head over heels right that minute. My parents had decreed that we were to pick brides, but I just didn't care. They threatened to disinherit us, and Henri took it seriously, but I knew that if we didn't meet someone that clicked, they were not going to force us into marriage without some feelings of affection. My parents were a rarity at the time in that they loved each other fiercely. I was pretty sure they wanted that for us as well They just didn't think Henri and I were paying attention to the girls who were good marriage candidates, as opposed to those who were unsuitable. They hoped by parading them in front of us, that we would find someone that intrigued us."

"That sounds awfully old-fashioned," Doris said, the sage voice of a mother whose son was about to be married. I had to hide a smile; obviously Aiden and I weren't an arranged marriage; we loved each other.

"Well, Henri had met this woman at the ball, and he was thunderstruck. She was pretty, well read, smart, engaging, and kind. After an hour, he was sure he had found the woman he wanted to spend the rest of his life with, but he still hadn't asked her name. Suddenly, she bolted, with no explanation. He tried to chase her down, but he couldn't catch her, and she was gone, with no trace, no name. All he had was the glass slipper she'd been wearing, that she'd lost in her hurry to leave."

Oh, crap. He's telling me that his older brother was the prince in the Cinderella story? That means, if I remembered the story correctly, that Cinderella became his sister-in-law. And if Clorinda was seeking revenge on her stepsister . . . what had Bert done to protect her? Was that why he'd been turned into a frog?

Bert watched my face intently as I worked it all through. "Janie, I think you've got it figured out, but let me fill in the blanks. Ella was the girl's name, but her stepsisters had named her Cinderella, because they made her clean all the cinders out of the fireplace and do other menial labor. They never thought she'd be able to make herself presentable enough to go to the ball, but she found a way; by making a deal with a faerie being that had owed her father a favor before he died. The glass slippers, the dress, and all the rest were part of that deal, but she left at midnight so she could beat her step-sisters home and thought they wouldn't know she'd made it to the ball in the first place.

"Ella had heard the clock, and knew she was running out of time to beat them home if she was on foot, and tripped on the way out of the castle. She'd lost one shoe, and slipped off the second to keep from breaking her ankle, but she kept the second shoe and the dress hidden when she got home. Clorinda and her other sister had been at the ball, but they hadn't recognized Ella out of the rags she normally wore to do work around the house. I always wonder what would have happened if Clorinda would have recognized Ella that night."

That would have been a sight. Had Clorinda seen Ella charming one of the eligible princes, what would she have done? After all, Henri wasn't the only prince, Bert was still available, but Henri would come before Bert in the line of succession. If I knew anything of Clorinda from the stories, capturing the younger prince would not be acceptable, because she would still be inferior to her stepsister in the hierarchy. So what had happened? I finished my lasagna and got up to slice the pie and serve it, waving Doris back into her seat.

Bert kept talking, and no one interrupted. "Well, you've heard the stories about the prince going door to door with the shoe, trying to find Ella. It took months. I went with him several times, and went on my own more than once. Henri was heartbroken that he couldn't find her right away. He was ready to propose on the spot. My parents didn't even say anything to me about not finding anyone. They were so concerned about him after the ball that I was off the radar for the time. The problem was that I was worried about him too. He wasn't sleeping. He wasn't eating right, and he was starting to lose weight. I made him stay home one morning and went out myself, hoping I'd be able to find her and reunite them and I'd have my brother back. I was starting to wonder if he'd waste away, because he was showing no signs of moving on. I went to the house where Ella, her stepsisters, and her stepmother lived. It was the last house I stopped at that day, tired and dusty from being on horseback all day.

"My father had decreed that anyone going out to look for Ella take the glass slipper and bring whoever fit the slipper back to the palace to meet him to discuss a royal wedding. Some took that to mean that it was a prize; fit in the slipper, get to marry a prince. The reality was that the only prize was the trip back to the palace, for my father to be able to ask my brother if it was the right woman. Even though I'd seen the woman in question, Father made me take the glass slipper, to be consistent with his decree. When I got to that house, Clorinda and her mother and sister had sliced off parts of their feet to try to make them slip into the shoe. They had bloody bandages on their feet, and could barely walk.

"They had a servant, who kept her face down, and didn't look up. I hate to say it, but I didn't always recognize or remember servants in those days. I'd grown up in a palace. If I'd seen her face, I'd have known her on the spot, and likely things wouldn't have gotten as bad as they did. If I'd just looked a bit closer, or insisted on the servant also trying on the shoe on that day, I still wonder if Clorinda would have been able to get past her stepsister marrying up and the loss of an eligible prince. It was like she seemed to think of a good marriage, politically, as her in-born right. And that isn't that far wrong from the cultural norms of the time, where men and women from higher class families were expected to marry for financial, political, and diplomatic gain."

Okay, so now we were beyond the story I'd heard as a child, although I didn't remember anything about anyone chopping off portions of their feet.

Walt Disney sure hadn't included that one in the movie.

CHAPTER TWENTY-ONE

"So, Bert, how did you figure out it was Ella and where she was?" Mia asked.

He smiled. "I played to my own strengths."

He explained that he did research. He was convinced he had somehow missed girls and that all the others sent out, including his brother, were making the same mistake. He just had to figure out what it was.

"Well, I hit the genealogy records. All the birth and death records of all the noble families who had received invitations to the ball. And I realized there was a noble woman who was unaccounted for in our search, who was about the right age for Ella; her father had been of minor noble birth, but enough that his family line was recorded. I found the record of the father's death, and the record of her birth, but no record of Ella being married, deceased, or missing. Our records clerks were always fairly thorough, I'd thought, so I started asking questions."

The clerks had told him they had been out to the house after the father had died, as he had a widow on record. They indicated the daughter had been there, and described her coloring, which matched the woman from the ball, and stated she had still been a child, playing outside with the two girls who had been the widow's children from a previous relationship. No records were available after that, as nothing had been reported and no new information had come in. As it was a matter of a minor nobility family, and the father was not alive to provide updates. The widow wasn't of noble birth, and neither were the daughters, so there was no reason to check up on them until the daughter was of marriageable age, which of course, had slipped off of everyone's radar.

Would she have been included in the invitation to the king and queen's ball?

Of course. In fact, she was invited, but the widow and her two daughters, not being of royal birth, might not have been eligible for the invite, as the daughters were not eligible for marriage to either prince under the kingdom's laws and customs requiring that royalty marry within royalty or nobility. That meant Ella was of marriageable status as well as age, and was single, as there was no record of marriage. So where was she?

Bert himself decided to launch an investigation, without telling his mother or father or brother. He decided to befriend the widow and her daughters hoping that more information would be forthcoming.

"In hindsight, I wonder if they were so welcoming because Clorinda still hoped for a royal marriage. Word had gotten out that my brother was laid up, some saying he was sick, others that he had lost his mind, still others that he had become feeble minded. If he was not available, then I was a good catch. I was an adviser to Phillipe and my father, and so I had some influence in domestic and foreign policy. Henri and Gerard weren't all that interested in what was going on in the kingdom, but it seemed to me to be important to all of us. We'd heard reports of citizens overthrowing governments and storming castles when they were unhappy with the use of power at the top. It hadn't happened to a king yet, but Phillipe and I were both concerned that if we didn't address the concerns of the citizens, it could happen to us."

To that end, Bert had been known for riding out into the countryside and speaking with the people of the kingdom, asking after their health and well-being, asking after their children, and how the crops were doing. While he hadn't stopped at that specific house in the past, he made a point of stopping and checking on the family.

He kept talking, telling us about visits he made, dinners he had with the widow and her daughters, never seeing the nobleman's daughter. We cleaned up the kitchen, loading the dishwasher and starting it to run, never interrupting him as he spoke. Even Allie was speechless, letting him weave a story around us, telling us his past.

How had we never asked him about all of this before?

"About the third or fourth visit, I'd stopped by to tell them I'd seen a fence down in the pasture behind their house, and that I'd set my valet to finding their stable boy so they could repair it. Clorinda answered the door, and it was very clear she was flirting with me. I didn't reciprocate other than just being polite, but she was making it very apparent she was interested. When I started backing toward the door, she started to unfasten her blouse, telling me I needed to stay, or she was going to tell everyone that I had ruined her and had to marry her. I had no intention of doing any such thing, and before I could explain that her ruse wasn't going to work. I wouldn't be allowed to marry her even if I'd stripped her naked and violated her in the town square. She wasn't noble-born or royal. It didn't matter what she pulled, it wasn't going to work. When I kept heading for the door, she started screaming. The servant girl I'd seen the first time I was there actually stormed into the room, brandishing a broom, and whacked Clorinda on the behind with it. Clorinda was so shocked, she actually shut up for a few minutes, and I got a look at the servant girl's face. It was, of course, Ella. I stepped forward and asked her to try on the shoe, which she did, and it fit perfectly."

Clorinda had been livid she wasn't going to marry a prince. He was grateful to have found his brother's love, and had her immediately moved to the palace. Bert told Clorinda to grow up and learn about life before she ever tried to pull anything like that ever again.

"She blames you, doesn't she?" Allie asked.

Bert nodded. "She believed that if Ella had stayed out of it and had done what she had been told, that she would have gotten me in marriage, and would have been able to manipulate her way to the throne itself. It never would have happened. To marry her, I'd have had to renounce my throne. Not that I was going to rule, anyway, but I would have been kicked out of the palace and would no longer have been able to advise Phillipe or my father. She wanted the power that comes with being a royal advisor, she didn't want me."

"So what happened?" Jonah asked. "Did she decide to come after you right away?"

"She disappeared for a couple of years. No one knew where she had gone. Her mother and sister stayed put, telling everyone how ungrateful Ella had been for their guidance growing up, but no one believed it; they'd all seen how she'd been treated for years. Ella, on the other hand, was loved by everyone, and never forgot a name or a face. She taught us more about everyday people than we'd known, and we'd always been pretty compassionate and caring rulers. She and Henri were married and expecting their first kid when Clorinda came back. She tried to get herself a place to stay at the castle, saying that Ella owed her, but I put my foot down and said, if anything, it was the other way around."

Apparently when that failed, Clorinda had tried to sneak into the castle, trying to poison Ella's tea, but Ella had a maidservant who was completely devoted to her and would not bring anything to her mistress that she had not seen prepared herself. That plan foiled, Clorinda actually killed two castle guards after torturing them for information on sneaking into Ella's bedroom. Bert had been alerted that the two guards were missing, and relocated Henri and Ella to another part of the castle out of an abundance of caution before they even learned that the guards were dead.

"Finally, we ended up concluding that Henri and Ella needed to disappear. Even in a heavily guarded castle, there was just no way to guard the two of them all hours of the day and night. Henri had friends in more than one other kingdom, and I was in charge of making arrangements for them to leave. I wrote five of his friends and laid out the issues with Clorinda, letting them know we would choose one once we were on our way, whichever seemed safest in flight."

They ended up nearly a week's hard ride away from the castle, and Ella made it just in time to give birth to unexpected twins, a boy and a girl. Henri was exhausted, but overjoyed, and Ella was happy to feel safe. Bert stayed until he was sure he had covered their tracks, and then journeyed back to their homeland.

While he had been gone, Clorinda had been terrorizing the neighborhood, demanding to know where they were. While Bert had been gone, his father had passed away unexpectedly, but probably from natural causes, and his mother had gone into a dark depression. Phillipe had taken the throne, and was trying to take control, but Clorinda was demanding that he hand over her sister or be killed. When she realized only Bert knew their location, she left Phillipe alone and began to threaten Bert.

"She threatened to kill the rest of my family, but the army was protecting Phillipe and Gerard and their families. She didn't have the power or the clout at the time to get around that. Henri and Ella were gone. My mother was losing what was left of her mind after losing my father, and she died just a month or so later. To be honest, I think she was lost without him, and would have been, regardless of when or how he went; they were so much in love in their lifetimes. The only person Clorinda could really get to was me."

Bert kept talking, his tones calm and even, but even so, I could still hear the regret in his voice. I wondered how he'd dealt with all the loss, knowing that he could be blamed for it. Not that it was his fault, but it was his own actions that had led to his family being broken up and surrounded by guards. I know I would blame myself.

He kept talking. "She captured me alone in the garden one evening, after court had been held for the people to air grievances and disputes. Clorinda demanded her sister's location, and I refused to give it to her. At that time, I didn't realize she had been learning magic; heck, I didn't even know that it existed. She turned me into a frog, thinking I'd give up my brother in order to get turned back. I don't think it ever occurred to her that I would prefer to stay a frog forever to keep them from being found. I think she knew they were living under assumed names, and that it was unlikely that, in the days before the internet and Social Security numbers and webcams and driver's licenses, that she would be able to track them down as easily as one would today. Instead, she was stuck with old fashioned shoe leather, and my brother and I had set up a set of coded instructions should she start getting close. We moved them three or four times until she was finally locked up in the dungeon for attempting to have someone else in the castle murdered. That time she was actually caught passing money to an accomplice who cooperated with us."

His family had been surprised, to say the least, when he'd been turned into a frog, but they had heard his voice and he answered questions showing that he was really who he said he was. They loved him all the same. Clorinda couldn't kill him, because no one else really knew where Henri and Ella might be hiding. Bert was careful to make sure that after the first move or so, their identities and their children's names were hidden, constantly changing, and that they never stayed more than a week in the same place, until Clorinda was locked up. Once she was locked up, they came out of hiding, and began to live their lives at a country estate owned by Bert's family on the other side of the kingdom. The kids grew up healthy and led their own lives, Bert's brothers and their families also grew and prospered and moved on. Once Henri, the longest living of his brothers, passed away, Bert decided to go his own way.

"Because sooner or later, being the family burden got to be old. I had to go see if there was more I could get out of life than just living in a corner of the family castle. That's when I went to Paris. And that's when I met Charles Perrault."

CHAPTER TWENTY-TWO

O kay, so we knew why Clorinda didn't like Bert, and why she might be after him, trying to get revenge for hiding her stepsister, but that didn't explain who was after the Perrault artifacts; it just explained why a specific witch was after Bert and why she wanted a particular artifact, the shoes that had shown up at the front door on Sunday.

But who had left them there in the first place?

We moved into the living room once we'd finished cleaning up from dinner, and Bert told us about meeting Perrault in Paris, by sheer accident, as he happened to come out of a brothel Bert had found shelter in. Apparently Bert had convinced one of the ladies working there to let him stay in her room when she didn't have a customer. He'd been out in the back alley while she was working, and Perrault, who worked as a tax collector for the Crown, had nearly tripped over him in his haste to get out of the building after his work was done.

Bert had apparently cursed at the man, as he'd been sleeping off the better part of a bottle of brandy at the time of their encounter, and Perrault had freaked out completely at the talking frog. I understood the reaction; it wasn't like any one of us hadn't thought we were nuts the minute Bert had opened his mouth for the first time.

Perrault had bolted out of the alley, but came back an hour later, trying to see if he had lost his mind. As Bert explained about magic to him, he began to realize Bert was a man in a frog's body, and wanted to know what he could do to protect other humans. The two of them struck up a friendship, and began researching, to try to figure out what might need to be done to protect themselves, and then their friends and families, and then the rest of the human race. Items began to pile up that seemed like they could be dangerous, like Ella's glass slippers, which Bert's family had been in possession of for years, and then more items began to surface.

That was when they started talking seriously about how to

protect those items, in order to prevent them from falling into the wrong hands.

"So what is the danger with the glass slippers?" I asked. "And what do they do other than being a really cool part of your family history?"

He shook his head. "I've never seen them do anything specific, but according to Ella, they were conjured, as opposed to forged. I'm not sure how anyone would make glass slippers like that. They were form fitted specifically to her feet, she said, even allowing for a small bunion on her right big toe that she'd had for years. Glass is formed by melting and blowing and intense heat from a furnace. There was no way that an individual would be able to stand having the glass poured over their feet to get that exact of a fit. They had to be made by magic in order to be so perfectly fitted.

"Are you sure?"

Bert shrugged, no mean feat for a frog. "Well, I've never seen them do anything else, but they haven't really been used for anything ever since Ella wore them to the ball where she met Henri. They were on display in the castle for a number of years, in a case where visitors could see them. It was a romantic story, and a number of couples got engaged in front of the case that held the glass slippers. It became a longstanding tradition for young people, which was a beautiful way to honor them. Henri and Ella thought so, too, even if they weren't around to see it."

"But Bert," said Aiden. "There's always a possibility that Clorinda got to the shoes if they were on public display. She could have put a curse on them, or well, anything like that."

Bert smiled. "She could have. Which is why no one ever wore them again. I'd really advise that no one actually put them on their feet, because I don't know what that would do, but as a piece of history, as a romantic item, as a tradition? They're priceless. But that's part of why they're so dangerous, because we don't know. It's why they were hidden away, though, when Perrault and I started to gather items to protect ourselves."

Something out the window caught my eye, and I looked away from the conversation, but I didn't see what it was. Maybe I was on edge from all the craziness that had happened over the last couple of days, but I could have sworn that something had walked through the yard. I shook my head. We were behind a threshold. There wasn't much magical that could get to us without us realizing we were under attack, given both the threshold and the salt and iron put down in a circle around the house. Aiden's cell phone went off. It was his father, wanting to come back to the house and give us some information, but being from the magical realm, Aiden had to help him past that circle.

Aiden talked to his father for a few minutes, before hanging up. Maybe it was a good thing we'd gotten Geoffrey a cell phone; otherwise, he'd have no way to let us know he was on his way, standing outside forever, unable to knock on the door when he showed up without someone to get him past the circle. We'd also been able to convince him that calling before he just showed up was likely a better idea than just appearing, since who knew what kind of magical emergency could be going on in our backyard?

"What's going on?" I asked, before looking up to see what might still be in the backyard. I still kept seeing something cross the yard outside of the window, but it could be as simple as a plastic grocery bag dropped from someone's car, and caught in the breeze.

"He says he remembers some things about the time period when Perrault had his geas cast, and wants to know when it would be a good time to come by and tell us about it."

It was already eight pm. Mia and I needed to get a good night's sleep, even more so if I was getting distracted by an errant piece of trash being blown around in the backyard. The boys also looked exhausted, especially Jonah, and they had at least another full day of yard work to go. I told Aiden to have his father come by tomorrow night.

Doris nodded at me, letting me know that, as tired as I was, the rational part of the brain was at least working enough to protect me from overdoing. "I'll bring dinner over again, Janie. That way you guys at least have one hot meal a day this week."

I tried to tell her that we were fine, but she wasn't taking no for an answer. Whether she was just over-momming us, or whether she wanted to be present to hear what Geoffrey had to say, who knew, and

I wasn't sure that I wanted to know either, at the moment.

The doorbell rang. It was Harold.

Now, that was timing. Harold and Doris had been seeing each other romantically ever since we returned from Wonderland. I kept wondering when they were going to tie the knot themselves, but if I said anything, they would laugh and joke and say they were in no hurry, as they had each other and plenty of time. I don't know whether it was all the wedding stuff going on in my life, but I kept wanting to give them the same thing that they were giving us; a day to celebrate their relationship just like we would have on Saturday.

Harold was there to pick up Doris. Apparently she had tried to tell everyone she would be okay driving home on her own, but Aiden and Harold were having none of that if there was a possibility of magical danger on the road on the way home. It was kind of sweet, even if it was rather overbearing and annoying at the same time.

He came inside and saw us all sitting around in the living room. "Uh, oh. This looks like a War Room meeting. And here I'd have thought Janie and Mia would have been resting, or checking out the cat that's hanging out in your back yard. Something going on?"

Oh, crap. That wasn't a grocery bag I'd seen in the window. A cat?

That could be nothing. It could be as little as the neighbor's cat getting out of the house, or a stray finding a peaceful place to get off the streets. It could be a kitten who ran away from home and got lost. Maybe we could take in a pet. Maybe we should take it to the animal shelter or Humane Society.

Or maybe it was magical. I remembered the Cheshire Cat we'd met in Wonderland. That was no normal cat. And it had been transformed not just by its own magic, but also because of the White Rabbit, using it for its own ends. Maybe we had a bigger problem than just calling the animal control officers to pick up a stray animal.

Don't we always?

CHAPTER TWENTY-THREE

I ran to the sliding glass doors in the kitchen. Why do I always head for those doors when the wonky stuff is going down? Well, because they offer the most expansive view of the backyard, of course. Also, because they were the least secured entry point of the house. Being glass, and large, they were the most vulnerable point to anyone who might try to get in. Magical beings probably wouldn't get past the protective circle around the house, but that didn't rule out their having recruited human help, or just plain destructive humans. And that glass hadn't been fixed yet. The boys had used electrical tape in small X's on the cracks to hold the broken glass together long enough for the house to be secure while we waited on the glass company to fix it.

In the backyard, there was a marmalade tabby cat, a big one. It probably weighed close to twenty pounds, and was dancing around as if it owned the joint. It didn't seem skittish or upset, or lost, like a stray. I watched as the darn thing rubbed its face over every piece of patio furniture I owned, over the legs of the gas grill on the edge of the patio, and on the concrete planter that had been there ever since I'd moved to the house as a kid. That planter currently held a large arrangement of flowers and decorative grass Jonah planted and was trying to grow naturally, without magic. That cat rubbed itself over every inch of everything in the backyard, even the rake the boys had forgotten and left in the grass.

Something was weird about this cat. And then I noticed that the salt and metal line, which didn't bother Bert, also did not bother the cat.

"Bert," I said.

He finally caught up to us in the kitchen, and made his way to the glass. "Hey, I know him."

My eyebrows shot up pretty high. That certainly wasn't the reaction I thought I'd get.

"Last time I talked to him, he was going by the name of Bob. Can you open the door, so I can talk to him?"

Huh? Something magical shows up and he wants to open the door? I was thinking that we should lock up and hunker down for the week, and he's going to open the door to a cat named Bob that isn't affected by salt and metal?

I didn't say anything, but he did.

"Janie, look, I know this cat. He's in a similar situation with me, in that he wasn't always a cat. He's probably still looking for his boots. He lost them in a poker game two hundred years ago, and has been swearing that he'd get them back ever since. He's good people, and he might have some idea of what's going on. It's worth talking to him. At most, he'd cost you a saucer of milk or so in exchange for his help."

A cat who was 'good people'? A saucer of milk. How cliché could you get? "Fine," I said. "Open the door." I went to the refrigerator. Luckily we had a bit of milk still in the fridge, and there was some heavy whipping cream in the door from Doris making whipped cream for the pie we had for dinner. I grabbed the cream, and poured some into a shallow bowl. "Bert, is this going to be insulting?" He'd been pissed when I'd poured tea in a bowl for him at our first meeting, as opposed to a mug or a glass.

He shook his head, turning to the door as Jonah opened it, letting in Bob the cat.

"'Sup, Bob," said Bert.

You have got to be kidding me. Really? I wondered.

"'Sup," said Bob the cat. "Seen my boots lately?"

"Naw, but I'm wondering if you've heard anything about Perrault's stuff in the last few weeks," Bert said.

"Got some milk?" he asked.

I held up the cream container and the shallow bowl, and then placed the bowl on the floor where he could get to it easily.

He pranced over to where I stood, his tail dancing in the air above him, and lowered his face to the bowl, drinking greedily. As the level in the bowl went down, I poured what was left in the cream container, and watched him finish that off as well. What was I going to do with heavy whipping cream? I wasn't spending time in the kitchen this week, the wedding was Saturday, and I was still really hoping that

Aiden and I would be able to get out of town and spend some non-magical-emergency time together as some sort of honeymoon.

It was a long ten minutes before Bob lifted his head from the bowl, with cream still dripping from his whiskers. "Thank you, ma'am. That was right tasty."

Um, he sounded like a cowboy the way he said that. He sounded like Jane, who we'd met last fall. Calamity Jane was a rough talking woman who had a heart of gold. She'd stayed behind in Utah, having struck up a friendship with Paul Bunyan after our trip out West. Last I'd heard, they'd made it more than a friendship, and were now dating and getting serious. I wondered if we'd have to make a trip west for a wedding in the near future. I rather missed her no-nonsense ways, tempered with cursing and drinking, but never when someone needed help. I jerked my brain back to the present and the aw-shucks talking cat in my kitchen.

Bob licked his face, and used his front paw to clean his whiskers. He sat down, and said, "So what's goin' on that you're askin' about that stuffed shirt?"

Stuffed shirt? Oh wait, Bert had said that he met the guy running out the back door of a brothel after showing up to collect taxes for the Crown. Had he really been there to collect taxes, or was he just so embarrassed to be there that he'd ducked out the back door to prevent anyone seeing him, even if it was for legitimate purposes. It was possible that he did fit that description. It just surprised me.

Bert sighed. "You remember when Charles and I were collecting artifacts and trying to find a way to protect the humans?"

"Ayup," was the answer. I took that as a yes.

"Well, someone's trying to get to those artifacts, and we're trying to figure out who it is and why. I'm thinking Clorinda's got something to do with it, but I can't figure the angle. And Maddy showed up the other night."

"Aw, shee-it," Bob said. "How'd you get all the snakes and frogs cleaned up so quick?"

"Snow Queen sent a team to deal with it."

"Crazy bitch don't understand just how unattractive her crazy mouth is. Even if it weren't for the snakes and toads, she's a nut ball.

Seriously psycho. She'll never get settled down, she don't learn herself how to control that damn mouth of hers."

Um, there was so much messed up about that sentence I wasn't sure where to begin. And while a part of me rebelled at the misogynistic statement, I had bigger things on my mind, like whether Bob knew anything about the geas Bert was under or not, and what he knew of the items that were being held. Should we be hurrying up about all this? Was there a ticking clock to find this stuff faster? We didn't know.

"I'd like to ask if Bob knows anything about the Perrault artifacts that Bert doesn't. I'd like to know if he knows anything that Bert isn't able to tell us. Or is he part of the same pact?" I asked.

Bob cocked his head from side to side, looking at me intently. "How much she know about what you were up to, Bert?"

"All of it," he said. "Or as much as I can remember at this point. It's been a few years, but everyone here is completely trustworthy and I would put my life in their hands. Heck, I've done it several times just in the last couple of years alone."

Bob nodded. "Good 'nuf for me. In fact, I came here looking for you anyway, Bert. You're in real danger, here, and I don't think you know all of what's goin' on."

I snorted. "When do we ever know all of what's going on? No, seriously. Every time we have something like this come up, we end up floundering around in the dark for a while, before we finally figure it out. So if you've got information that can help us, don't dance around it. Let us know what we can do to protect him; and ourselves from whatever is out there."

"Well, of course, Clorinda would love to get her hands on you, Bert, but she's a big stick. Someone is waving her in the right direction, but there's no doubt in my mind that there's someone way more subtle pointing her towards you. There's a bigger plot afoot, being orchestrated by someone planning way more detailed and sophisticated and long term."

That had Evangeline written all over it. She definitely could plan long term. She'd been married to my father for more than ten years while she worked to kill him, not realizing that his death wouldn't give back her power. She had to cause mine. And it was when she realized that and started to plot against me that Bert showed up and helped to protect me. Would she seek revenge against Bert for helping me thwart her plan? Absolutely, but Aiden had been more visible than Bert had been in that situation. Would ruining our wedding have the added benefit of hurting him as well as me? Sure, but just ruining the wedding didn't get her back the power my ancestors had stripped from her. She'd have to kill me, and she knew that now. Was she planning on all of it in one fell swoop? Very possible.

Of course, that didn't mean that Evangeline was the one responsible. I had to remind myself she wasn't the only bad guy out there, and that just because she could do it, didn't mean she actually had.

I'd just be really surprised if it was anyone else.

CHAPTER TWENTY-FOUR

Bob, obviously, had no idea what I was thinking about my stepmother. He hadn't been around for all of that, so he couldn't know, but that didn't stop him from continuing to talk about the Perrault artifacts and the vow Bert had taken.

"Dude, I'd never have made that stupid vow. How does it help anyone if you can't talk about what you know when that's the exact information that could get you killed? And all your friends are in danger. Heck, I'd think I was in danger, too, if they find out I've been here. And someone is definitely watching you. Don't know who, don't know how, but no question there's something a bit wonky going on here." Bob was making me paranoid even as he was making a lot of sense.

Someone watching us? Here at the house? I wasn't aware of anyone being able to watch us inside the house, and we'd had Geoffrey contact the Snow Queen on a mirror that was in a room no one slept in. Even if she could use the mirror to watch us, that door was normally shut to save on heating and air conditioning costs since it was an unused room. There wasn't much that could be seen from that mirror if the door was shut all of the time.

Was there another way to see inside the house? Or did they just have a surveillance team watching our comings and goings?

I asked Bob. "What do you mean that someone is watching us? And how?"

He shrugged. "Whoever it is seems to know what's going on. I mean, I hear Maddy has slipped her guard in the magical realm and was here at the exact time you all were."

That could be coincidence, but then I also hear nothing has happened here with Bert out of the house. Was someone watching to see when he left? How would they have known that he left when he was inside of my purse this morning, without seeing him actually go into the bag itself?

All good questions, none of which we had answers to. But it was helpful to know someone might be watching, even if we didn't know how closely. That could be used against someone; if we could set it up without being seen to do so.

Now how were we going to do that?

"So the next question, Bob, is what do you know about Perrault, and about the artifacts that he tried to hide?" Jonah asked.

"Well, just like anyone else, Perrault had a family, and he was worried about protecting them. He had kids, and a brother, and the brother had a family. He was worried. I couldn't blame him," Bob said. "Look, his wife actually was killed in a freak accident, and he never figured out what happened. He never found out what killed her, and when he learned that magic was real, he was convinced her death had something to do with magic, even though he never figured out whether it did or not."

"Was it?" Aiden asked.

"Never did find out for sure, but I never heard that it did. Perrault worked for a long time for the French government, in various departments. When he was forced out due to some internal politics, his wife was already dead, and his children were grown. He didn't want to miss out on things for his children, and for their children, and devoted himself to writing about Christianity, and then to writing his fairy tales. His work regarding the artifacts came just before he was forced out of his position with the government. Some flunky's son wanted Perrault's job, and he was ignoring it to work on the magical stuff. I don't know that he saw it as a true loss; he got more time with his family and he got the time to work on his book of fairy tales, which he saw as warning letters to the public. I think he was obtuse enough not to get into concerns about exposing magic to the general public, but no one took it as warning. It was just seen as an amusing children's book. It was where the Grimm brothers started when they began their work, but at the same time, Perrault didn't get the warning out to the public the way he wanted. Come to think of it, the Grimms didn't either."

I nodded. "Tell me about it. Heck, I didn't know anything about all of this being real until Queen Eva decided that I needed to die, and began to move against me."

"Anyway, Perrault and Bert, and a few others, began to amass what magical artifacts that they found, and storing them in a locked vault in the palace at Versailles. Everyone figured that it was the safest place to store them, as there were so many royal guards in and out of the palace on a regular basis, and security measures in place to protect the king."

It made a lot of sense. "So, I assume that they were moved," I said.

"They were," Bert jumped in. "Since the Versailles vault was the subject of multiple attempts at break-ins, we didn't feel like they were safe. Also, word had gotten out in the magical community the items were there. While some of the items have intrinsic magical powers, some don't, and some, well, we just don't know. Better that they be housed someplace anyone didn't know about."

"So you had a mole, someone in the know who was letting information leak to the magical community, who would have tried to get the items back." Mia guessed.

"No, we don't know that. You see, probably ninety percent of the magical community are just like ninety percent of the mortal community; they just want to live their lives. Go home at the end of the night, raise their kids, and have their normal, everyday lives. It's the ten percent on each side that get a little more ambitious, and those are the ones who cause problems for one hundred percent of both sides. Most of the trouble makers in the magical courts are in the court nobility, and most of what they're up to is currying favor with their leaders, or political maneuvering for their own gain, or to advance their own agendas. Mostly, though, they're carrying out someone else's plans, like their queen."

Which went along with my idea that my stepmother was in charge of the whole shebang. Even though she'd been knocked off her throne by my own proof of her deception, I was sure she still had her followers, whose political ascendancy was linked to her own. Some of them had to be working to get her completely freed, and placed back on her own throne. I'd already heard whispers of those who saw the Snow Queen's role as temporary. They saw her as a guardian of the court, keeping everyone in line until Evangeline had served enough penance for her falsehoods and was able to take back the reins responsibly. Quite honestly, I wasn't sure enough time would ever pass for that to happen. Of course, I was a bit biased, but I sure slept better knowing she wasn't in power, even if she was getting a day pass for the wedding.

And maybe that was another question for the Snow Queen. Was there a plan to restore Evangeline to her throne, or was the Snow Queen prepared to run the court for an infinite period of time? Would my stepmother ever be able to regain her throne? I guess I'd always assumed it was a permanent deposing of a queen, but I'd never asked the question, and I felt like an idiot for not asking sooner.

"Well, guys, we have a lot of work to do in figuring out the next step, but Mia and I have got to get some shut eye for tomorrow, or we'll be worthless tomorrow night, and I have a funny feeling we're going to be trying to work all of this out some more then. The guys have more yard work tomorrow, and there's still a ton of wedding stuff to get done. Bob, you are welcome to stay with us tonight. Bert, he can stay in the study with you, can't he?"

"Of course," was the answer.

The doorbell rang, however, just as I was trying to herd everyone to bed. It was Geoffrey.

With information about the casting of the geas that comprised the Perrault Vow. That he said couldn't wait until tomorrow.

I was never getting to bed tonight.

CHAPTER TWENTY-FIVE

Geoffrey was awfully wound up when he came in, his normally immaculate hair sticking up more like his son's, as if he'd been running his hands through it over and over in frustration.

"I just can't believe what I've found." That didn't sound good.

"What did you find?" Bert asked, sounding worried.

"Donkeyskin," he said. "One of the people who knew about the Vow, about the magic of the geas, stole the donkeyskin out of the pile of artifacts being protected, and they used it to hide from everyone else while they watched the ritual. It bound only the people who participated, and the person who hid didn't participate. They know the location of the artifacts; and they know there are two ways to get to it. One is by human means. They've hired excavating crews to dig and look and try to see what they can get to by crane and backhoe and all the rest. But there's a magical way to get there, which is faster."

I looked at Bert, who nodded, before his face froze up involuntarily. Apparently there was some issue with whether or not he could confirm or deny information already available, but his short nod before he stopped was enough. So whoever it was knew where it was hidden in the mortal realm, and was possibly still looking for where it was hidden in the magical realm. I wondered if they'd also put a layer of magical protection on the human route, as well as a human means of security on the magical route. It made sense to me to protect such items like this; many magical beings would never think of security doors made of steel or iron grates over windows, and that would stop many of them from even coming close to getting inside. Such things couldn't be touched by magical beings, so it was another layer of protection keeping them out, just like magic could keep out a human spelunker or explorer stumbling upon just the right cave or cavern.

Smart.

"So, Geoffrey, where is the human side excavation going on? Is it somewhere nearby?" I asked. We didn't have the time this week for a big expedition, so I hoped it was within the state.

"Oak Island, near Nova Scotia," he said. Again, Bert gave a forced half-nod, before his face froze up. If he could keep doing that, it would help.

Canada. That was a good day, if not two, to drive there and the same amount of time back. We had no way of knowing exactly where on the island to find them, but there was not enough time to drive there, find it, figure what we needed to do, and drive back with the bar exam this week.

We needed to figure out the magical route in. If all else failed, I could break out my emergencies-only credit card and send one or both of the boys to Nova Scotia, but I couldn't miss the last two days of the bar exam and hope to pass; it just wasn't going to happen. And I needed to pass the bar exam on the first try, so we could start to set up our practice and get more money coming in.

Jonah piped up. "Hasn't there been some kind of television special on Oak Island lately? That sounds familiar." Sure enough, a quick internet search on my laptop showed a television show on the island, showing the progress, or non-progress, of an investigation to show what exactly the island was hiding. At least we could see what was going on without having to travel all the way there.

Bert and Bob indicated they could volunteer to watch the show while the rest of us did what we needed to; fixing the door and the yard, taking the bar, prepping wedding supplies.

"So what about the magical route?" Allie asked. "That's got to be a more direct way of going about this. And even if we were able to just move the items for a short period of time, we could do that to protect against someone getting a hold of them and using them for nefarious purposes during the wedding. If we found out it was safe, we could always just turn around and put them back. No one would expect that."

"But anyone who got through all of the security once to find the items gone, would surely go back if they heard that the move was only temporary, and then they've already learned how to beat your system. Seems to me that moving them like that would only make things less secure, not more, and make ourselves an even bigger target, if we haven't already done so," Doris said.

Practical, that was our Doris. And she was right.

Geoffrey shook his head. "Unless there's a portal somewhere nearby, I can't imagine that it would affect us."

My jaw dropped. He'd said the magic word. "Portal." Evangeline had used a portal in the basement to take me to the magical realm against my will, or, at least her son Hansel had. That portal had been closed by the Snow Queen a couple of years earlier, and I wasn't aware of any other portals in the house. A portal was how F.A.B.L.E.S. got access to the magical realm for secure meetings and for some minor magical working of their own, if they were able; they'd fixed my Rapidly-Growing Hair problem, which they had told me was Rapunzel Syndrome, with such magics and a disgusting potion on the other side of a magical portal.

"So is there another portal around here somewhere that we don't know about?" I asked.

We all stared at each other, rather dumbfounded. "Hello," I said. "Is there another portal that I don't know about?"

There were some guilty looks on a couple of faces in my living room. Allie, Bert, and Bob, all looking a bit sheepish and, well, like they were going to confess to just about anything. If one of them told me that they'd kidnapped the Lindburgh baby, I'd have been less surprised than for what they were about to say.

"Well, there is another portal, other than the one that was closed," Allie said. "It's in the attic, where you never go, and none of us have ever used it."

"I can't get up there on my own, so I haven't seen it, but I can smell it." Bert added.

"You can't smell anything," I retorted. "You've said that before."

"You know what I mean, Janie. I smell it like I smell magic. Maybe taste it is a better word, but I can sense it. It seemed like it had been used a couple of times, but no one ever came out of it." Bert seemed a bit defensive.

"*And you never said anything about it?*" I shouted. "I was kidnapped through a portal, I was kept captive, and she *wanted to kill me.* And there was a portal above my head, above where I slept every night, and you never told me about it?" There wasn't a whole lot of doubt, now. I was wide awake, nowhere near ready to call it a night now, and ready to tear their heads off for keeping me in the dark. "All the things we'd been through, all the dangers, all the adventures, all the heartache, and no one had told me that I was sleeping every night underneath a portal to a magical realm that I knew nothing about!"

Everyone was dead silent when I finished screaming at them. Maybe they thought I had a right. I knew I wouldn't have stopped until I'd gotten the entire thing out.

Aiden looked pissed. Well, he slept beside me every night, and it looked like he was in the dark as well. Jonah and Mia looked baffled, as if they'd had no clue. Doris looked stricken, as if she'd realized the danger her son had been living in. Geoffrey looked surprised.

"So where did it come from?" I asked, softer. "When did it get put there? Did someone move it there?"

No one said anything. I heard the hallway clock ticking, and then striking the hour. It was ten in the evening at this point, and why was it that everything happened when I had to get something else, including sleep, done?

CHAPTER TWENTY-SIX

The ticking of the clock went long enough that I felt like we could have had a commercial break if we'd been a television show.

"Who in the world gave permission for a portal to be moved into the house? I mean, there wasn't one there three years ago when I moved my dad's trunks out of the attic. So, somehow, someone got into the house to do this, or someone living here gave permission for someone magical to come into this house and cast what magic they had to cast in order to create a portal in my attic. So how did they do it without any of us, who have experience doing so, failing to smell the use of magic in the house?

It didn't take long before Bert spoke up. "I did it," he said, in a small voice.

"WHY WOULD YOU DO SOMETHING LIKE THAT?!?!?!" I yelled. "What happened the last time you made a deal behind our backs, giving up a little of our security?"

He hung his head. "I know," he said, in a smaller voice.

He'd traded away the location of where the portal we'd had in the basement went to for potion ingredients to make himself human, because he wanted to impress a girl. And in doing so, he could have gotten that same girl, Mia, killed, at the time that the Seawitch was targeting her and her father. He'd taken the potion, and failed to win her over, but had saved her life by jumping in front of a spell that had been designed to strip Mia of her humanity, her human life. It had instead stripped Bert of the humanity returned to him by the potion, and he'd returned to his frog form, worked through his broken heart, and become her friend, as well as Jonah's friend. His relationship with Allie was relatively strong, I thought, so why in the world had he done something like this?

He sighed. "Marie-Jeanne L'Heritier once asked me why I was willing to be an immortal and carry the burden of Perrault's secret with me the rest of my life. I told her that keeping these items secret were more important than my life, than her life, or anyone's life, no matter how long or short that life might be. She predicted that I would be the one burdened with this; that I would be the one who would be in charge of security for this when everyone else was gone. She was right."

"Who is Marie-Jeanne L'Heritier?" Jonah asked.

Aiden answered. "Charles Perrault's niece, she also wrote fairy tales in French that were published at the time. She, as well as Madeleine de Scudery, Madame d'Aulnoy and Henriett-Julie de Murat, was also involved with several French intellectual salons at the time, and all of them published similar types of tales. Perrault's were the most popular; his were published as the Mother Goose tales in France."

Bert nodded. "They were all involved in the casting of the geas and the finding of the artifacts. The publishing of the fairy tales and the participation in the salons were their covers, how they explained their activities as they were putting it all together."

Aiden jumped in, playing professor again. "They spent time with Fouquet, Moliere, and even King Louis XIV. They used to play a parlor game where they retold classic fairy tales as if they were creating them spontaneously, making every character a member of the gentry by birth, or shepherds or shepherdesses in pastoral settings, but the sheep tenders were secretly royal or noble and their innate nobility was not hidden."

He'd been studying under my father at the University of Dayton, in linguistics and folklore when Dad had died, and he had taken time off from his studies after an injury in Wonderland had affected his memory. He really needed to get back to his studies, and this reminded me of how good he was at it.

"So, Bert, if you were the immortal being in charge of keeping this secret and this security, what would have happened if you had become truly mortal two years ago, when you turned back into a human? How would you have handled it at that point?" I asked. Maybe I was being a bit nasty, but it was a legitimate question.

He shrugged. "I wasn't the only immortal keeping the secret at that point. There was another being involved, who appeared to be immortal as well. I was wrong. He died two weeks ago. That was when I agreed to move the portal to our attic, so I could watch the entrance."

The ramifications floored me, in more ways than one. I was still pissed that he'd done it without talking to me, although I was starting to understand why he didn't feel like he had the option of saying no, or allowing me to say no. I just wish we'd had some prior knowledge that it was there, although I'm not sure what I would have done differently in the last two weeks. Would I have made sure someone was always home? Would I have lain awake at night worrying about what might come through, or would I have just assumed he had broken his promise to me not to endanger us again and kick him out? Would I have been able to do it, to follow through and put him on the street, when he'd saved my life so much in the past, or would I be unable to trust him and unable to kick him out, constantly living under the idea that someone in my house was a liar? And what did that do to the idea of him becoming human again and having a life with Allie?

I looked closer. The shrug I'd seen earlier seemed to have been covering true emotional upset with feigned indifference. He was crying softly, angling his face to hide the tears in the play of light from the table lamp that sat just high enough to cast a shadow in his direction. He must have been truly conflicted at the idea of doing this; but felt like he didn't have a choice. He wasn't even looking at Allie, who seemed to be staring at him in dumbfounded silence. I wondered what she was thinking, and figured that a woman who was willing to run away from everything and everyone who cared about her to protect them, and found that such an action didn't work, might not be too far off on standing with him when this kind of decision found its way to his lap. She looked shocked, so I was pretty sure she hadn't known about it, and it was likely she'd have words for him later on keeping secrets from her if I didn't miss my guess, but I was fairly certain she hadn't known about the portal.

"So how did you keep it hidden from us?" I asked. "Most of us know how to smell for magic, and we'd notice if someone was slinging it around heavy enough to create something like that in the house. You've cloaked it somehow. How is that?"

"It's accessible from the other side, but that's only if someone got there by burrowing through the excavation needed to get to it from the mortal realm. If that didn't happen, then it closes until it's activated. If it's not activated, and it's not open from the other side, then it's not throwing off the scent of magic."

"How do you activate it?" Doris asked, quietly.

"It's an incantation, followed by a specific ingredient tossed on a rune on the floor," he explained.

"There's a rune painted on the floor of the attic and you didn't tell me about it?" I asked.

"No, there's no paint. It's about knowing the specific spot on the floor, and tracing a rune with your finger on the wood. It's about knowing the exact amount of the ingredient to toss on the rune after it's traced, and it's about knowing the exact cadence of the words to be spoken in the incantation."

Well, that sounded oddly specific. Wait a minute. The geas hadn't stopped him from telling us where it was. Did that mean the actual rune and ingredient and incantation were banned but not the location because we needed all of that to access it? Did that mean he couldn't open it in front of us? If that was the case, then moving it here was probably the smartest thing he could have done. Casting anything to open it would bring all of us running. Us being present would prevent him from finishing the casting if he was unable to reveal how to get there. So even if some black hatted villain kidnapped one of us and held us at knifepoint in the attic, he couldn't open it. Hiding it in plain sight, a brilliant move.

Or was it?

I was hoping for something to get slightly easier this week, but it didn't look like that was going to happen anytime soon.

And then I thought of something else.

"Bert, you said that the glass slippers that were left for us were one of the artifacts Perrault had hidden away. And yet they appeared on the front step the other day, as if a gift for us. Almost as if someone was leaving it as a wedding present. So if the slippers were taken out of hiding, and the hiding place is in our own attic, who in the world would have left them on our own front steps, and why?"

CHAPTER TWENTY-SEVEN

"I don't know," said Bert. "I don't know who left them."

That was a scary thought. "Is there a way you would know if someone had gotten to the items, wherever they were held? Some kind of warning system, or alarm in your head that would sound to let you know things no longer needed protecting, or needed a whole lot more protecting?" Aiden asked.

Bert shook his head. "I was told that the only person who was able to send that kind of signal was dead. That's why I had to move the portal, so I'd be able to keep an eye on it."

"Who was that?" I asked.

"Gabriella," Geoffrey said. "You're talking about Gabriella. You're saying Gabriella is dead?" His face, oh his face, was full of pain. Even if they hadn't had a relationship that had lasted, he had said that they had been friends. Losing a friend is still painful, and learning about it unexpectedly, even more so.

"That's the information I got," Bert said. "I obviously didn't see her body, if that's what you're asking. I don't know how. I don't know when. I got the information two weeks ago, and pulled what strings I could to move the portal as fast as possible. I couldn't wait for official confirmation through channels, although I've asked for it. I had to make sure the portal was protected as fast as possible, because I didn't want there to be a magical emergency while the girls were taking the bar or preparing for the wedding, and look what's happened now; exactly what I was trying to avoid."

I sat back on the couch, putting my hands behind my head. There was a lot to take in here.

"Guys, at this point, I don't know where to even start addressing all of the information we've gotten tonight. I think it's smart for all of us to go to bed. We've got to sleep on all of this and come up with a plan. Obviously there's information we need to double check and process, and there's still plenty of work to do. Anyone who doesn't live here full time is welcome to stay, provided they don't invite anyone not already living here into the house or stay past five in the afternoon tomorrow. And no one tries to open any portals or speak through any mirrors anywhere in the house. This information stays here until we get back from Columbus tomorrow, and then we'll figure out what we do next. Sound like a plan?"

Everyone nodded. That was good, because my brain was full, and I wasn't real sure I had room for much else until and unless we were ready to move forward with the next step. Doris agreed to sleep in the spare room with the mirror Geoffrey used to contact the Snow Queen. Geoffrey agreed to sleep on the couch in the living room, where everyone could see him, and for his part, he promised to stay downstairs, so no one could accuse him of trying to contact the Snow Queen or try to open the portal. Bob headed for the study with Bert.

Mia and I went into the kitchen to pack our lunches for the next day in silence. We cleaned out the water bottles we'd taken to stay hydrated, washed out our travel coffee mugs, and packed our lunch coolers without saying a word. As we put everything together where we could grab it all first thing in the morning, Mia finally commented.

"I think we need to give Bert some slack."

"Slack? Aren't we right back where we were at two years ago, with Bert doing the same thing he did then, making decisions and negotiating behind our back and putting us in danger?" I couldn't help it. I was pissed.

"Look, Bert screwed up back then and he knows it. That was about his own personal gain. What does he gain here? He loses. If he really is the guardian of the items now, then what chance does he have with Allie for lasting happiness? I really think that's the last thing he wanted, and that he never thought it would ever happen."

She was probably right. Heck, I knew she was right. Bert had learned his lesson, had stopped drinking, and had cleaned up his act pretty well in the last couple of years. I knew he never would have done it if he thought he had a choice. How much had he felt his back against the wall to do this? What choices would I make to protect my friends, how much would I keep from them, if I felt it would protect them? It was pretty clear I'd do the same, if not worse, to keep those I loved from harm. I nodded at her. "We all just need to sleep on it. I know I need to shut off my brain long enough to get some sleep. I'll feel better after I've had some sleep. We can talk more in the car in the morning." She agreed.

I went upstairs, where Aiden was waiting, with my heart heavy, worried about Bert. Aiden met me at the door, ready for bed himself in a pair of Scooby Doo sleep shorts and a University of Dayton Flyers t-shirt. He gave me a kiss and wrapped his arms around me.

"You doing okay with all of this?" he asked.

"I'm worried about Bert," I said.

"What do you mean?"

"The guy takes things very personally. He almost trashed everything to impress a girl two year ago. And now, I'm thinking he might be trashing any chance he has at a normal life, even one where he might choose to become human again, in love with a girl who loves him back, and he's willingly setting things in the way of that relationship to protect all of us. He's gotta be wondering what he did wrong to deserve this."

"I agree. He has to be feeling like the universe hates him. I know I would be. I also know that if I were in his shoes, I'd have to do the same thing, and Janie, you would too. It's part of why you love him so fiercely; you know he feels the same way we both do, and you know it's killing him inside." He squeezed me tight.

I pulled back. "Yeah, you're right. I'd totally do the same thing, and when I calmed down from being angry with him for not telling us about the portal, I realized exactly that. So what do we do about the whole thing?"

"I have no idea."

"I don't either."

"So sleeping on it?"

"Yeah."

We shut the door and went inside, pulling back the covers and plumping up the pillows in silence for a few minutes.

"So how can we support him? How can we make this better for him?" I asked.

"I think a lot of that is up to Allie."

I heard muffled voices down the hall, coming from the direction of Mia and Jonah's room. Apparently they were also discussing the night's events. I wondered where Allie was, and what she thought of all of this, but I also knew she probably needed some time to consider her own thoughts. If I felt overwhelmed at all of this, what about her? Then again, her entire existence had been dictated by people who wanted to manipulate her and her mother, wiped her father's memory of her from his head, and made her feel like she was an extraneous piece of trash. She escaped because of the sacrifices of her mother (which made me think she'd understand the whole thing) and then was abused by the men who took advantage of her inexperience and her naiveté (which made me think she wouldn't). Then she did exactly what Bert was trying to do, sacrifice herself in order to save her friends, us. That didn't work so well, so I could see her trying to talk him down, because we hadn't let her do it on more than one occasion. I was swinging on a teeter totter, trying to figure out what her stance was going to be, and was no closer now that I'd been thirty minutes earlier.

I laid in bed next to Aiden, and realized how lucky I was. I realized that somehow, through all the crazy events of the day, through all the ups and downs of our relationship, we were on the same page on most issues without even asking each other. That hadn't always been the case. Just last year, I'd been convinced he was working up the courage to leave me, when in fact, he'd been working up the courage to propose marriage.

"Aiden, should we postpone the wedding?" I asked, quietly.

He took a minute before he answered. "You want to postpone the wedding?"

"No, I really really don't. In fact, I think I've maybe been reckless at forcing us to get married this week, so fast after the bar exam. And now this with Bert? If we postponed the wedding, then we'd take the legs out from under whoever was targeting us. I think its Evangeline. I think she's going to use the wedding as an excuse to get in the house. In other words, somehow she knows that the portal was moved here. And if it's not her, which I highly doubt, then word's out that it was moved here. I'm wondering if whatever markers Bert called in to move it leaked the location of the portal."

"But you heard the conversation down there. It takes the tracing of a rune, a certain ingredient, and an incantation in order to open it. Someone sneaking into the house isn't going to have the right information on how to do this, will they? So the real question is whether there's any other way to open a portal, and whether or not that information is available to the public, or at least available to anyone who might be looking for it."

"Good question," he said, lapsing into silence again for a few minutes before answering my original query. "Short answer? I'm not sure that moving the wedding date, or just postponing it, will do anything to keep anyone safe. Longer answer? I don't want to move the wedding date. I want to be married to you, and I want it to happen as soon as possible. But at the same time, whether we're married today or tomorrow or Saturday, or a year from now, a piece of paper and some cake is not going to change what we mean to each other. It's not going to change who we are, or that we love each other. If we moved it, there's a chance the invitation still stands for any wedding guests, so we wouldn't solve the problem, we would just be postponing the wedding.

"There doesn't seem to be a reason based on our relationship, to postpone. We're still good. I've got no complaints. If you have a complaint, or something we need to talk about regarding our relationship, then we need to talk about it, but there's no indication that changing the date keeps anyone safer. Postponing is an excuse. We don't need to start our lives together with an excuse.

"I say we go ahead with the wedding. If nothing else, it gives us a great story for the grandkids. And if nothing happens, then we've gotten married. All the work is done. It will be more work, and more detail to get it moved at this point than to go ahead, unless you have cold feet unrelated to the current crisis."

And right there, right on his face and in his rationale, was why I loved him. "No cold feet. Just worried about keeping everyone safe and whole."

"Then we're getting married on Saturday. There's no reason to delay. I love you."

Chapter Twenty-Eight

The next morning came awfully early. There wasn't going to be enough coffee to make me feel fully prepared for the day. I yawned as I filled my travel mug, Mia behind me waiting to do the same.

"You sleep much last night?" she asked.

"Some. Not as much as I probably should have with the bar exam, but I kept turning everything over and over in my mind. There's really no good answer for any of this, there's just putting our feet one in front of the other and keep going." I handed Mia the coffee pot, and we grabbed our things, moving a little on the slow side after all the events of the night before. "I just hope that we stop getting new information quite so fast. We still need to figure out how to handle the information that we got last night. I mean, are we just supposed to ride out the week and hope everyone goes away after the wedding and leaves us all to live in peace? I think we both know that will never happen at this point. So what do we need to do in order to prevent this from becoming a bigger issue?"

She nodded. We went out and got in the Escalade, purposely not taking Bert with us this time. If he was the guardian of the attic portal, then he needed to be there to, well, guard the portal. Besides which, Allie had decided to call in to work and use personal days for the rest of the week, to deal with wedding stuff and so that she wouldn't be leaving the house. I know she'd planned this prior to Bert's revelations, but staying home to work out whatever issues they might have as a result of Bert's secrets didn't hurt, either.

I was driving again, as we headed towards Columbus. The drive was about an hour long; just long enough to be a pain; but almost the entire drive was highway, with open cornfields making up the scenery, so it was pretty, and traffic wasn't bad until we hit the outer loop. Like the day before, we'd left early to try to beat much of the rush hour traffic hurrying into the city. Again, we got to the parking lot early enough to get a decent parking spot and have the car close enough to the door for a quick escape if something happened. A few more people had gotten into the parking lot at that point; at a guess, I'd have to say people had learned the lesson of not wanting to park so far away they needed to take the shuttle afterwards to get to their car. Of course, the traffic had been heavy getting out of there the night before, but I still much preferred the idea of sitting in my own car in gridlock to standing on a corner and waiting forever for a shuttle and being dependent on that shuttle to get me to my car.

Like yesterday, we waited for a while in the car, then went inside and took up position at the tables where we'd sat yesterday. Most people were settling back in at the same tables they'd sat at the day before. I noticed a few empty tables. Had people really not come back for the second day? It was a lot of money to pay to take the test, and it was only given twice a year. Even if I'd felt totally overwhelmed the day before, I'd still finish the test, because even if I failed, I'd have a better chance of knowing what to expect the next time.

The proctor stood up again, waiting for us all to be seated and quiet down. I knew I was ready. I'd studied the material. There wasn't much else I could do to prepare for this. The butterflies in my stomach, however, weren't quite so comfortable, and I was pretty sure they were going to pretty much explode in my guts. Or make me throw up. Or both.

Either way, it wasn't going to be pretty.

I reached into my bag and pulled out a piece of gum, slipping it into my mouth and trying not to be obnoxious about it. I wanted to see if the mint from the gum would help settle my stomach. It was just starting to help when the proctor finally started talking.

We had another morning full of essays, and then the afternoon would be the multi-state multiple choice questions. The multi-state test covered general legal principles that apply in most of the United States, as opposed to Ohio specific information in the essays we'd been writing. We'd taken dozens of practice tests, and none of them had been easy.

When I'd been a kid, I'd always thought multiple choice tests were the bomb, because the answer was in front of me. I didn't have to remember all the details. I just had to recognize the right answer that someone else had already written. In this case, the problem was recognizing the most correct answer, as opposed to one right answer versus four wrong ones. Here, all of the answers could be correct to a certain degree, so just recognizing something as correct wasn't good enough. Worrying about which was the best one could be agonizing, and there was a time limit imposed as well. When we'd first started practicing there were many times we hadn't finished the entire section within the time limit; now it was real.

I couldn't be watching for anything magical going on if I was concentrating so hard on the test. I was starting to regret leaving Bert at home, but I wasn't sure I had the heart to ask him to watch my back when his seemed to be the one in danger. Either way, I couldn't dwell on it, so I picked up my pen and started into the next essay.

After an uneventful lunch, we came back inside to take the multi-state test. The test booklets were passed out, and I sat at my table, taking deep breaths and trying not to panic. A proctor slid a test booklet under my gaze, and when I lifted my head slightly, there was a tiny pair of boots placed right beside my test booklet.

Boots. Smaller than that worn by a newborn baby. As if they would fit an animal. Like a cat.

Like Bob.

I jerked my head up, but the proctor had moved on. In fact, there were three proctors passing out tests. I had no idea which one had done it, and no time to go ask questions or narrow it down; I had to take the biggest multiple choice test of my life, and the magical emergency craziness was affecting me even here.

I didn't have a choice. I made a mental note as to which proctors were possible, and started in on the test. It didn't take long for me to realize I needed my entire brain to pay attention to what I was doing. If I did otherwise, then I would fail, and all of my work over the last months, if not the last three years, would be down the drain until I could take the test again in February.

I couldn't afford to take this test over and over again. I had to pass this thing as fast as I could. I had to do it now, and I had to get past it so that I could protect everyone else.

I also had to let go and let the others help.

I trudged through the test, slogging through each question, watching the clock to make sure that I wasn't wasting time, even as I was answering each question carefully and deliberately, reading slowly and forcing myself to think through each step. Finally, I completed the last question, and double checked to make sure that I had a filled in answer on every single question on the answer sheet. I went through briefly to make sure my answers all corresponded with the right questions, and took a deep breath. The hardest part of the test, at least, in my mind, was over. Tomorrow would be a half-day, with only the practical application portion to do.

Writing a brief or a motion or a memo, that they were providing me with the research? I could totally do that.

Now, to take a quick restroom break and see if I could find the proctors who might have given me Bob's boots, and I'd be doing well. A quick glance around told me Mia was still working on the test, and I had enough time to do what I wanted. I slipped the boots into my purse, picked it up, handed in the test booklet and answer sheet, and headed for the ladies' room. I saw a proctor standing nearby, but he wasn't one of the three I had thought to ask. He smiled at me and I pointed to the restroom. He nodded.

I went inside and did what I had to do.

When I came back out, there was a different proctor standing there. I whispered I had turned in my test already, but that I had a question. He waved me to the outer chamber, where we had walked into the large room, and where we wouldn't be bothering anyone else still concentrating. I knew how much I'd had to concentrate on what I was doing, and I didn't want to be a distraction to anyone else.

"When the test booklets were being handed out, someone left these on my desk. I used to own something like this, and they look like they're mine, but I just wanted to know who it was, so that I could thank them." I was concerned that if I didn't lay some claim to them, the proctor would confiscate them as lost and found items. I was pretty sure they belonged to Bob, pretty sure they were related to the whole magical mess that we were in, and pretty sure we would regret it badly if I allowed them to get too far out of our sight while we were in midst of a magical emergency.

The proctor's eyebrows went up pretty far; it was clear he didn't know anything about them. "Wait here," he said. "Let me go ask around."

I waited for a few minutes. He must have had to ask more than one person, because he was gone for several minutes. Finally, he came back with an older woman. "This is Clarissa. She says one of the other test takers picked up the boots at lunch yesterday near where you were sitting and turned them in, pointing you out. She's the one that gave you the booklet and the boots earlier."

I looked at her critically, and her eyes seemed slightly out of focus, almost as if she was fuzzy about what she was doing. It crossed my mind someone might have be spelled her to get her to bring the boots to me, much like someone had brought the glass slippers to my front door, but who would do such a thing?

I didn't know anyone, mortal or magical, who would just randomly have strangers bring footwear to me. I didn't know anyone, friend or foe, who would send such a thing without having some way of my knowing who had sent what. And given the wedding presents and the amount of thank you notes I'd have to figure out, most were putting a card or a note with them to let me know who had sent them. The slippers and the boots? Not so much.

"So who gave them to you?" I asked.

She shrugged. "Don't know. The woman just said she'd seen you sitting there and found the boots when you got up to leave, figured they were yours, and asked me to give them to you when I saw you. They were still in my pocket when I was passing out tests, so I just went ahead and gave them to you before I could forget."

Mia walked up right behind me, having just turned in her test as well. "What's up?"

I handed her the boots by way of explanation, and shook my head, trying to communicate to her silently to keep her mouth shut while I did this.

Apparently she understood my wild eyed expression well enough, because she didn't say anything else.

"Can you look and see if that woman is still in there taking the test? If she's already gone, then I've missed my chance to thank her, but if she's still in there, I'd like to wait and tell her that in person."

The proctor nodded, and said, "I can't tell you her name, but I can tell you if she's still here or not. I'm not sure what I can tell you if she is, but let's find that out first."

I nodded, and she went inside. She was gone for a few minutes, while Mia and I stood there and watched other test takers walking out for the day as they finished as well. I almost hated waiting, because the longer we stood there, the more likely we were going to be caught in gridlock and be stuck in traffic just trying to get out of the parking lot. I wanted to get home as soon as possible, but I also wanted to see if I could figure out who was leaving me magical footwear. The desire to see who it was won out over the hurry to get home; so we waited.

It didn't work, though. The proctor came back and reported the person was not inside taking the test. That meant they had either already turned in their test by the time I finished and was long gone for the day, or they weren't there to take the test at all, and had just shown up to deliver those stupid boots.

I was voting for the latter. I just have that luck.

CHAPTER TWENTY-NINE

We ended up in the car heading home, with Mia driving this time, and me staring at the boots I'd gotten from the proctor. They seriously looked like a fancy pair of cowboy boots, with alligator skin, silver toe tips, and if I wasn't mistaken, they had spurs.

Honest to goodness spurs.

How in the world did a cat from a French story end up with the most flamboyantly cowboy pair of boots I'd ever seen? There was even a Texas Longhorn insignia on the top of each foot. And then there was also the drawl that Bob had talked with last night. As I thought about his voice, I was pretty certain that these were his boots. Who else could they belong to?

As we drove home, I kept turning the boots over and over in my hands, looking to see if there were any identifying marks that might tell me the name of their owner, but there wasn't any. There were scuffmarks on the side of the right boot, and creases at the ankles, showing that they had been worn, and worn a lot. How long had it been since they had been worn?

"Huh," I said. "So if these are actually Bob's boots, how in the world did they end up looking like something out of a cheesy Wild West show? I mean, these boots have got to be older than the idea of a Wild West show; they've got more years to them than Texas statehood. So how?"

She laughed. "Janie, you know as well as I do that magic can change things over the years. Look at the Galoshes of Fortune that I ended up with a couple of years ago. They currently are rubber rain boots with smiley faces on them. You think that was their original state? There's no way that the technology to make those boots was around when Hans Christian Andersen was writing his stories. Stuff changes. I don't know whether it's the magic inherent in them, or if it's just an adaptation reflex, but magic changes things. Of course they're Bob's boots. Who else would fit in them?"

I smiled at her. She was right. Not everything adapted with the times like the Galoshes, or like Bob's boots, but it wasn't the first time we'd seen something like that. Sometimes it was amusing, like looking at all the threaded detail on Bob's boots, or the smiley faces on Mia's galoshes. Other times, well, let's just say that I was starting to worry about Bert, who had been transformed by magic so many years ago, and had been living with it ever since. I was concerned that it could affect his mind, his personality, his very soul. Was that why he used to drink so much?

We rode the rest of the way home in silence, Mia driving on the interstate, me watching out the windows and whipping my head back from time to time to check behind us for threats. It wasn't like we were paranoid or anything, but the obvious lack of threat made me more uneasy, not less. I didn't like being on the lookout all the time. It made me worry that I was missing something, and waiting for the magical bad guy to appear never was my strong suit. I've always said patience was a virtue only when I didn't have to wait for it.

I just wanted them to come out into the open and do whatever it was they were going to do; and to heck with waiting any more. I was tired of always feeling like we had to play detective, like we had to piece together what was going on with old books and dusty old memories.

We got home to find the boys sweaty and exhausted, lying in the grass and staring up at the sky.

"What do you guys think you're doing?" I asked. "Isn't it enough that we could be attacked at any time? Why are you out here instead of behind the threshold, or at least behind the metal and salt circle?" I hadn't even waited for Mia to park the Escalade before jumping out and running towards them, hoping to shoo them into the relative safety of the house.

"Why?" Aiden said. "There's been no sign of anything today. We just got done working as you pulled in. We're taking ten minutes to enjoy the work we've done. Take a look."

I shut my mouth before I could argue with him, and looked around.

The grass was level, green, and lush, with no divots, gouges, or holes that someone could get a heel stuck in and trip, which had been my concern for wedding guests, never mind the groom. The flowerbeds were mostly back to normal, with flowering plants and decorative shrubs and grasses growing like gangbusters; they looked even better than they had a week ago, given the hot July weather. The side of the garage that had been damaged looked good as new with a fresh coat of paint, and the only thing left to fix was the sliding glass door, scheduled for tomorrow. I took a deep sigh of relief, because it looked like we were going to be able to host the ceremony after all, instead of having to find an alternative location and then get more people to guard the house. After all, guarding the house had gotten ten times more important, given the portal in the attic.

I smiled as I looked around. I could visualize the chairs and the ribbons that Doris and Allie had organized, set up in the back. The boys had painted a very small gazebo to put up in the backyard and use for an altar during the ceremony, which would become a lasting keepsake in the yard to commemorate our wedding. I could imagine the guests sitting in the chairs, and me walking down the small aisle, and it was all going to be beautiful. We just had to survive long enough to get there.

Doris came outside just as I was taking it all in. Harold and Geoffrey were right behind her, bickering about who was going to use the grill to cook the plate of chicken breasts she held. She ignored them and started up the grill herself, letting them argue as she waited for the grill to heat up.

I grinned at them. There didn't seem to be any chance that Doris would ever get back together with Geoffrey, but Harold looked like he was getting jealous that Geoffrey was spending time at the house this week. Harold was normally the even-keeled, rational guy, but he looked a little panicked as he and Geoffrey argued about which one of them would do justice to the chicken breasts Doris had been marinating all day. It did my heart good to hear it, because it was normal jealousy, as opposed to magical insanity. I hoped Harold knew that she wasn't going anywhere. It was obvious to anyone who saw them together that they were perfect for each other. Was Geoffrey just out of sorts that his former girlfriend, Gabriella, had been killed? Was that why he was hanging around so close, and dancing attendance on Doris? Was he just worried about her, or was he having some sort of existential crisis and worried about anyone he had been romantically involved with?

No way to tell at the moment, and we did have to tell everyone about what had happened that day and give Bob his boots. And see what else needed done.

Jonah looked tired. Not just from a hard day's work, which I assumed had been the case anyway, but he looked like he was ready to drop. How much magic had he been slinging around to get all of this accomplished today? Should we be worried about him? He had dark circles under his eyes and his eyes were red, as if he'd been awake all night without benefit of caffeine in the morning. And I knew I'd left a full pot of coffee ready for the boys when we'd left. There wasn't a soul living in our house that wasn't addicted to caffeine. I knew better than to leave an empty coffee pot. So why did Jonah look like he was running on empty?

Mia was fussing over him. I assumed she saw the same thing, and left her to it.

Aiden and I went over to the bickering beside the grill and sat down on the patio furniture, watching the entertainment that Doris seemed to be ignoring, even if it was for her benefit.

If we didn't have the magical conundrum, the upcoming wedding, one more day to the bar exam, and a concern about Jonah's wellbeing, it would have been a typical summer evening, grilling on the patio. All we needed were some beers and some corn on the cob, a radio playing in the background, and maybe some kids chasing lightning bugs to put in mayonnaise jars with holes punched in the lids.

Someday we'd have to do exactly that, when Aiden and I had a couple of kids running through the yard, with Doris and Harold and Geoffrey here to enjoy them, and Mia and Jonah here as honorary aunt and uncle. I smiled at the thought, because I was willing to do a lot to get to that point. The only problem?

Figuring out where the other people missing from that scene would be. The other honorary aunt and uncle, who had earned their rights to enjoy that kind of scene as well.

Bert. And Allie.

CHAPTER THIRTY

So I asked.

"Where are Bert and Allie?" I leaned forward on the chaise lounge on the patio, trying to see into the sliding glass doors to see if they were coming.

Doris looked sad. "I heard them arguing earlier today, but I haven't seen them for a few hours. I know they're both still here, though; I never heard the front door open and close, and that's how Allie leaves when she's taking the bus to work. Besides, I thought she had the day off."

"She does." I stood up, heading inside to go check on everyone. I still had my purse, with Bob's boots inside. I was hoping he hadn't gone too far, either. I'd like to see what he had to say about them.

Allie was inside, sitting by herself in the dark, in a corner of the dining room.

"What's wrong?" I asked.

She didn't say much at first, quietly standing up and wiping her eyes.

"You okay?" I asked, worried about her.

"I'll be fine." She got a very determined look on her face at that moment. "I'm done crying. I'm going to kick that frog's ass."

Good for her, I thought. It was exactly what Bert needed. "So, what happened?"

"That jerk decided to break up with me because he thinks he can never be a human, because he's got to safeguard that portal for all of eternity. He thinks he would have to give up his humanity forever so that he can be a martyr to magical interference for the rest of his life. He won't even try to come up with an alternative plan. He won't even explore options. I'm going to kill him myself; magic won't even have to."

Aha. I'd called it. Bert was going to sacrifice his relationship with Allie to be the guardian of the portal. And I didn't disagree with him.

I'd do the same thing if it was Aiden and I, with confidence that Aiden would agree, which he had last night.

But obviously Allie didn't agree. One look at her determined face had me thinking that we had it all wrong; we were thinking about magic and protecting everyone else, but we weren't thinking about whether we hurt the ones we loved most. I took one look at Allie's face, and I knew we were wrong. It was wrong not to even look for another option, to completely give up hope. As long as we were all alive, and safe, and the portal still protected, it wasn't over. There was no reason to have him just hole up and forget that he was alive.

Just like there was no reason to postpone the wedding.

Just like there was no reason to postpone taking the bar exam.

Just like Bert had no option but to move that portal to try to prevent me from feeling like I had to do exactly that.

"Do you have a plan, Allie? He's pretty stubborn, and he probably thinks he brought this on himself just from being involved with Perrault in the first place and not finding a better way to hide all of this. He's going to try to sacrifice himself if he can, to protect all of us. I'll bet he's even thinking since he's the last one to hold the secret, then there will be no one that can enter the portal if he's gone. He might be looking for the way to end it all, if that keeps us all safe." Looking at Allie's face, I realized she hadn't thought all of that through, but she wasn't contradicting me.

"I don't have a plan, yet, but that frog's got to do a lot more than just hurt my feelings to get me to walk away from him when I know he doesn't actually mean it. I'm not giving up yet." She headed for the hallway, stalking towards the study, where Bert liked to hole up when he was melancholy or morose. I was betting he had at least one bottle of liquor in there with him.

I'd have made money on that bet. When we walked into the study, Bert was sprawled out on the pillow he used as a bed, his mouth hanging open, and drool dripping from his mouth. A half empty bottle of Jack Daniels sat next to the pillow. Bob welcomed us inside with a very boozy, slurry greeting, and when I got inside, I saw Jack had friends; a bottle of Jim Beam and a bottle of Jose Cuervo rounded out the collection. He was going to hurt in the morning, I decided. If the hangover didn't kill him, Allie left him alive, and whoever was after him let him live through the weekend, his butt was mine.

It smelled like vomit, but when I looked, it appeared that he had thrown up in a glass ashtray instead of on the hardwood floor. That was good news; it wouldn't ruin the finish on the floor, and the ashtray could run through the dishwasher.

"Hewwo," sang Bob the cat, in a cutesy, sing-song baby voice. "Didju find me boots? What's a cat without boots, I tells ya?"

Some of the cowboy seemed to have disappeared from his voice, but there was still an odd cadence to his speech. I assumed it had something to do with the shape of his jaw and the amount of alcohol it appeared that they both had imbibed.

I hoped the cat hadn't thrown up anywhere, and if he had, I hoped that it was somewhere that I would be able to find it easily. I'd had a cat when I was little, and I still remembered Dad flipping out when he'd found a hairball or something that was old because the cat had brought it up somewhere that wouldn't be found right away, like under the couch or behind a bookshelf.

"I think I did find your boots, Bob. Someone brought them to me today." I pulled them out of my purse, and set them down on the floor.

His mouth hung open, and he tried to hurry towards them, stumbling over his feet as he did so. "I owe you forever, my friend. I will do you any service, or any work you deem appropriate. I owe you a debt, and I am not sure that I can ever repay you. What can I do in service to you?"

Yeah, um, kinda drunk. "You can start by not throwing up in my house."

He looked a little embarrassed. "I must confess to being sick in your waste can."

In the trash? I didn't think I even had a trash can in the room. When I looked confused, he pointed to a large vase in the corner. Luckily, it didn't have anything in it, and it was glazed ceramic; it would wash out with the hose outside, if I could get Aiden and Jonah to help me move it. It would take all three of us because the thing was fairly heavy, but it was still doable.

"That's okay. We can take care of that. Just don't do it again, eh?

Oh, and encouraging the frog to drink is not a good idea. I've cleaned up more frog vomit than I'd like, and I'd prefer not to do it again."

Bob looked over at Bert, who was unconscious on his pillow. "It was his idea. Something about his heart being hurt."

I bet it was. I bet that he felt like he was tearing his own heart out by the roots in order to hurt Allie the way he had in order to get her to even consider letting him get away with it. And he must have had her at least partially convinced, to have her sitting in the dark and fussing over it. I wondered how long she had been sitting there, working herself into a right fury.

I knew he'd met his match in Allie. She was going to take his hide off when she saw what he had done to himself, but for the moment, there wasn't much else we could do, except to remove the liquor from the room and leave Bob and Bert to sleep it off. I made Bob tell me if there was any other liquor in the room they had access to, and he pointed out a small bottle of Woodford Reserve whisky sitting in a corner near the sofa. When these guys drank, apparently, they didn't go for the cheap stuff that college students went for. They went for the liquor that could cost anywhere from thirty to fifty dollars a bottle, and they had four bottles they'd put a good sized dent in.

Well, I guess I should have been happy they weren't going for cheap beer. Cleaning up frog and cat pee wasn't on my list of fun to-dos tonight, either.

I got Bob to promise there wasn't any more alcohol in the room, and promise not to drink any more that night, so that he could watch Bert, to make sure he didn't drink anymore, and choke on his own tongue (as a frog, this could be a problem). It was time to let the others know what I'd found out, tell them all about Bob's boots, and see if they had any more solutions to the problems we were facing this weekend.

And, hopefully, get a better night's sleep tonight than we had the night before.

God, I was tired.

CHAPTER THIRTY-ONE

When I got back to the kitchen, the others were already inside, setting the table and getting ready for dinner. The grill was off, and the others were dishing up marinated grilled chicken, spinach salad, baked potatoes, and Doris had made a Boston crème poke cake, with pudding poured into holes poked in a yellow cake, with chocolate frosting on top. We demolished dinner fairly quickly, stuffing ourselves silly. For some reason, everyone was exhausted, and everyone was starving. It had been a long day for everyone.

Mia and I began clearing the table and loading the dishwasher as we told the others about Bob's boots, about the woman who had handed them to me, and an inability to figure out who had tried to hand them over. I told them all why Bob and Bert weren't joining us for dinner, and we all had a quick laugh at Bert's drunken escapades before it died to an awkward silence with one look at Allie's face.

She was pissed.

Royally pissed.

In an overly calm voice, she said, "I would like to ask you all to help me come up with a better solution for this situation than Bert has come up with. He doesn't seem to think he's got a better option. I think there is, we just have to find it. So, I know we've got a lot going on this week, but we need to convince him that his life as he knew it is not over. I'm willing to stand by him as long as humanly possible, and I think he actually wants to become human again, if it's possible. But he's given up, saying it's his duty and his responsibility to do this. He's not considering any other avenue, any other course of action, or any other possibility."

"Allie, of course we'll help you. I know he just doesn't want you hurt." I didn't have the heart to tell her that my reaction would have been the same as hers, but my heart hurt for her.

"Too late. He just hurt me more than any magical being ever could have. I'm going to have his hide for this. And then I'm never going to let him go."

My heart cracked into a million pieces, breaking as I saw her heart break. I met eyes with Aiden, and the look on his face was priceless; it looked like he felt the same way I did. Of course, we'd all felt a fierce desire to protect Allie from the moment we'd met her; she just inspired that in everyone. But she didn't need protecting, because she was more than capable of taking care of herself, as we were seeing.

Bert didn't stand a chance.

"Okay, so there's some weirdness going on here." I brought up the shoes from the Perrault treasure showing up at our doorstep without anyone seeming to be able to access the portal. "If the portal was already here, and Bert's the only one who can access it, then either the shoes were already outside of the Perrault location, and someone is playing a joke, or someone already has access to it, and is targeting Bert. I know Bert thinks he's got to protect it, but if someone's already got access, then the silver lining is that he may not have to be the guardian of it for all eternity. The concern is who has access to it. If the shoes were already outside of the portal, then why would they target him? Someone would have had to have gotten them out, and known his connection to them. But if they knew the connection, why leave them on the front step? Why not package them just for him, and not left where any one of us might have tried them on?"

Doris nodded at me, putting the leftover cake into the refrigerator. There was no way we'd have finished it; it was so rich that a small piece still had me satisfied despite my overwhelming love of dessert. Doris closed the refrigerator door. "Allie, you're talking to a number of people here who have either had to fight for a relationship affected by magic, or who have left a relationship behind due to the conflicts in the relationship due to magic. We all understand what you're going through. And you have our support, no matter what happens."

Geoffrey looked stricken. Yeah, their relationship hadn't survived, due to the conflicts between his magical life and her mortal one, but they'd gotten Aiden out of it, and so they'd stayed in some contact. It was always hard to tell with Geoffrey, but it seemed to me that he kinda regretted the way all of that had happened. In their case, though, his court responsibilities kept him in the magical realm quite a bit, and as a mortal, she could not have lived full time in that realm without going mad. For them it was a practical matter of location. And it looked like Doris had moved on, having married previously and had other kids. And now with Harold, it looked like she'd found someone to spend the rest of her time with. So was Geoffrey just sad over the road not traveled with her, or was he genuinely still interested?

Then there was Aiden and I, who had not had the world's smoothest road to the matrimony we hoped to join this weekend, and Mia and Jonah were still ironing out some kinks in their own relationship, given his magical heritage and his monthly obligation to meet with his many times great-grandmother out West and practice his magic, working to restore her homeland to its former glory. That wasn't going to be an easy feat, as there seemed to be little in the way of water or arable land to support their work in trying to bring back enough plant life to support a return of the people who had once lived there, but he seemed to be optimistic.

Speaking of Jonah, his ancestor, Frog Woman, was another one who'd seen a magical relationship wither and die. She'd tried to have a relationship with Johnny Appleseed, but they'd had different goals and different plans to use their magic with plants, and they'd split before she'd found herself pregnant. She'd given up the child for adoption, and many years later, Jonah's own biological parents had done the same with him. It was only years later that he'd learned of his heritage and started trying to figure out how to use it responsibly.

"So, you'll all help me?" she asked, looking very small and very fragile, no matter how angry she was.

"Of course we'll help see what other options are out there, Allie. And then you and Bert together will have to make the best decision for you. That doesn't promise you a happy ending, though; you do realize that, right?" Geoffrey said, carefully. Of course he was being careful about making promises, he didn't want to break one. That was a big taboo in the magical world.

She nodded, although she didn't look happy about it.

"So what do we do about the shoes?" I asked. "I'm sorry to be insisting, but is it possible that someone has gotten access to the Perrault treasure through the excavation in the mortal realm, and placed them there to play mind games with Bert?"

"Not a chance that we've been able to find," Jonah said. "The excavations on Oak Island, where we think the treasure is, haven't found anything yet as far as we've been able to determine. There's absolutely no sign of any recovered treasure or artifacts. We've found no record anywhere, although they are finding more and more information on the different phenomenon on the island. I was trying to see if I could find a phone number for the researchers, but all I could find was one for the guy who's producing the television show. And they wouldn't speak about anything that hadn't been revealed on the show itself. I don't blame them for keeping a close hold on those details. After all, they don't know if I'm trying to leak some sort of spoiler that could wreck their ratings."

No question Jonah was an actor; I wouldn't have thought of that. He'd done some local television lately, but was still working on breaking in. Still, it was more his field than mine, and I trusted his judgment.

The doorbell rang.

"Anyone expecting a guest?" I asked. I hadn't invited anyone over today, and I was really hoping no one else had, either. Then again, an expected guest would, hopefully, be less dramatic this week than the unexpected and potentially magical guest.

No one volunteered that they had.

Oh, shit.

CHAPTER THIRTY-TWO

There was an older woman on the front step when I answered the door, Aiden right behind me with an aluminum baseball bat for protection. Was it sad that we felt like we had to keep the bat by the door and answer it ready to swing for the fences? It was just the way it was this week. I just hoped she wasn't the new Avon lady, or someone from the neighborhood watch group, because that could get entertaining to explain down the road.

"I need help," she said quietly.

"And someone sent you here?" I asked. This could be magical help, or just someone who needed to use the phone to dial for a tow truck. Either way, with the wedding just days away, and having just cleaned up the last magical catastrophe, I was not inviting this woman into the house.

She nodded.

"So what can I do for you?" I asked.

She glanced around. "Can I come inside?"

Oh hell, no, I thought. "No, but I'll walk you around back. We have a patio there that's visible to the street. We could talk privately there."

She looked surprised, but nodded. I stepped out of the house, and asked her to follow me. She did, her head down, staring at the grass all the way around the house. No matter what I said, or what small talk I initiated, she didn't say anything at all until we got to the back yard and I showed her the patio.

"And no one can see this from outside your yard?" she asked.

Wow, was she paranoid. Made me glad I hadn't invited her in. "Well, let's put it this way, in order to see into the yard enough to see what's going on, we'd see a head poking around the edge of the house. There are no holes in the section of the fence near the patio that could be seen from the neighborhood, and the rest of the fence is far enough away that with a radio playing, there no way to eavesdrop without jumping the fence, which we'd see. It's not perfect, but it's as secure as I can make it without taking you inside, and we're not doing that at this point. I don't know you." The neighbor boys were playing something on the radio just on the other side of the fence, which neatly solved that problem.

She nodded.

I sat down on the chaise lounge on the patio, and waved her to the chair. "How can I help you?"

"I was told to come here and ask for help, and I have done that. I am Griselda. I was told to ask for help as they wished me to gain access to your house and to place a magical device within your house. If I am not given access to your house, I cannot place the device, and will have to return it."

My eyes widened, staring at her in disbelief. "Are you saying you wished to harm us?"

"No," she said, frantically. "Never. I don't wish to harm anyone! I was just asked to place a device within the home, and leave. They didn't tell me anything other than that."

"Who is they?"

"I don't know."

"How do you not know who told you what to do? Was it over the internet, or were they wearing a mask, or what?" Aiden asked. He had a point. If someone was standing in front of me asking me to do something, I should at least be able to describe them.

"I don't know because they didn't ask me personally; they asked my husband, who told me to come do this for him. He's my husband. I have to do what he told me to do."

Was I the only one who heard the metaphorical nails on a chalkboard in the background when she made that statement? Yikes! Talk about living in the last century . . . or maybe the one before it. I cringed, and I couldn't hide it. Might as well run with it. "You don't have to do what your husband says just because you're married."

"He's my lord and master," was the answer.

I was now hearing screeching tires in my head. I don't think I'd ever heard anyone say something like that unless they were one of the women at Allie's shelter. I saw Allie through the sliding glass doors, in the kitchen with the others, and I wondered if I could catch her eye. She had some training in speaking with women who had been abused, even if it was only emotional abuse, and not physical harm. I didn't have that kind of training. I tried to get Allie's attention, but it didn't work.

"No matter who you're married to or who they are, you are allowed to make your own decisions. You are allowed to say no. You are allowed to ask questions."

"No, I am not. My children are gone because my husband wished it; if I want them back I cannot go against what he says. He has told me they will be killed if I go against his wishes. He has ordered them killed before, and only sent them away to make me think they were dead."

Holy shit, I thought, saying a silent prayer of thanks that Aiden was nowhere near what this man was. My soon-to-be husband would never put up with such a thing, and would come out swinging at anyone who tried, and not just with me, but with any woman, or man, or child, for that matter, who needed it. I took a shaky breath, and tried again. "Then you need to get help rescuing your children and you need to leave your husband. What's your name?"

She ignored my first question. "My name is Griselda."

I spoke to her for quite a while, trying to get more information from her about her children. She answered some of the questions, but when I started pushing her to leave her husband, she clammed up. I finally asked her to wait a moment while I asked a colleague to join me. I was out of my depth with her. I needed help. She nodded, silently.

I slipped inside.

"Allie, I need your help outside." I outlined what I was hearing from Griselda.

"Has she said why she told you about it?" Allie asked.

"What? We need to help her leave her husband." I exclaimed.

"Has she asked you for help with that?" Allie asked, in a quiet voice. "Has she said one thing that tells you that she actually wants help with that issue, or have you even asked her what she wants? It's obvious that she wants something from you, but I haven't heard you say what she actually has asked for."

"How could she not want to leave someone who threatens her children?" I exclaimed, frustrated.

"Look, we can ask around and see what we can do to help the kids no matter what, but she may have made the decision not to leave him, for whatever reason. In fact, you've said that he's been controlling and manipulative but you haven't said that he's ever actually put his hands one her. A lot of women won't leave because they don't think it's abuse if there are no injuries."

I didn't understand that.

I must have made a face, because she didn't stop there. "Look, Janie, you take on everyone's battles for them, and I love you for it, but you have to ask yourself if it's a fight that they want you to take on."

"What are you saying? If I hadn't fought for you in Wonderland, you'd still be hiding in that realm, hoping it kept us safe. Who knows where we would be?" I crossed my arms, and leaned back against the counter in the kitchen.

"And Aiden might not have had his memory issues, and he might not have almost died."

"And you and your mom might not have reunited." I shot back.

"Look, we can do this all day long. Bert got sick, Aiden could have died. I feel bad about that every day. Your relationship was fine until after you came back from Wonderland and Aiden had his memory issues. You guys could have lost each other."

"But we didn't. We would have found our way back to each other again if we had lost our way."

She snorted. "You were preparing yourself for the possibility of his leaving you while we were out West last year. I heard some of your discussions with Bert, and he told me the rest. You were going to let him go, because you thought that was what he wanted. You were willing to forgo the fight for your relationship because you thought he wanted to give up. That was out of character for you. You aren't someone who ever gives up, or when to give in, and I love that about you. But Aiden was willing to fight. He forced you to fight for your relationship."

"Yes, which is why I'm standing here, saying we should fight for her, even if she isn't asking me to. She needs someone to fight for her."

"The point is that you weren't going to fight. You might believe that you were wrong, but it was your decision to make, and you made it. You were going to give him up, and you were trying to do it with dignity. She has to decide what she wants to do in this kind of situation, and we have to support her in doing it, and tell her that we are ready to help her when she is ready for the help."

I tried to let that sink in. "Why the hands off approach? She seems to think her children are in danger."

"And she may be doing exactly what she thinks will keep them safest. She knows her situation best, not us. And someday she may come to us and ask us for help. We have to let her know we will not judge her at all, regardless of her choices. It might be the difference between her asking for help or not. If we let her know we're a safe place for her to ask, and not feel judged, then she's more likely to come ask for help down the road if she's not ready for it now. If you act judgmental, you might not ever get her back asking for help."

Well, if she wasn't ready now, I certainly didn't want to scare her off from asking for help in the future. I just wanted the future to be in five minutes, I thought, as we walked back out onto the patio.

"How can you feel okay about what might happen to her in the meantime?" I asked. It was kind of mean, but it was an honest question. How did she do this every single night at work and stay sane, and not worry about each and every person that she talked to if they didn't stand up for themselves right that moment? I knew I would blame myself forever if something happened to her or her children in the meantime, before she was "ready" to ask for help.

"Well, Janie, first of all, she's an adult. She is able to make her own decisions and her own choices. You might not agree with them. You might think her choices are dangerous or stupid, but they are her choices. And from what I heard of your arguments in Wonderland, you agree with me. People should have their own free choice to decide what to do with their lives and their businesses and their families. They should be allowed to go where they want, engage in free trade, and spend time with those they want to spend time with. If you truly believe that, then you have to let people make their own decisions, whether you like the decisions or not."

She was right. She had a very strong point. And no matter what I did or said, Griselda was a grown woman, with the right to make her own decisions.

"And the kids?" I asked.

"That's a separate issue. If it was a mortal family, I'd call children's services; I'd have to. It's mandatory for us to report them for investigating potential abuse or danger to the kids. In fact, we could be charged with a crime if we don't report it. So, you and I will look into what's going on with the kids. It could be that he's threatened them, but that they aren't even in the house any longer, which means he's not as big of a threat, and we maybe just keep an eye on the situation. If they're still there, then maybe we see who can intercede for them in the magical realm. Most faerie court royalty takes a dim view of harming their own children; they don't have very many."

I felt a little bit better at that. I had way no problem owing a debt or a favor somewhere to save some kids. "Okay. Will you talk to her? You have more experience at this than I do. I'm afraid I'll scare her off."

Or maybe I already had?

We went outside in a hurry, hoping Griselda was still there, and I didn't see her at first. She wasn't sitting on the patio any longer. Instead, she was looking at the plants in the backyard and checking out the back fence.

She heard us approach, and turned around, smiling. "Well, you have a lovely backyard. I miss gardening. Before my children were born, I liked to breed roses. After they were born, I just didn't have the time. Children do that to you; make you re-evaluate your life and make different decisions."

Was she trying to tell me something? Maybe Allie had it right, and Griselda was making choices based on what she thought was the safest course of action for her children. If that was the case, then there was no judgment there. It made her a concerned and scared mom, not an idiot. I tried to revise my internal opinion of her, but I was just having a hard time doing so.

"Thank you so much. We've been working hard on the yard. I'm getting married back here this weekend."

"It will be a lovely wedding," she said, and seemed a little sad.

I wondered if she was thinking of her own wedding. "Thank you. Griselda, I have some questions for you. This is my friend, Allie. Are you okay with her listening to this conversation?" I asked.

She nodded, looking a little shocked that I'd asked.

"Why did you tell me that someone wants to plant a device in my house?" I asked.

She smiled. "You asked the right question. Someone asked my husband to have the device planted in your home. He owes a favor, but he does not wish to be involved, and he's heard what you did to your stepmother. He does not wish to anger you, but he felt he could not say no to the person who made the request of him. He sent me to try to plant the device, but he made no promises regarding secrecy so I am here telling you that I was sent to do so."

Cagey and smart, I thought. And, just in case I was mad at her husband for sending someone at all, he sends his wife, which any research on me would show me to be sympathetic. And I wouldn't hold it against his wife, if she's the one warning me that someone's trying to plant something in my house. "Do you know who had him send you?" I asked. "What were they trying to plant?"

She shook her head. "Some sort of device that records a voice and is set on a timer," she said, describing the device, which she took out of her pocket.

I took the device. "Do you mind if I keep it?" I asked.

She smiled. "Even better. I can tell them that it is at your house, since I'm handing it to you at your house."

"And if they ask you where it is in the house?" Allie asked.

"Have you picked up your mail today?" she asked.

No. Allie ran to the front of the house and grabbed the mail out of the mailbox, bringing it back to where we stood in the backyard.

Griselda placed an item in the stack of envelopes. I probably wouldn't have seen it right away if I'd grabbed the mail, myself. "I'll tell them the truth. I didn't get in the house when I knocked, so I put it in your mail, and then watched you get your mail, so that it would get into the house when I couldn't get inside." She smiled. "This makes everyone happy."

"Except the person that wanted this in my house," I said. "They're going to be disappointed."

"What you do with it when you find it in the mail isn't my problem." Griselda squared her shoulders and walked toward the side of the house, leaving in the same direction that we had come from the front door. "I appreciate your concern, and I appreciate your cooperation. Maybe someday we'll speak again." She winked, and walked away.

Allie and I stood there.

"Well handled," Allie said. "Couldn't have done it better myself."

"So why do I feel like we let her down?" I asked.

"Look, it's not going to take much to make some inquiries. I betcha that Geoffrey would do it like a shot, if it made him look good, and to be honest, even the Snow Queen probably wouldn't keep you on the hook for information like this. She would want to act on it fairly quickly. Sounds like Griselda was trying to send you a bit of a message with that wink and her closing remark. She's considering coming back to you in the future, when all of this isn't hanging over her head. To be honest, she probably knew about the wedding. Likely this served a second purpose, to check you out while she did her husband's errand for him. It was an excuse for her to continue to appear compliant and obedient and patient and size you up at the same time. Betcha five bucks she calls you back within a month."

I hoped that she was right, and I made a mental note to ask Geoffrey to check into looking after those kids. Maybe I would have enough business to make a go of this after I got my bar results. Of course, first I had to pass the test.

Chapter Thirty-Three

We went back inside. I had the random thought that I needed to start making up business cards for our future business, though I'd have to figure out what to call myself. I couldn't say lawyer until I actually passed the test and got sworn in, but I could start handling negotiations on magical realm issues prior to that; there wasn't a bar exam to take for that, it was pretty much trial and error, diplomacy, and plain common sense. Maybe I needed a business card for magical clients and one for mortal realm clients. I wished I'd done more for her, even putting a business card in her hand, but I wondered if that would have endangered her. I don't know, just having that contact information might have been a comfort to her.

Or it could put her in danger if her husband thought she was considering something else? What about her kids? I'd have to talk to Allie about how to handle situations like that. I had a funny feeling I would get more cases like that in the future.

I was still worrying about Griselda, but I wasn't silly enough to take whatever she'd slipped in the mail inside the house. The garage, on the other hand, was separate, and had its own protective circle. I asked Allie to run in the house and ask Aiden to join me in the garage, without saying anything to anyone else. She nodded, squeezed my hand, and headed back to the house.

I flipped through the mail as I walked to the garage, and when I went inside, I saw that I still had a gym bag sitting on the side bench. I opened it while I waited on Aiden, and found what I was thinking of; a cheap ear bud set of earphones, ones I used to wear to the gym and listen to audio-books while I walked on the treadmill. I sighed. I needed to start doing that again, but for the moment, they would serve my purpose. The item that Griselda had brought was a digital programmable recorder. I wanted to hear what was on the recorder without activating anything around me, without starting a spell, or otherwise causing more magical mayhem.

Aiden walked in just as I set down the mail and began fussing with the recorder. There was one recording on it, and I handed him one of the ear buds so that we could both listen.

On the recorder was my voice, inviting someone into the house. Damn.

Planting a recorder with a timer on it, meant that technically they were rigging an invitation into the house for a specific time. I looked; the timer was set for five minutes after the ceremony was supposed to start on Saturday. Someone was looking to engineer an "invitation" into the house while I was otherwise occupied. Aiden and I looked at each other, horrified.

"So apparently we are being watched," I said. "There's no question about it now. So how did they get that recording?"

Aiden shook his head. "Well, Janie, if it were me, and I wanted that recording, I'd wait in the bushes in the front by the door and wait for someone to show up that you were expecting, record the entire conversation at the door, and then I would edit it down to what I wanted. It wouldn't even be hard to do. I'd say this is magical, and someone truly wants inside this house at all costs. I don't smell anything magical about the recorder, though. It looks like it's on a simple timer, set for Saturday. But we caught it. I'm almost half convinced they wanted us to catch it; like they wanted us to leave it in the house, thinking we caught it and turned it off. Makes me think there's a magical catch to it, so you're smart to have only brought it into the garage. I think it needs to stay here. It should never come into the house."

I agreed with him wholeheartedly. I didn't like the idea people were trying to smuggle things into the house. And then I had a really nasty thought. "Aiden, should we be worried about the wedding presents that have shown up so far? I mean, that's a more likely way of ensuring that something would actually get into the house, to show up in a box from one of the stores where we registered for wedding gifts."

From the look on his face, it appeared that he hadn't thought about that either. We looked around in the garage, and it appeared that there wasn't going to be room in the garage to store them unless we moved one of the cars out of the garage and parked it in the driveway for the rest of the week, not something I normally liked.

Allie didn't drive; she took the bus if one of us couldn't take her somewhere. Jonah and Mia each had cars, but they parked on the street and they only used their cars if they were going somewhere alone. Mostly, the Escalade was our mode of choice; it fit all five of us and a frog, and a lot of times we were all headed in the same direction. The fact that it was parked in the garage behind a protective salt and metal circle meant there could not be any magical interference with our primary mode of transportation, and the vehicle we used most during magical emergencies. While the car did have a steel frame, and most of the parts were made of metal (meaning that magical folk were not likely to touch the car or its parts), there was nothing to stop them from pouring sugar into the gas tank, or honey in the gears, or just puncturing tires. Puncturing a tire would be fairly obvious, but it would definitely work to screw up my day.

The other car in the garage was the Buick that Aiden now drove. It was a heavy tank of a car, with a steel frame as well, but it was several years old. It had been my Dad's car, and then mine when I'd started law school after his death. After Aiden had crashed his own car, yet again, we'd decided he'd start driving Dad's Buick. It was just safer for him to drive something less likely to crumple with him inside.

We made the decision to park the Buick outside and keep the Escalade in the garage, protecting it as Mia and I needed it in the morning to make it to the last day of the bar exam. Aiden was planning to stay home, as he'd taken the week off to work on wedding stuff, and he'd taken the week after the wedding off for us to have a bit of a honeymoon. Yeah, speaking of that, we still hadn't decided where we were going, but even then, we planned to take the Escalade and get out of town. The Buick could sit and need repairs until after we got home, and no one would be hurt.

Aiden went for his keys, and I rounded up the others to start carrying the presents that were taking up space in the dining room. Mia insisted on putting down an old tablecloth to protect the packages from any grease stains or fluids that might be on the floor, even though I didn't see anything like that, and said so, but I couldn't talk them out of it. Boxes from Amazon and from Macy's and from Walmart were piling up. I hadn't realized we had so much, because we'd just been piling it in the dining room. Aiden ran to get his magical detectors and the rest of us tried to get some organization to the pile.

"At least we have the dining room back," Allie said. "If we keep having extra people to dinner, it gets cramped in the kitchen. It's just not made to seat that many people comfortably."

She had a point.

I was definitely ready to call it a night. It had been a long day, a long drive home, and now, a long evening of drama, worry, and now manual labor. Was it time to call it a night yet? I was ready to crash.

And then one of Aiden's magical gadgets started going off, screaming a warning through the evening air, loud enough to attract attention from the neighbors, or well, anyone in a five block radius with reasonably decent hearing.

Holy crap.

Aiden tried to shut the thing off, but it just shrilled louder. We tried every switch on the thing that we could find, but there was no shutting it off. One of the neighbors came by, asking if we were all right; he couldn't figure out how to shut it off, either. My head was starting to hurt from the noise; and I saw Mia and Allie rubbing at their ears; apparently it was affecting them as well.

And then the cops pulled up.

That was all I needed tonight. I hoped it was just a noise complaint. I wasn't sure I could handle anything else.

CHAPTER THIRTY-FOUR

The gumball lights on top of the cruiser were flashing as the police pulled into my driveway. Aiden was ripping pieces off his detector, trying to shut it down without destroying it, but finally, he didn't have a choice; he ripped it in half just as the cop got to the garage.

He was young, I thought, to be a cop.

"I'm Officer Gearheardt. We got a noise complaint for this residence. I take it that gizmo was the culprit?" He nodded at the pieces in Aiden's hands.

My fiancé nodded. "I tend to do some robotics and model building as a hobby. I was working on this out here in the garage, and it suddenly started making the noise you heard. I didn't even know it could. I tried to shut it off without destroying all of my work, but as you can see, I took it apart. The noise shouldn't be a problem anymore, officer, because it will take me weeks to repair the damage, and I might not even be able to do it."

The officer took a look at the bits and pieces lying all over the place, and the giant pile of wedding presents sitting in the middle of the garage. "Well, I wonder if there's some electronic gift in there causing feedback."

Aiden looked surprised. "You know what, I never even thought of it. Well, I'll just have to wait until after the wedding to experiment with repairing all of this, once we know what's in all of the packages. There's no reason to risk ticking off all of the neighbors when it might be as easy a solution as that."

The officer smiled. "So who's getting married?"

Aiden explained we were getting married on Saturday, and then leaving for our honeymoon, but that we had roommates that would be living in the house while we were gone. He asked a few questions about the house, and our security while traveling, then told us congratulations and to have a nice trip.

"Officer, I am sorry that we've created such a nuisance in the neighborhood. Please convey my apologies to whoever called it in; we normally live pretty quietly around here, and some of the neighbors are even invited to the wedding reception on Saturday night. We certainly didn't intend to cause anyone any issues. We'll happily pay the noise ticket if you feel it's necessary."

The officer considered for a moment. "I think your neighbors were more worried than anything, said you've had a lot of visitors over the last few weeks. Heck that many delivery people coming by could explain that. I won't write a ticket, but will write this up as a warning. You don't need an extra expense with a wedding this week, and I daresay that the neighbors will understand, but you will get a noise citation and a fine if I get called back out here on a noise complaint this week. Understand?"

Aiden and I bobbed our heads in unison. "Thank you, officer," I said. "There will be no more trouble with noise this week. I promise."

The young cop smiled, and shook Aiden's hand before heading back to the cruiser and pulling away. I breathed a sigh of relief. We really didn't need to add making up with the neighbors to our list of to-dos for this week. Given the tendency to have a ton of oddball visitors and late night happenings at our house, it was important to me to stay on the right side of the neighbors, and we lived in a neighborhood with a lot of people who tended to call the police at minor concerns. They had an active neighborhood watch group and they were constantly on the lookout for problems, concerns, and criminals.

I'd thought that this was a good thing when I'd moved back into the house; the neighbors did generally care about each other quite a lot, and I knew quite a few of them. Many of them were older, and retired, which meant they had all day to sit in their homes and watch out for each other. That was my backup; that word would get out in the magical community that there were that many people watching my house and that it would not be smart for anyone to try to sneak up, because I would be warned and magic could be exposed.

So they'd tried to sneak something into my house. Likely twice, if the detector Aiden had pulled apart could be believed. In fact, we'd only caught it because of the second attempt. What would have gotten past us if we hadn't checked? How had we been so naïve as to not run some kind of magical detection as each gift showed up at the house? And how were we going to handle that at the wedding reception on Saturday night?

I mentioned the concern with Aiden.

"Janie, as soon as Jonah and I finish the work on the house we'd planned before the wedding, I'm thinking that Alfred and I need to talk about security. I think I can rig something up to detect magic, or at least to keep harmful magic at bay in the backyard. I think we can handle this."

But yet another thing was coming up to make the wedding difficult. Maybe we shouldn't do this . . .

No. I had to keep going forward. We'd fought too hard and too long to give up. So why did I constantly think that I should give up, and yet it was not appropriate for me to let Griselda make her own decisions on whether or not to fight back? Or was I just emotional with the upcoming wedding and all the stress from the bar?

I was voting the latter.

I so had to get a serious grip on my horses. I was a basket case.

I took a deep breath. "Okay. We can handle this. I'm going to go inside, and try to get some things together for tomorrow. Will you lock up the garage when you're done?"

He nodded.

"Thanks." I walked back into the house, breathing slowly and carefully around the panic that was running through my bloodstream like a bunch of squirrels on Mountain Dew and pixie sticks. I needed to take a break, and breathe.

I hit the kitchen door to a roomful of people all asking questions at once. Doris had a question about the cake. Allie had a question about our conversation earlier today. Harold wanted to know when I wanted him to show up on Friday and set up folding chairs for the rehearsal. Geoffrey wanted to know when I wanted the flowers to be delivered, because the florist had called; and Bob had wandered in to let me know that Bert was no longer inebriated and did I want to talk to him about his duties at the wedding.

I ran past all of them, heading for the stairs. Voices followed me as I went, and I slammed the door on them as I ran to my bedroom. It was quiet there, with no wedding craziness, no cops rolling up on a noise complaint, no magical conundrum, no bar exam, no emergencies, and no houseful of people every night for dinner and to worry about what was coming. I loved everyone so much, but I was tired, and I just wanted some time to myself before I started screaming. It was all too much, and it felt like all the walls were closing in on me.

I flopped down on my bed, and threw one hand over my eyes. Yeah, it was a little Southern belle drama queen, but I needed a break.

Apparently I really needed it because I fell asleep. I woke up an hour later to Aiden coming in to get ready for bed.

"Feel better?" he asked, in a mild voice.

I felt bad immediately for ignoring everyone. "I'm sorry. It's just all a bit much. What was I thinking to schedule everything so close together? Not saying I want to move anything, but thinking we should have thought this through better before we planned all of this?"

He laughed. "You're just overwhelmed. Just think, the bar exam is almost over. You only have a half day tomorrow, and the test is over."

"For now. If I failed it, I have to retake the test."

"Janie, I'll be very surprised if either you or Mia fails this test. You were ready for it. I've heard you guys cramming for months, and remember, I've been here for the whole process over the last three years. We're forty-eight hours away from the wedding, and you are hitting the last minute detail panic. I'm honestly surprised it hasn't hit you earlier than this, especially with the magical stuff coming up as well. You feeling better?"

"Wait a minute, you expected this?" I asked. "Why didn't you say something? I've felt like I've been losing my mind!"

"Janie, my mom's been around weddings for a long time. She's done wedding cakes and catering, and even did some wedding planning for a while, during my time with Dad. You know how many horror stories I've heard about brides completely losing their shit right before the wedding?"

"Oh, yeah," I said, rolling over to look at him. "So on a scale of not that bad to calling off the wedding bridezilla, how bad did I rate?""

"Given the givens, and everything going on, truthfully not that bad. Just take a deep breath, and remember that in two days, we'll be married, and in three days we'll be on our honeymoon. The bar will be over, and you'll be able to relax for the first time in probably three years."

He was right.

"So how much do I need to go down and deal with?"

"Nothing. I took care of it. Look, Harold and Stanley will be here with the folding chairs on Friday afternoon at around four. The rehearsal is at five and the rehearsal dinner is at six, so there's plenty of time to set up; there's not that many chairs to set.

"I made the executive decision to go with raspberry filling in the extra cake that Mom made, because she's worried for some reason that there won't be enough, but Mom always over plans and overestimates cake. We probably won't even use it, and I know you like her raspberry chocolate layer cake, so it's done.

"Bob and Bert have been assigned to patrol the house tonight, under strict orders not to touch any booze in the house for any reason, so you can sleep better knowing we've gotten the presents that might be magical traps out of the house, and someone is keeping an eye out. Bert has had some coffee, and solid food, and he seems better. Allie had to go ahead and go in to work tonight because they're slammed, so she's going to be there for the night shift. Mom is in the guest room, and Harold has already left for the night. Dad is on the couch downstairs, willing to give Bob and Bert a break if they need it."

Wow. He had neatly handled everything.

"Thank you," I said. There was nothing else to say. He'd done everything I'd have done, and even thought to set up sentry duty for tonight to make sure that someone was watching for us while we slept. I couldn't have asked for better.

I knew there was a reason I was marrying him.

CHAPTER THIRTY-FIVE

The next morning dawned bright and clear. I actually felt more rested than I'd felt for the last two days. Maybe the breakdown of the night before and the nap before we all crashed for the night did what I needed it to do. I relaxed enough to let go of some of the anxiety I'd been carrying around.

Mia and I were up again, headed to Columbus. I did feel some jealousy against my classmates, many of whom were probably just waking up at about the time we got onto the highway, having stayed in hotel rooms over the week, with no other outside stressors or people showing up for dinner, or wedding paraphernalia all over the house. I wondered if that would have been the right way to handle this, but it was too late now.

Yet again, we showed up early enough to park fairly close to the door, to allow for a quick getaway if possible. We went inside and took the same seats we'd had for the last two days. In fact, my rear end seemed to be molding itself to the metal folding chair I'd been sitting in for so long.

The last part of the exam was started, and we opened our test booklets and blue books and started writing. The assignment was to write a persuasive brief arguing the exclusionary rule relating to a violation of *Miranda vs. Arizona*, a question of custodial interrogation. I knew this stuff, and dove in. An hour later, I glanced up at the clock, gauging the amount of time I had left, and saw a shadow pass behind the proctor's announcement stand. I stood up and stretched, being very careful only to look either at my paper or at the proctors, but I didn't see it again, so I sat back down, concentrating on the test itself. Finally, we finished our exams, Mia and I at almost the same time, and headed to the front of the room to turn in our tests. We both left the last of the bar exam in the tray in front of a proctor by the door, gathered our things, and headed outside.

It was a beautiful summer day. The sky was a clear light blue, the clouds were white and fluffy and pillowy, like cotton balls sprinkled through the sky. As we got in the car and headed for home, I kept getting distracted by the beauty in the flowers at the side of the road. I'd never seen flowers that looked quite so brilliantly colored, or so welcoming and summery. I had to keep reminding myself to pay attention to the drive, but there wasn't a lot of traffic on the road once we got outside of Columbus, and we weren't in a hurry. I was enjoying the drive.

I couldn't decide if I wanted us to stop for a cup of coffee, if I wanted us to go visit some friends, or if I wanted to go home and sleep for a week straight. My brain was on overload. Mia apparently felt the same. "It's all so pretty. I feel like I should be on some kind of attention deficit medication; I can't stop looking around. Things are so pretty and bright and clear, and I don't know where to look next," she said.

"I agree. Or is it just that we are so tired and stressed, and have been for so long, that we've missed noticing things like pretty flowers and blue skies. Isn't this part of what we're trying to protect?" I asked. We needed to stop and smell the roses from time to time, or what were we fighting for?

"You know, we have enough stuff going on in the next couple of days that we do need to remember to enjoy the moment, as opposed to just worrying our way all the way through the weekend. How many times will you marry Aiden? Just the once, I hope," Mia said, a grin playing at the corners of her mouth. "So are you going to regret not enjoying the one wedding you have, or are you going to just grit your way through it and hope to enjoy renewing your vows in twenty or thirty years, and hope no magical emergency comes up at that point? Because I gotta tell you, it doesn't seem to me to be a good plan."

It didn't seem like a good plan to me, either.

I was feeling a bit nostalgic, so I took the scenic way home. We stopped for coffee and bought a dozen donuts to take home to the others, and I drove past my childhood home.

I'd sold the house when Dad died; he'd maintained it as a rental property after we'd moved in with my stepmother when I was nine. It was the proceeds of the house that had paid my way through law school. As broke as I'd been as a student, I'd graduated with almost no debt, and what debt I had was from putting home repairs on a credit card. Those were almost paid off, as well, so there wouldn't be much left. We'd start our law practice and I wouldn't have much of anything I still owed.

As we pulled up in front of the house, a Craftsman style two story brown and tan home, I saw a kid on the front lawn, sitting on a red tricycle, while the whine of the lawnmower sounded from the side of the house. Almost twenty years ago, that had been me; playing in the yard while Dad was mowing. Why didn't I remember what Mom was doing? I still didn't have a lot of memories of her because she'd disappeared when I was pretty young.

I'd originally just thought she'd taken off on us, and never really gave her much thought; but after Dad had died, Mia and I had found Dad's journals and some newspaper clippings that told us a way different story. She'd disappeared, and no trace was ever found at the time, although her body was found two years later by the side of the highway, with marks on her body that the police never figured out. Dad had committed himself to an institution for a while, convinced he was losing his mind after Mom was gone, seeing magical creatures and imagining they were there to snatch me away., He wasn't crazy; there probably had been magical beings showing up to cart me away on Evangeline's orders, though I couldn't prove it.

What were the marks? I wondered. I had enough experience now in the magical stuff that I might be able to solve it myself. I snorted. Like I didn't have enough to do with everything going on this weekend. I'd have to see what I could find out after the wedding, when we were back from the honeymoon.

I wondered what kind of life I would have had, if Mom had not died. I wonder what she'd think of my wedding, and whether she'd have been Momzilla, or whether she would have been crying as I'd picked out my dress, and as I got dressed on Saturday morning. I wondered what details of the wedding she'd have been involved in, and what she would have thought of how my life had turned out. But would it have turned out this way if she'd been around? It had been her disappearance and death that had been the catalyst for

Evangeline's entry into our lives, and it had been Evangeline who had introduced the reality of magic for me.

I shook my head. I'd hoped when Evangeline's memory fogging magic had worn off, that more memories of my mother would come back, but I hadn't gotten much. I remembered the smell of her perfume (White Shoulders), and the smell of her shampoo. I remembered her singing to me when I woke up scared of a nightmare as a small child, and I remembered her reading me nursery rhymes. They weren't bad memories to have. I wondered if I could get a bottle of White Shoulders and wear it for the wedding; it would make me feel like she was close to me that day. I mentioned it to Mia.

"I think Mom's got some of that," she said. "No reason to buy a whole bottle. I'll call her when we get home."

I smiled. That was exactly the kind of thing that Mia kept doing, finding easier solutions to problems that I hadn't figured out how to solve. It was why she was definitely my best friend as well as my maid of honor.

It was time to head home and start concentrating on wedding details. The bar exam was over. We could relax until the results came out in October. We'd have some down time, enjoy the wedding, and start figuring out what to do with all of Bert's new circumstances, and try to help Allie, before we got too bogged down with the starting of our law firm and working life.

I was looking forward to it.

For the first time in three years, I felt like I didn't have a care in the world. I was relaxed. I felt like I had done the best I could have on the bar exam, given the situation, and felt mostly comfortable with my answers. It was always possible I'd done something completely wrong, but I wasn't obsessing over how I'd done, like some of the other students we'd talked to before leaving Columbus earlier.

Wedding prep was now the order of the day.

"Shall we go home and see what the boys need help finishing?" I asked.

She nodded. "Let's go home."

CHAPTER THIRTY-SIX

We got home to find the yard work done, and the boys were in the midst of housecleaning. It made me happy to watch them finishing up with the vacuum and the dust rags; maybe I'm weird, but I'm more relaxed when my house is clean and organized. It doesn't have to be perfect, but it just made the house feel more homey when we didn't have piles of stuff and dust bunnies all over the place.

"Thanks, guys," I said, and really meant it.

"We have a surprise for the two of you," Aiden said. He handed me an envelope. "Tomorrow morning, the two of you are going in for massages, facials, and a manicure and pedicure. It's on Jonah and me. We love you guys, and want to say congratulations for making it through the bar exam. It's our way of saying, indulge yourself. You've earned it."

Inside the envelope were gift certificates for all of the things he'd just said; the massages, the facials, and the manicures and pedicures. I'd never had a facial before, and I'd only had a manicure and pedicure when I'd been a bridesmaid for some of my college friends. I wasn't going to say no, though, or complain. It was my own wedding, and I wanted to feel pretty.

I gave him a giant smacking kiss, wrapping my arms around my fiancé and squeezing him tight. It was a thoughtful way of getting me to relax, but I already felt more relaxed than I had in a long time. If I relaxed more, would I be comatose? I laughed aloud at my own thoughts, and heard Mia kissing Jonah as my arms were still around Aiden. It had been so long since we'd done anything girly. I was looking forward to the morning.

Allie came in at that point, looking exhausted, but I saw a smile on her face when she saw Mia and I hugging the guys. "They gave you your gifts, huh?"

"You're not going with us?" Mia asked.

She shook her head. "I've got an appointment to get my nails done for the wedding, but I'm still on call tonight. If I have to go in, then I'd be asleep during all of it. It seems like a waste of time and money for me to sleep through that much pampering. I'll join you for the manicure later in the morning, but otherwise, I'll be here, either setting up, or sleeping."

I understood her choice, but I definitely didn't want to leave her out. "Are you sure? You could use a girl's day, as well." I wondered if it would help her feel better to relax in the morning.

"Rain check, then, Janie. When all of this is over, we'll take a whole day and do a spa thing, even if we do it at home, with bubble baths and doing each other's nails."

You know, that didn't sound like a bad idea, either. "I'll hold you to that," I said.

She smiled, but the smile didn't go all the way to her eyes.

Bert and Bob came into the living room. I noticed that Bert was purposely avoiding looking at Allie, and as relaxed and as happy as I was, my heart broke a little for them. We had to see what other options there might be.

Bert cleared his throat, and I let go of Aiden. No sense in making him jealous when we knew that he was hurting from the end of his relationship with Allie.

"You find something, Bert?" Mia asked. She'd done the same, letting go of Jonah's neck.

He nodded. "I think that the shoes were left as a warning. I think that someone's after a bigger prize, and whoever it is, might be using other magical allies to distract us. I don't know how they got the shoes, but I keep thinking that maybe the shoes didn't actually make it into the stash of items to be hidden, since they didn't actually have any known powers at the time, and any curse would have been after they were made, and not documented."

It did make some sense, but there were still holes in his explanation. "Why warn us?" Aiden asked. "Why leave the shoes as a warning? What were the shoes supposed to be warning us about? The warning is no good if we don't understand the message."

Bert nodded. "I think it was a warning to me. I think it was a warning that they are coming after us, and that it's my fault."

"Your fault? Because of your involvement with Perrault?" I asked.

He nodded.

"Okay, let's call that Theory Number One. Theory Number Two is that maybe we've got more than one bad guy here, and they're all doing different things for different reasons, and maybe we're making a mistake in thinking that it's all related. I mean, Evangeline's coming to the wedding. Clorinda seems to possibly be poking around, and Madeline is looking for her sister, Gabriella. Why do we think that they are all working together? I haven't heard anything tell me that the three of them have anything in common, except for wanting something from us. That's not exactly proof they are working together."

I could tell that Bert wasn't completely convinced, but even he had to admit that it was possible.

Or was there a Theory Number Three that just hadn't occurred to us yet? If so, I was hoping that it made more sense than Number One or Number Two. I didn't say anything out loud, but I was kind of thinking we were reading all of this completely wrong.

Bert said he wanted to do some more research. Bob immediately volunteered to help. Bert seemed a bit taken aback, like he'd been planning to research the bottom of a whisky bottle alone, but he had the good grace to accept. Bob winked at me as he followed Bert back to the study. I knew Bob was still taking it as his duty to keep Bert sober, so I nodded at him. Keeping him on task, and doing actual research would do all of us more good than cleaning out another vase or ashtray in the morning. The guys had already taken care of the vase that had been violated the other night, and I kinda wanted to keep the house in good shape, even if we weren't inviting anyone inside for the wedding ceremony itself. I guess it was like when mothers told you to wear your good underwear in case you ended up in the emergency room; in case anyone did come in the house, I wanted it to look decent. And no, I wasn't thinking to clean the house because Evangeline might come in. I had a couple of aunts and uncles who had never seen the house (and hadn't come over when Dad was alive because of Evangeline), and I wanted them to think the place looked nice. I had a funny feeling they'd be stopping by before the weekend was over, even if it was for a morning-after brunch.

"Aiden, what are we missing about all of this?" I asked. "I feel like there's more to all of this than we've realized. Is there something I'm not thinking of?"

He shook his head. "Let's have one night to relax and enjoy the fact that you survived the bar exam. Let's just chill out. Bert and Bob will do research. Let's just watch a movie and talk about this weekend, and see if we can all just go to bed early and get a really good night's sleep. The brains will all work better if we get some rest."

He had a point. I was tired. And I was worrying. I needed a quiet night, I knew that; I just couldn't seem to bring myself to relax when I knew there was something out there that was coming for one of us, if not all of us.

"All right, Aiden. What movie would you like to watch?" I asked.

Jonah piped up. "Something with explosions," he suggested.

"Yeah, with Bruce Willis or Steven Seagal or Mel Gibson," said Mia. "And lots of guns."

I guess we were watching an action movie. I smiled. For some reason, movies like that relaxed me, too. I guess they were good distraction from everything else going on. Aiden went to get the movie set up, and made a few phone calls.

Doris and Harold showed up with Chinese takeout that evening, and we all stuffed ourselves silly while we talked about the wedding and watched Mel Gibson and Danny Glover proclaim that they were not too old for that shit, as explosions and fire and gunplay and funny come back lines relaxed us enough to call it a night fairly early.

There would be enough going on in the next couple of days that a little relaxation would go a long way.

CHAPTER THIRTY-SEVEN

A good night's sleep did a lot for me, and apparently Mia felt the same way. Aiden and Jonah woke us early, cajoling us out of bed with coffee to take us out to breakfast prior to our girl's day out, and then they hurried back to the house to work on the gazebo that we'd use as an altar for the wedding. It needed some last minute work to place it in the yard, and to secure the base of it so that a strong wind wouldn't blow it over at the last minute.

I felt rejuvenated; ready to face whatever was ahead, but I was also looking forward to a nice relaxing day ahead.

Too bad it didn't stay that way.

We headed to the spa, where I was ready to be pampered and treated like a queen. I didn't expect what we did get.

The massages were wonderful, and every muscle in my body felt like it was oozing with relaxation in a puddle of massage oil. The masseuse had magic hands, it seemed, and I felt more relaxed than I'd felt, well ever. I was wrapped up in a fluffy white terrycloth robe, with paper flip flops on my feet after having the skin on my feet buffed to a high shine and my toenails painted some shade of pink somewhere between Blush and Bashful. My face was polished and scrubbed and cleaner than it felt like it had ever been. All I had left was my manicure.

Mia was already in the manicure room, and a woman was already working on her cuticles as I sat down and put my hands on the manicure table. Another woman, around my age, came in and sat down at the table across from me. She picked up my hands, placing them in a small bowl of water and some sort of chemical that she said would soften my cuticles and moisturize the skin. I started to enjoy her massaging my hands and fingers, until she pricked the tip of my finger with one of her instruments.

"Oh, shit," I exclaimed. "I know why they want through the portal. I've figured it out."

Mia gave me a concerned look. "Um, Janie, can you table this conversation for later? We're kinda in the middle of something at the moment, and then we can talk about it on the way home."

Dammit, she was right. I had to keep my mouth shut and get through the lovely manicure that my fiancé had paid good money for. I sat there through the entire thing, and twitched so much that the lady had to repaint my left thumbnail three different times. Finally, I thought she was done with it and stood up. I was wrong.

She grabbed my wrist and yanked me back down into the chair so she could sprinkle glitter dust onto my nails. I thought that was it, until she picked up the bottle of clear lacquer to put over the glitter dust. It seemed an eternity until she finished with the last final brushstroke. I stood up, blowing on my nails until the nail tech shrieked at me. "You'll ruin the finish! I've never had a bride act like this on the final set of her nails. If you don't let me finish this the right way, you might as well shred your nails on a cheese grater and paint them with watercolors!"

Wow, she was a little hyper. I had to sit with my nails under a special light, and then sprayed with a special fixative, and then sit immobile for ten minutes with my fingers up in the air, sporting jazz hands.

I was practically whimpering by the time we were done. We got changed out of the terrycloth robes and got our clothing on, ready to head home. The nail tech was still complaining about my not caring about my appearance at my wedding, but to be honest, I didn't really care if my nails looked like dinosaur talons at the moment. I thought I had some stuff figured out, and I really wanted to get this craziness behind me.

Finally, we got to the car. I didn't even have the door closed, much less the key in the ignition, when Mia turned to me and asked, "What is your problem, Janie? What in the world could you have figured out while we were sitting there?"

"The nail tech jabbed me in the finger with one of her tools, and I pieced it together. What's the one fairy tale that we haven't seen come up, that involves someone getting stabbed in the finger? The curse was supposed to be for death, but the severity was mitigated by another fairy to a sleep for a hundred years."

"No," Mia said. "It can't be. You mean Sleeping Beauty? Okay, so yeah, getting stabbed in the hand might remind me of the spinning wheel spindle, but how does that compute to what we've got going on in our lives this week? I haven't seen a spinning wheel, and I haven't seen a faerie queen with horns. Didn't the bad faerie in the Disney movie, and that one with Angelina Jolie, didn't they have horns? So what does that mean for us?"

I smiled at her, and started the engine. "Look, if Perrault was stashing away dangerous artifacts, and hiding them to protect the humans from them, what's the most dangerous item in his collection of stories? Well, the worst I've thought of is the spindle. What I don't know is if the curse is still active, and whether it still carried a curse of death, or if it was a curse of sleep, and if it was sleep, is it one hundred years, or just until one receives true love's kiss? So if that's the most dangerous, or one of them, what could you do with a spindle, just walking around with it, especially at a crowded wedding reception? A spindle can't be that big."

Mia didn't say anything.

I started driving home, and kept talking. "So if Evangeline, or Clorinda, or Madeleine, any one of them, got a hold of such a thing, think of what they could do to any of us. If they had a specific target, they could get us while we were doing the Hokey Pokey, before any of us could turn ourselves around."

She snorted.

"Yeah, bad joke, I know, but it's still true. We wouldn't know who did it unless we locked down the reception and searched everyone, and how would we even begin to do that?" I asked. "A big portion of the reception guests don't have a clue about magic. How could we possibly explain why we have to search them? And how do we keep people from leaving while we search? It's not practical."

"Okay," Mia said. "I get why this could be dangerous, but why do you think that's what the goal is? What do you think about the red riding hood, or the boots for the cat, or about the glass slippers in the first place? Wasn't there a discussion about shoes you couldn't take off, that made one dance themselves to death, at one point? Or what about a big, bad wolf?"

I winced. "There's part of me that says not to give them any ideas if they're actually spying on us. I think we have to see what we can find out about that spinning wheel spindle, and see if Bert knows anything about what it actually does. And then we need to start asking around and see if we can figure out who's working together and who's just after us, and why. We need to know who's on what team, or if they're all completely unconnected. If that's the case, then we might be able to use them against each other."

"The enemy of my enemy is my friend?" she asked.

"Something like that," I said. "That, and self-interest. All of them have blind spots to what they're trying to accomplish. I'm sure each and every one of them would have reason to stop the other. Evangeline on the throne would be a one-track goal to end me, rather than think of the court's interests. Clorinda wants to take out all the humans, and well, Madeline's power is just kinda yucky. I mean snakes and toads all over the place just as she talks? Ugh. Not my idea of a dinner companion."

She laughed. I did, too.

"Yeah, if I get cursed, I'd rather just about anything but that. I'd stop talking for the most part, and just wear one of those dry erase boards around my neck to write down anything I wanted to say," Mia said.

"That would certainly be cheaper than going through pieces of paper over and over and over again and throwing it all away. And eraser crumbs everywhere would be annoying." Now I was just being silly.

"You know what, though," she said. "We should really try to enjoy the next couple of days. I mean, let's not forget what we could be facing, but at the same time, this is, hopefully, the only time we have to take the bar exam. You'll only marry your first husband once," she gave me a wink. "And every day is a day that you never get back if you spend the whole day worrying."

She was totally right. So, of course, we stopped for ice cream on the way home.

Graeter's ice cream. Because Black Raspberry Chocolate Chunk would just make the day that much better. And what the heck? We were celebrating, no matter how small the dish of ice cream might be, we had earned a celebration. And Graeter's was on the way home.

Or, rather, I made sure that it was.

CHAPTER THIRTY-EIGHT

The guys were waiting for us at home, and I explained my revelation about the spinning wheel spindle. Aiden and Bert immediately agreed that it was the perfect tool for an assassin; small enough to be snuck into a large gathering, powerful enough to wreak havoc without much effort.

As I thought about it, this was personal. Someone truly wanted a personal revenge. That could be anyone, especially the three that had been unhappy with us lately. I still wasn't convinced they weren't all working together toward a common goal, but we had a ton of details to finish up today.

I ran up to the attic, since I had an hour or so before we had to go to the reception site at the Marriott, near the University of Dayton campus, to make sure everything was set up for the next day. We would then meet Harold with the chairs, to finish set up in the backyard, and then we would have guests coming for the rehearsal and dinner later that night. I was looking forward to the rehearsal dinner; I'd picked my favorite place for dinner on the weekend. Aiden loved the place, and Mia and Jonah had fallen in love with it as well.

It was the Dublin Pub, an Irish restaurant and pub at the end of the Oregon District. I was looking forward to pub fries; a house specialty with a white sauce, bacon, scallions, and cheese over French fries. I figured if I made it to Friday night, I could splurge a bit on my diet, or lack thereof. I'd been running around so much that I didn't think one dinner would make my dress too tight. I also thought it would be my reward after the week of crazy that we'd just endured. I'd made a table reservation on the patio outside, and there was supposed to be a band playing later that night, a local band, Homeland, that played their own version of Celtic rock. They were one of my favorites.

I was still daydreaming of pub fries when I opened my father's iron trunk to check for his journals. I remembered seeing a reference to the Sleeping Beauty tale in one of the later volumes. I cracked it open and started reading, hearing Aiden coming up the stairs behind me.

"*I found a reference to the Sleeping Beauty tale in a volume of references from Versailles. It appears Charles Perrault was involved in something that was displayed there, and that this was a popular story at the time. I haven't yet found if there's anything to the story that Perrault was the head of some commission to store, restore, or locate artifacts related to folklore, but it appears he might have been. Funny, the French are normally more records conscious than this, but this kind of record, relating to stories and artifacts prior to Napoleon, could easily have been destroyed during the French Revolution and the Terror that followed. Too bad; I rely on those kinds of records for much of my research anymore, and I just hate thinking of all the history an angry mob can, and has, destroyed over the years . . . but I digress. It's the prerogative of a scholar to lament the lack of sources, especially those destroyed by human hands.*

Evangeline has shown some interest in my research lately, which is unusual, but it has been an interesting couple of weeks while I've worked on this project. She's been more interested, and we've had more detailed conversations than I remember us ever having in the past. Sometimes I wonder how we ended up married; we just don't have all that much in common. Janie would love hearing about my research, but Evangeline never cared, and now that Janie's in college, I just don't have someone who wants to hear about the off the wall topics I end up reading about. It's been like reconnecting with someone I'm not sure I ever truly connected with in the first place. Yet again and again, I keep wondering what brought us together several years ago. I'm enjoying all the conversations, but at the same time, I'm also wondering what strange magic love truly is . . ."

He wasn't kidding. Evangeline had to have cast some sort of spell, not just to get his attention, so soon after my mother disappeared, to get him to marry her so fast, and to get him to suddenly stop paying attention to so many of the things that had meant so much to him over the years. He'd suddenly stopped talking with his friends, stopped pursuing his hobbies, and just worked all the time. I never really saw them together; he spent all of his time in his study, and she spent all of her time on various committees and fundraisers and society groups.

I'd expected that it had gotten worse when I'd moved out of the house in college, but it sounded like me out of the house had been bringing them closer. If they were talking more, did that give her more opportunity to cast the curse on him that ended up killing him? Would she have been able to do that if I'd stayed home while I was in college, commuting to campus every day instead of living in the dorms and only coming home when Dad insisted? Had that stepped up her plan, or had she just had better access? When did she actually start cursing him? Was it right after the wedding, or did she wait until I was out of the house? I'd never know, but I'd always wonder if my freedom at getting out of the house had come with such a price. If so, it was too high to pay, and I'd have done it all differently if I could have. But hindsight is always 20/20, and I would never have guessed in a million years that she was doing such a thing. Even if I'd suspected it, I never would have believed it.

I kept reading.

"... I did find a reference, however, to the idea that there may be a spinning wheel spindle related to this story that may still exist. If so, it's supposed to carry the curse that sent Princess Aurora to sleep for a hundred years. I'd love to see this spindle, but at the same time, I'd be very careful touching it. Maybe I'm being overly cautious, but why risk it? I wonder if latex gloves would prevent the curse from affecting the person handling it? I'd probably pick it up with tongs, just to be safe, because you just don't know what something like that is capable of."

So did Dad believe in magic or not? I couldn't tell for sure, but here, it sure looked like he was at least considering the possibility that it was very real and very dangerous. His earlier entries had seemed to intimate that he was convinced manifestations of the magical world were actually hallucinations and that he was losing his mind. He was even committed to a mental institution for a while, and took medications, trying to banish such visions from his brain. And yet, there seemed to be some indication that he still saw them, even after he was treated and medicated for the issue. So did he start to think it was real again, or had he convinced himself that it was the crazy coming back out?

Well, I knew for a fact that magic was real, and if Dad hadn't known, then he'd certainly been killed by the nine-hundred-pound gorilla in the room. Evangeline had slowly cursed him to death. I wasn't sure if it made me feel better to think Dad and Evangeline had connected somewhat in those last years, so that Dad had some companionship in the end, or if it made me madder that she had used his interests to get closer to be able to kill him faster. Of course, the journal entry seemed to allude to whether Dad was starting to wake up from whatever fog Evangeline had him under; he was starting to question how they had even gotten together in the first place. Was her spell that was killing him more powerful than the one fogging his brain, or maybe the two couldn't be active at the same time? Or was it a ruse to get him closer to her to speed up the process? I didn't know, but it was starting to look like Dad hadn't been as clueless as it had originally seemed.

That made me feel a little better. I mean, I'd never thought about my dad being clueless, and I'd felt better when I'd realized my evil faerie stepmother had been fogging our brains and our memories for years, because my dad was actually a pretty smart guy. Heck, he'd have to be to be a college professor, or at least I'd thought so.

I flipped through the last couple of journals and found the other reference to the spindle I had remembered seeing.

"So I believe Evangeline is up to something, and I don't think she's having an affair. She is holding meetings both day and night, with rather odd characters, as if she has a bigger plan afoot. I've heard the name Perrault in her meetings, as well as Grimm. When I first heard her, I thought she was talking about me; as we'd spent a bunch of time talking about my recent research. The longer I listened, however, the more I was convinced she was talking about something else. I still don't know what she is up to, but something tells me she's got a secret, and it's one that I need to discover.

"When I asked about her late night meetings, she wouldn't answer, and when I kept asking, she exclaimed she would not rest until she found it, but wouldn't tell me what it is. When I eavesdropped on

her next meeting, I heard them talking about a spinning wheel and a spindle, and talking about it like it was a rare antique. I thought it was a discussion with an antiques dealer at first. She was always collecting antiques and spending money I didn't know she had to collect things that were important to her for some reason I never understood. I started to walk away, thinking it was just another antique hunt, when I heard the words Perrault and curse, and I knew she was after something more than just a run of the mill antique. Alas, I never found out if she got it, and I still haven't heard exactly what it was or what it was supposed to do.

Oh well. It's not like any of this stuff is real. Possibly I'm hallucinating her discussions, but at the same time, I can't be altogether sure she isn't doing something truly strange. After all, why would she care about a spinning wheel and spindle? It's not like she was ever going to spin wool into yarn or anything else. I'd never seen Evangeline do anything even remotely domestic; yarn craft was well beyond her normal activities. Why in the world would she want something like that? She never bough furniture unless it was named after a French king, or elaborate enough for a formal sitting area. It just wasn't her style, even if it was for decoration only.

It's times like this that I miss Abigail. Abby was more straightforward, and told me why she wanted something, and we talked about all of the decoration choices in the house without either one of us feeling like one was running roughshod over the other. She never kept secrets from me, and we talked about everything. We finished each other's sentences, and we never wanted to spend time apart unless it was necessary. I think it drove Abigail nuts from time to time that she felt the need to spend all her time with me, because she was quite an independent woman, but it seemed like the need to be with me overruled all of that; even if we were doing our own thing, we were generally doing it in close proximity to each other. With Evangeline, it's completely different. Sometimes I think we're married in name only. If I was actually somebody, I'd think she married me for some kind of advantage, but I'm not rich (she has more money than I do), I'm really a nobody, and she really gained nothing socially from marrying me. I'd hoped she would be a better mother figure to Janie but the two of them truly hate each other."

He had that right. I'd read for years that mothers and daughters fought like cats and dogs during the teen years, but Evangeline and I had put that to shame. I'd been a lost little girl hoping for a new mommy when they got married, only to turn into the sullen, hateful teenager who wanted her evil step mom to go away in just three short years, and it never got any better. Everything that went wrong in the house was always my fault, and Dad just told me to try to get along with her. I'd hotfooted it out of that house the minute I could without causing a problem for Evangeline's social standing. College had been an escape hatch, one that worked better than any weekend at a friend's house, because I knew I didn't have to go home to her at the end of the weekend.

I handed the journal to Aiden, who had come up the stairs behind me while I read. He read the entry with some interest. "Okay," he said. "I'm starting to believe that Evangeline has a hand in what's going on this weekend, especially if the spinning wheel and spindle are involved. I wasn't convinced before, but now I'm starting to believe you. Is there anything else in here from your dad about the spindle or the spinning wheel?"

I shook my head. "I don't remember seeing anything else, but of course, I could be wrong. Let's go through and look."

I sat down, as if getting ready for a long research session. I'd spent hours going through Dad's journals, but I hadn't gone through them for references of what was going on in my life, or about certain type of folklore or fairy tales. I'd been going through them for personal recollection and just trying to remember details that Evangeline's magic had somehow dulled or erased from my brain. Maybe a thorough re-read would bring to light certain facts that weren't clear to me at the moment.

He laughed. "Janie, we don't have time for that today. We've got a truck full of chairs showing up, a wedding ceremony to set up, a rehearsal, a rehearsal dinner, and a good night's sleep to get before tomorrow. You can't tell me you haven't read those journals something like four hundred thousand odd times in the last three years, just to try to hear your dad's voice again in your head. If there was another mention, you'd remember it."

He had my number, and he was right. I had read those entries something like eleventy-billion times. I'd remember it, and in this case, I was pretty sure it didn't exist. That didn't mean I didn't want to check again.

Is it sad that I started thinking then that it would be in our best interest for me to color code and index the references in my book, like the Bibles in the church down the street? Would it help if I could flip faster through Dad's journals when an emergency was staring us in the face?

Of course it would, but Aiden was right. We had way too many things to get done to stop and start a research project now. Even if it sounded more fun to do than setting up the figurative orange blossoms and white satin.

But I was getting married. The next couple of days needed to be about my future, not about my past. It was time to move on.

"Good bye, Dad," I whispered to the ghost of my father that resided in those journals. "I wish you could have been there with me this weekend, but I'm going to make you proud, no matter what I run up against."

Did I just imagine it, or did I hear Dad's voice whisper, "You always make me proud."

I wasn't about to question it. It was exactly what I needed to hear.

CHAPTER THIRTY-NINE

I just barely made it downstairs before the doorbell rang. It was Harold with a pickup truck full of white wooden folding chairs from the rental equipment place on the edge of town. He and the boys unloaded the truck, and Mia and I agonized over how to place them for the greatest impact. Finally, we decided on just two rows of five chairs each, on either side of a small aisle, where we would put down a white runner coming from the back of the house, leading up to the gazebo that would hold a unity candle and would stand behind the pastor, who I'd known since I was a kid.

Pastor Jenkins, who was the pastor at the local United Methodist church in Kettering, had been the pastor who had conducted Dad's funeral service. He'd been supportive and caring in the days leading up to Dad's death, and he'd tried to, as he said, "heal the rift" between Evangeline and I. It hadn't worked, obviously, but I also hadn't been back to church in an awfully long time. When we'd needed someone to conduct another funeral service, for Tobias, Mia had let me call Pastor Jenkins, and while we'd been at the wake afterwards, he'd asked where Evangeline had moved to.

I'd told him that she'd decided to do some traveling and that she had deeded the house to me so that I'd have a safe place to live while I was in school. He'd raised his eyebrows pretty high, because our house wasn't exactly cheap, and it was far from a starter house or a college dormitory, but he hadn't said much at the time. He'd called once or twice, inquiring about how school was going, concerned about how I'd reacted after Dad's death, and once or twice more, checking on Mia after her father died.

I was pretty sure he didn't believe our story about Tobias being in a hiking accident on a camping trip. The truth was, that we didn't think we could talk much about him being mauled by Bigfoot as he was running after an emotional Paul Bunyan. That one would have taken a lot of explaining.

Pastor Ricky Jenkins arrived just after the chairs did. He was a middle aged man, with a funny tuft of red hair on the top of his head. He had been through the weddings of all of his sisters, and then had gotten married himself many years ago. I could tell he loved his wife very much because his voice got sad when he mentioned her. I'd heard that she'd died a long time ago. I'd never met her.

He had a few minor suggestions, and we listened carefully. I said yes to widening the aisle, and to only letting the runner go back about fifteen feet, stopping about thirty feet from the house. He suggested that when I'd mentioned my desire for no one at the ceremony to go into the house, but he'd seemed surprised when I'd been so adamant about it.

"I'm just concerned about security that day. And there's one or two people who I'm sure are coming just to snoop around in a truly older relative, none of their business kind of way. I'd be less stressed if we just keep everyone outside. No exceptions, sorry, sir. We've actually rented a port a john, so not even to go to the restroom."

His eyes widened. "That seems harsh, Janie. You won't even let your few guests pee inside? That seems decidedly un-welcoming."

"And we had a visitor try to run off with four rolls of toilet paper a while ago," I said. I didn't mention that it was Geoffrey, who'd had too many cups of coffee and didn't know if he'd make it back to the faerie realm without, well, paper products. "I'd rather not restock the whole house just because I'm getting married. All of this has been expensive enough as it is."

He laughed. "Janie, this is not an expensive wedding. I think you've probably spent more for the reception, but then again, if you didn't mind people in the house, I'm sure you would have just hosted the reception right here. You've got the space, if you could rent enough tables to hold it all."

"I also don't want the mess, if Aiden and I are going to go on a trip after the wedding. We can't leave until it's cleaned up, and I just figured we'd be too tired, so why not just nip that in the bud before it can be too overwhelming."

I could tell he wasn't completely satisfied with the explanation, but I figured he was likely to be quiet about it until a time later when we were all a lot less stressed. Or at least not under wedding stress. The man was a pastor, after all. He was familiar with how wigged out people could get in the midst of planning and pulling off weddings.

We got the chairs set up, and Aiden came outside with a large bag of salt. The pastor's eyes widened considerably when that appeared. "What are you planning to do with that?"

"It's just a decoration," I said, as I poured a circle around the right hand side chairs.

He didn't say anything until I went to the left side and poured a circle around the front row only, leaving the back row uncircled.

"That's just a decoration?" he said, looking like he had some idea what we were doing.

"Yes," I said. "It's just something that Aiden and I have joked about, that the people we loved the most should be encircled in salt."

"But you left out some of the chairs. Why aren't they all inside of the salt?" he asked.

Good question. "It's a specific design, Pastor. We could add another circle at the top for you, but otherwise including all of the chairs ruins the design." God, I sounded like a lunatic.

He looked puzzled, but said, "Don't worry about me. I'm good. Wouldn't want to ruin your design."

My true purpose was to protect my few wedding guests from the ones I didn't want to invite. If Evangeline was going to try something, she was going to have to do it before or after the ceremony; I didn't want her to have a chance at hurting someone in the middle of the ceremony. I'd have Aiden spread some tacks or nails on the circles as well, just to be on the safe side, but there were only four guests at the ceremony that would be affected by salt and iron. Geoffrey would understand if we warned him ahead of time, but not too ahead of time . . . we didn't want him to spill the beans to Evangeline or feel like he was obligated to do so.

We'd had that problem before.

I turned and saw Doris with clothing on hangers for Harold and for herself for the rehearsal dinner that night. I looked at my cell phone in order to check the time, and realized that the afternoon was slipping away from me quickly. I ran upstairs to run a brush through my hair, put on a bit of mascara, and change into the sundress I'd bought last month to wear for tonight. I ran into Mia and Allie in the hallway upstairs, doing the same thing; the last minute readiness for the evening.

"You ready for all of this?" Allie asked, with a smile on her face. "No matter what else is going on, this is a happy occasion, and I'm so glad for the two of you."

"Thanks," I said. It was clear that no matter how heartsick she was, she was genuinely happy for me. I reached out and squeezed her hand. I appreciated the fact that she was putting on a happy face for me. I wanted her there, because she was a big part of the reason why I was alive and standing and ready to enjoy my new life with Aiden.

The three of us girls all met at the top of the staircase, and linked arms to head downstairs. "Ready?" Mia asked.

"I'm ready," I answered, and we skipped down the stairs much like Dorothy Gale and her friends skipped down the yellow brick road. Was it sad that the metaphor in my mind went straight to someone who almost had her day ruined by a witch?

CHAPTER FORTY

We headed outside, giggling at each other, and saw Aiden and Jonah talking with the pastor and sitting in the chairs. Aiden shook his head at me as we walked up, and I mentally translated that into an inability to put down the nails and tacks yet, as the pastor was still sitting there. I did notice that the pastor was not sitting within a salt circle; but maybe he felt that there was some religious issue with doing that. If it was, apparently it wasn't stopping him from performing our ceremony, which was good; it was a bit late to find a replacement.

Doris and Harold were coming out of the kitchen as we came up to the chairs. Geoffrey was standing off to one side. I had a random thought; maybe having Geoffrey hold a guest book for people to sign would keep us from having to tell him about the chairs until the last moment. I knew I had a simple moleskin notebook inside, and we had all kinds of quill pens as well. We even had a ballpoint pen that had a quill on it, and I figured that would be the one we'd use. It made me think of the iron gall ink I'd thrown in Evangeline's face a few years ago, and I wondered if that could be an excuse to have some around, but I wouldn't put something like that in Geoffrey's hands without warning him, and running the risk he would accidentally spill something that would be the equivalent of acid on himself. Geoffrey wasn't exactly a klutz, but his son certainly was, and there was just enough possibility of Aiden tripping coming down the aisle that I didn't want to endanger anyone on purpose. Could I put a small vial in a pocket, or hold it with my bouquet so that I wasn't completely unarmed at the time I said "I do"?

The pastor took charge, instructing us on where we would stand, and what we would do, who walked down the aisle first, and in what order. Allie sat in the front row of chairs, with Bert inconspicuous in a large handbag on her lap, and silent as to the next step. I could tell she was happy to sit with him like that, but from the small grunts and half-whispered words I heard from the handbag, I knew he wasn't happy. Whether it was about being in the bag, about being that close to Allie when he was trying so hard to push her away, or about being involved in something outside of the house at the moment was hard to say.

As Geoffrey got to the chairs, I stepped in front of him and stopped him from sitting down in the chairs as Harold and Doris sat down together. "I've got a job for you, Geoffrey," I said. "It's a wedding day thing, but since we're here for rehearsal, I figure we better rehearse everything. You won't actually get to the chairs until just moments before the ceremony starts, so we'll just have to put up a sign reserving one for you."

He puffed up a bit that he would have a role so important that he wouldn't be able to sit down right away. I started thinking that this was even smarter than I'd thought. I could dictate which seat Geoffrey sat in by putting a sign on a specific chair, to keep him away from the salt circles. He felt important, and needed at his son's wedding, and that was worth a lot, to me, anyway. As annoyed as I could get with Geoffrey, he was soon to be my father-in-law.

"Geoffrey I've got a moleskin book and a quill pen that I'd like to set up with a stand for you, so that you can get guests to sign the book as they arrive. We'll set it out at the reception, too, so that we know who came to help us celebrate. Someday we'll all look at each other and wonder who came to what, and this way we'll always have a record."

He seemed genuinely happy to have a wedding day kind of task. Yeah, he'd been the tailor for the boys' suits, but that work was done, and he'd have to just stand there and hope that they didn't wrinkle or stain anything that he'd done so much work on. Everyone else had wedding day tasks, and for some reason, I hadn't thought about Geoffrey needing something to do that day. It was perfect.

"Okay, look, your sole job is to get the guests to sign the book when they show up. That's it. If they ask for a restroom, you are to direct them to the port a john by the garage. If they complain about bees, there's insect spray in the garage that you, and you alone, can go get the spray out of the garage. No one is to be invited into the house, for any reason. You do not have the authority to let anyone into the house. Got it?" I asked him.

He nodded, a bit overeager to get started. Maybe I'd created a monster, but he'd do that job really well, greeting people and getting them to sign in. Of course, normally there would also be the job of corralling everyone at the last minute, keeping the groom on task, and, of course, getting people seated, but with a private ceremony, limited guests, and well, Jonah and Bert, I thought we were pretty well covered.

We lined up, and walked through the ceremony a couple of times, to make sure that everyone was where they were supposed to be. Allie kept Geoffrey busy talking with Bert about something not related to the wedding, and we blew through all of the rehearsal preparations fairly quickly. Before long, it was time to head to dinner.

Mia's mom was joining us, as well as the pastor, Harold, Doris, Aiden, me, Allie, Bert, Jonah, Mia, Geoffrey, and a couple of out of town cousins, named Eunice and Minerva.

Eunice and Minerva were each pushing ninety years old, and they were first cousins to each other as well. They were meeting us at the Dublin Pub in another thirty minutes or so. I hadn't expected a rehearsal that was so quickly handled, but at the same time, we had been thorough, and I hadn't expected us to be done on time in order to get to the restaurant on time and still have a clue as to what we were supposed to be doing the next day to actually make it from the house to the actual clothing and the actual words being spoken and the vows actually being said. I guess I hadn't realized the importance of actually practicing such things, but Aiden had insisted, to try to cut down on the clumsiness he might feel the next day, when he was nervous; and I had to say that I felt better knowing that he was more relaxed. I hated to admit it, but familiarity breeds confidence when it's something you've never done before.

Suddenly, we were all buckled and bundled into cars, and headed to the restaurant. I was suddenly starving, and realized that I hadn't eaten lunch today.

Pub fries, here we come.

Aiden and I rode alone in the Escalade, a rare moment alone together. We hadn't had much of that all week.

"How are you doing, Janie?" he asked.

"I'm good. How are you?"

He was driving, something he didn't do much when we were together, but this was a special night. Aiden very deliberately used his turn signal, merging off of the highway onto the exit ramp heading towards the Dublin Pub. "I'm good. I'm looking forward to tomorrow. Are you worried about something happening?"

I thought about it long and hard before I answered. "I am. Look, we've laid down salt, and you'll put down iron nails before you leave to head to your mother's tonight. I'm not worried about something happening during the ceremony itself because of that. Alfred and some of the Wonderland folks will be standing guard at various places throughout the house to prevent anyone from coming in before and after the ceremony. We've made the house as secure as we could. The place that is totally not secure is the reception. We have enough magical guests that we can't lay down salt and iron there. Our guests would be uncomfortable, and many of them wouldn't be able to stay long enough to eat any of your Mom's food. I know a couple of them are really looking forward to the cake, so that's pretty crappy to make them feel so unwelcome."

"What can we do?" he asked.

"I've been thinking about it. I think that we can arm as many people as we can with small bags of salt and maybe some small metal items, and possibly even plant a few weapons at the reception site? The problem is that the reception site is the reception tent outside of the Marriott; it's not all that secure. Anything we left there tonight could walk off before we even got there. There would be no guarantee we would have the things we needed when we actually needed them. Of course, it's hard to steal what you don't know is there; if no one saw us plant them, there would be no one who would know to steal them."

He sat a minute, thinking furiously. "I've got it. We can wrap up a couple of weapons as wedding gifts. Mia and Jonah and Allie and my mom, and the F.A.B.L.E.S. members can bring them in just before the reception starts, as if they are just one more present piled up on the table. The trick will be remembering which box has what in it."

It was a good plan. I liked it. It would work. I wouldn't risk any of the weapons that Dad had left me, sitting out in the open over night, but they might still be available to us in case we needed them, in case of a magical attack that required weapons. I liked it. But what about an attack that didn't require weapons, or an attack with something as small as the spinning wheel spindle. Would it work on more than one person at once? I'd not heard of its magic working on more than one target at a time, but had it ever been used on anyone else? I didn't think so. Did that mean that all of its magic was gone, like it was a one-time-use item? I wouldn't think that the amount of magic it would take to cause such a curse would be wasted on something that could only be used once, but just because it wasn't logical to me, didn't mean a magical bad guy didn't think that way. I mentioned it to Aiden.

"You're right. So maybe we have Alfred and the others secure the house after the wedding and come to the reception to keep an eye on everyone?" he said.

"No, I think someone needs to stay at the house in order to prevent someone from breaking in while we're doing the Electric Slide with the Snow Queen." I winked at him. He'd been really worried about dancing at the wedding. I'd let him off the hook, by telling him that most of the dancing would be slow dancing and there were only a few times he'd need to dance with a crowd. I caught him three weeks ago, practicing in front of a mirror to make sure he could do the Electric Slide without landing on his rear end in front of everyone.

"Thanks, Janie," he deadpanned. "I'd stopped thinking about the dancing part, and was just thinking about having fun when you brought up dancing. I hope everyone has good insurance."

Yeah, I was bad. I laughed out loud. "No one is going to be laughing at you. There will be enough people there who don't know those dances, and you practiced."

It felt good to laugh with him, but the magic of that relaxed car right ended pretty quickly when we got to the Dublin Pub; it wasn't a very far drive.

It was a beautiful summer night, with a clear sky. The heat of the day had cleared off some, and it was slightly cool as Aiden parked the car in the lot and we walked up to the door. I saw Mia and Jonah already sitting at the patio, but we had to go through the restaurant to get to where the tables were, and where some of the others were already sitting.

We joined them, looking over the menus, ordering drinks and appetizers. I asked for a hard apple cider, something alcoholic to celebrate, but most of the others ordered beers, Guinness, Harp, Bass, and other imported brands. We ordered appetizers and waited for the others to show up, laughing and joking about the wedding the next day. Pastor Jenkins was in that crowd as well. He accepted the offer of a Guinness, thick and foamy at the top.

The band wasn't yet ready to play, but we were definitely settling in for a good night. No one drank more than two drinks, the food was filling and good, and we were all telling stories on each other; although most of them centered around Aiden and I. Dad would have loved to have been at this, and I got a little teary eyed as I thought so.

Even though it was a good night, with shepherd's pie and beef boxty and Rueben sandwiches and Dublin pub fries, as well as good beer (and cider), everyone was getting tired. I know I was.

It was going to be an incredibly long day the next morning. Still, it seemed like I didn't want the evening to end. I was yawning by the time we all piled back into the cars to leave.

Aiden jumped in with his mother, having already taken his overnight things to her house earlier in the day. Mia and Allie and Bert jumped in with me; Jonah was driving his car to Doris's to stay with Aiden and ferry him around in the morning, like a good best man was supposed to do.

The ride home was fairly quiet. Bert didn't say a word, neither did Allie. Mia was driving my Escalade, and we were headed for an early night.

For the most part, the night had gone as well as it could. So why was I still waiting for the other shoe to drop?

CHAPTER FORTY-ONE

W e got home to a quiet house, but Alfred was there, and some of the other Wonderland folks, setting up with binoculars and different types of surveillance gear. They were really getting into their roles, and I was grateful, but it was time to go upstairs and call it a night.

I resisted several offers for a cup of coffee (Mia), tea, or cocoa (Allie). Instead, I went upstairs and took my dress from the hanger in the spare room, as well as a box of vanilla wafers. I was still hungry, but not enough for an entire meal. I sat on the bed, munching on vanilla wafers, and staring at my dress. It was real, and I was actually getting married in the morning. I'd made it through memory fogs, and the loss of friends, through portals and curses and evil step moms.

Now I just had one more day to get through. And then I'd be married to Aiden, and we'd be gone on our honeymoon. I couldn't wait.

Of course, we still hadn't said where we were going. And a lot of it depended on whether we had any major last minute expenses for the wedding. We hadn't made a reservation anywhere, because we weren't sure we'd be able to pull it all off and still actually have money left over to go, but we hadn't ruled out anything just yet, and I was hoping to at least leave the state.

I was ready. I'd survived the week from hell, and as weird as it was to curl up in bed without Aiden right beside me, it was even weirder to do think I'd be married the next day. I lay down on the bed, and curled up on Aiden's pillow, where I could smell his shampoo, and looked around the room.

My dress was hanging in my room, with the small train spread out on the floor to prevent wrinkling. My shoes, a pair of ballet flats with memory foam in the soles, were sitting on a chair beside the dress, and my under things sat on the dresser beside the chair. My dress was simple, an A-line dress with spaghetti straps, with vintage looking lace overlaying the white fabric. I had a simple veil that would hang from the bun I'd planned to put my hair up in, and I was going to carry a bouquet of simple daisies and wildflowers. The name of the game was a backyard and casual wedding; while the boys' suits were slightly more formal, it would all work together.

I was picturing the whole scene, and it was going to be beautiful. I smiled. I was looking forward to it, and I wasn't even thinking about the magical conundrum we were facing in the morning. What was going to happen? Was my stepmother going to object to the wedding? Or would she wait until the reception, where she might have more allies there to help her wreak havoc? Could I count on her obsessive need to stick to proper etiquette to prevent causing a scene, or was this going to be a problem throughout the day?

I knew I was going to be worrying about it throughout the day.

I feel asleep, finally, at about two in the morning, after my mind finally slowed down enough to shut down and sleep. I didn't know that my brain could run in circles, but it was definitely chasing its own tail.

I woke up in the middle of the night hearing footsteps in the hallway. At first, I wasn't sure I heard it, and thought it was part of a really strange dream involving Roger Rabbit, a glass of wine, and a bottle of hot sauce, but I kept hearing it, and finally woke up.

But the footsteps were still there.

I hopped out of bed, grabbing my robe. I shoved my arms into the sleeves as I opened the door and went out into the hallway, but there was nothing there. I walked down the hall towards Mia's room, but there was nothing in the hallway, and I cracked open the door to her room. She was in bed, lying on her stomach, with her face towards the door, mouth hanging open and drool dripping from the corner. She obviously hadn't heard anything.

I went back into the hallway, where no one else was up and moving, and walked towards Allie's room.

Like I'd done with Mia's room, I cracked open Allie's door, to find a lump under the covers, with one bare foot sticking out of the blanket and hanging over the side of the bed. I recognized the color of the nail polish as the one Allie had picked for her toes earlier. The lump moved steadily, with the rise and fall of her breathing, and I could tell that she was out cold.

So neither one of my friends had had anything to do with the footsteps I'd heard.

Doris had gone back to her house with the boys for the night, and Harold had gone with her. Geoffrey had gone back to wherever it was that he went when he wasn't hanging at our place, because he hadn't been able to come up with a good excuse to go with Doris and Harold and try to keep them apart at her own house. I still wondered what his deal was; they'd been broken up for years, and there had never been a hint of Doris wanting to get back together with him, or he with her, but he was suddenly very aware of their relationship, and acting like he had a problem with it. I hoped he got over it soon; it had been pretty clear, at least to me, that Harold wasn't going anywhere, and Doris was happy.

That, however, meant, that the only others in the house were Bert and Bob. I slipped back into my room and grabbed my slippers, then padded my way down the stairs to see if they were okay. I was pretty sure the footsteps had been a full sized human, but I'd been asleep, and magic was unpredictable. I made my way through the house to the study, where Bert and Bob had been sleeping, and found Bob asleep and purring, curled up into a tiny ball of marmalade colored fur in the corner of the sofa. I had to stop myself from reaching down to pet him; he was extremely cute when he was asleep. As the light shifted from a car's headlights going down the road and shining through the window, I saw that he had his boots on the sofa with him, standing up against the back of the sofa cushions, right near his head. It was extraordinarily cute, and it made me smile. I turned my head towards Bert's cushion, where he'd slept for the last couple of years. It was empty.

Bert wasn't always a sleep-through-the-night kind of frog. He had a tendency to prowl the house while we were sleeping, but it was rare for any of us to catch him, and he certainly wasn't one to make the kind of noise I'd heard going down the hallway; he just wasn't big enough to clomp that loudly. So where was he?

I left the study, leaving Bob asleep, and headed for the living area and the kitchen. Not a soul was moving in either place, the dining room was still eerily empty after moving all of the presents that had been piled up there for so long, and I didn't find anyone else downstairs. I headed back upstairs, checking on Mia and Allie again, and heard footsteps again.

There were only two areas left that hadn't been checked; the former servants' quarters that my stepmother's rapidly revolving selection of maids had lived in when she'd been in charge of the house, and the attic. None of us used the servant's quarters. I'd started thinking that Aiden and I could eventually knock down some walls back there for playroom space when we got around to having kids, giving them a huge space to play inside, especially during the winter. But none of us went in there. And Dad's trunks were in the attic, along with the portal that Bert had moved to this house.

I headed for the attic, being the more likely place for him to be pacing around and checking our security.

When I got to the attic, I was very surprised by what I saw.

I certainly hadn't expected to see purple, swirling air in the attic. It was a portal, and it was open.

I was going to kick that frog's butt.

CHAPTER FORTY-TWO

W ho had opened the portal? I wondered. Certainly Bert wouldn't have left it open. Would he have gone through it without telling any of us? Did it go where he thought it would?

I looked around, and I didn't see him anywhere. I wondered if there was a way to close it. I felt vulnerable and alone sitting there and looking at it and not knowing what might come out of it. Had someone gone inside? Or had something come out?

I was worried.

So what should I do?

I looked around, poking around the corners of the piled up items in storage in the attic, hoping Bert wasn't hiding anywhere up here. No one was watching, and no one was around. I checked my pockets, making sure I wasn't carrying metal, since I was going in voluntarily. Faerie beings tended to see bringing metal into their realms on purpose as an insult, especially if it was something that could be used as a weapon.

I stepped through the portal in my robe and my fuzzy bunny slippers. And I was very surprised at what I found inside.

The inside was a small apartment. I had just stepped into someone's living room. It was warm and cozy, and I could smell chamomile in the air. The apartment was something I'd have seen on one of those tiny house shows; with a loft bed and a small galley kitchen, and not much space to the living room. I could see almost the whole apartment from where I stood just inside the door.

Why in the world would someone have an apartment in a portal? I wondered. And the kitchen seemed to be pretty updated; where in the world would someone have gotten granite countertops if the portal and such were created in the days of Perrault, several hundred years ago?

Or was this the living space of the guardian of the treasure? It made me feel a bit better for Bert; if he really was going to be cursed to living forever and taking care of all of this, at least he'd have a nice place to stay. And this place was really nice; in fact, everything was updated to the newest, greatest, and latest.

But there was a door in the back of the galley kitchen. At first, I thought it was the bathroom while I was standing there like an idiot, looking around at someone else's house, and one that I hadn't been invited into. I had to shake my head and remind myself I wasn't magic, and therefore didn't require an invitation to enter someone's house.

I walked through the kitchen, and as I got to the door, I realized that the bathroom was actually to the left, just behind the kitchen. So what was the door?

I opened it. Hey, I was already trespassing. Might as well get a few answers while I could.

Inside the door was a dark storage room. Apparently this was the storage we'd been looking for, where the Perrault items were held. I saw a table on the other side of the room that looked like it would be a workspace for whoever was living here, but what would they be working on? A thick leather journal sat on the table, but I didn't go read it immediately; I was struck by the bushel baskets sitting around the room, and filled to the brim with stones.

And not just any stones. On closer inspection, it appeared they were unpolished diamonds and rough pearls. I looked around and saw a light switch.

Saying a quick prayer, hoping to be alone, I turned on the light. And my jaw dropped.

The room was the size of a football field, and the bushel baskets of those stones were piled up everywhere. I don't think I'd ever seen so many.

I don't know how long I stood there, taking it all in. There was enough in monetary value here to pay for all of our retirements, all of our expenses prior to retirement, and still have so much left over that we would have no idea what to do with the rest.

I sat down, rather heavily, on the floor.

So Gabriella had lived here with the treasure. And she wasn't here now. So Bert had been right, that she was gone.

"What the hell are you doing here?" I heard a voice behind me, slightly hoarse, as if it wasn't used very often.

I turned around to find a very pretty woman, with blond wispy hair piled up in a messy bun on top of her head. She was dressed in a very bohemian style, as befitted someone who was into the tiny house living that I'd seen on television. There was a small pile of stones on the floor in front of her, and as I watched, one fell from her mouth on her last word.

It was Gabriella, Geoffrey's former girlfriend, who we'd all assumed was dead.

I couldn't help it. "You're alive?"

"Who are you?" she asked.

Her voice was raspy, as if she didn't use it a lot, but if the room behind me was any indication, she did speak from time to time.

"My name is Janie Grimm. The portal to your apartment is now located in my attic. It was open, and I stepped through."

She lit up a bit as I said that, and then I noticed that she had a dry erase board on a string hanging from her neck. Was that how she normally communicated? That seemed like it would be hard. How many years had she lived like that? She grabbed her marker and wrote, *Glad to meet you. Congratulations on your wedding.*

"Thank you." I smiled at her. "Wait, are you here to guard the portal? We thought there was no one left to do that."

The marker came out again. *I was not part of the geas that protected the location and how to access it. Bert got notified that the last member of the pact besides himself is deceased. He believed it was me, and it was safer for him to believe that.* She grabbed a small kitchen towel out of a pocket in the side of her skirt, and wiped off her writing after she saw that I'd read it.

"Why?" I asked. "He's ready to give up everything he's worked for to protect this portal. He's willing to give up his own happiness. Is it worth all that?"

In a word, yes. It's not just the items that Perrault hid that are here. There's also the fact that I could be an asset to a magical enemy, due to the material value of the other items that are here.

"What other items? Don't worry, I don't want them. I just want to know what someone might be breaking into my house to go after."

She seemed to consider this. *This isn't the only room here.*

There's a vault behind this room, and many magical artifacts are hidden there. Some are minor, some are dangerous. I've rounded up a number of items since this portal was created, and have hidden it from the humans, because I wanted to protect them, but I also didn't want them to have the power behind those items. Hiding it all seemed safer.

I couldn't disagree with her. "Is one of those items a spinning wheel spindle? I think someone might be after it. And I think that they might try to use it at my wedding to hurt one of us."

I think you're right, was the scribbled answer. *I think someone is after you, and that's one artifact that they might use to do it.*

"What do you know about the spinning wheel and spindle?" I asked. "Is it usable on more than one person at a time? Were you the one walking around in the house? How did the portal get opened? Where's Bert?"

She laughed, and then whipped out the marker again. *I know everything about the spinning wheel and spindle. It works on one person at a time, but only if it is being used for revenge. It puts the person who is pricked by it into a deep sleep, like a coma, and that sleep will last a hundred years, if it is not interrupted sooner. If someone is not awoken in one hundred years, they will die.*

"That's a twist! I thought the curse was supposed to be death and was lifted to a hundred year's sleep. So how do we break it if someone gets stuck?"

True love's kiss. It must be someone that is truly in love with the person unconscious, and that love must be reciprocated by the unconscious person.

"Wow, so if the person who is attacked with the spindle isn't in love with someone, they're screwed?"

Pretty much. Oh, and yes, I was the one walking around your house. I opened the portal to see where it had been moved to a couple of weeks ago, and have been moving around your house when everyone was asleep, or when no one was here.

"Why?" I asked.

Because I don't have internet access in my apartment. I took my laptop and went to your empty rooms, the ones you never use, and was

looking to see if there was any news on the internet as to what might
be after the items I care for.

"Did you do that where the portal used to be?"

Yes. There was a coffee shop under the apartment where I was at
in Paris. The gentleman whose apartment I was at was the man who
died, the last one of the geas. The coffee shop had wi-fi.

"Did they mind you using their wi-fi?"

I'm sorry. I was trying to lay low here. I should have asked.

"Not what I meant. I don't care if you use my internet. I'm more
concerned about someone prowling around in my house while I'm
asleep."

She grinned. *I'm sorry. I just didn't want anyone to realize that I*
was still protecting it. I was trying to draw out who was after me. The
man in Paris was killed. Bert was notified and yanked the portal. I
didn't let on that I was alive because I didn't want to be targeted
myself.

"Your sister has already shown up here looking for you."

She winced. *I am sorry about that. She is . . . unpleasant.*

"So if word's out that you're alive, and here, then you don't have
to hide anymore, right?"

My sister is not the only one after these items.

"You don't have any magic of your own?"

Other than these crazy diamonds and pearls, and the ability to
stay young and alive for pretty much forever, I don't have any other
magic. I do, however, have the ability to bear metal, unlike most
magical beings, and therefore, I have a gun, which will do nicely
against both magic and human intruders.

She had a point. "But Bert doesn't have that kind of magic, either.
Gabriella, you were risking an awful lot."

I knew Bert lived with you. I figured he had enough contacts to
get the portal moved, and that if he didn't, you did, and he'd know how
to contact someone in the magical realm to help.

Well, that could have been entertaining. I didn't say it out loud,
but I did wonder which would have been more surprised, Geoffrey
learning that his old girlfriend was alive and well, or the Snow queen,
who could always have her own agenda that wasn't necessarily

aligned with our own interests. And for someone who wanted to keep these items away from both magic and the humans, neither sounded like a good idea.

"I guess that makes sense. But why not let Bert in on it?"

Because I didn't know who was after me. I didn't know if they were after Bert, too, and I figured he would be safer not knowing.

Damn every single one of us for trying to protect each other by keeping our mouths shut. How much would be easier if we'd all just talk to each other instead of just trying to grin and bear it in the name of protecting each other?

CHAPTER FORTY-THREE

"So what in the world are you going to do now? You're just going to live in the portal in my attic?" I asked.

That's something that you have to decide, and I would have come forward and talked to you about it, after the wedding.

"Um, thanks?" I said. "But what if we were all killed leading up to the wedding? What if someone got to us before then? Someone is definitely after something. I think we do have someone that is going to try to disrupt the wedding." I quickly summed up, bringing her up to speed on the number of people that seemed to be hot to get into the house, or had acted to try to force us to do something we didn't necessarily want to do.

You have been busy. But your wedding is tomorrow. Shouldn't you get some sleep?

"You're going to drop all of this on me and then tell me to go to sleep? Are you kidding? I doubt if I could fall asleep now."

She laughed.

"Seriously, though, I have another question. If you open the portal, and creep through the house at night, what's to stop someone from going in, like I did, while you're gone? What if it's someone who wants to steal an artifact, or to cause you harm, or to steal from you?"

She grinned. *But nobody knows I'm here. Bert moved the portal so fast that there's no way that the others have any idea that I'm here; or that I'm still alive.*

"Hate to burst your bubble, but I think word's out that you're here. We have a decent threshold, and there's a salt and metal ring around the house, but if someone wants in here bad enough, they're going to get in. We don't have a security system, and it's not hard to break in when there's no alarm."

I knew that because of the number of times I'd broken into my own house as a teenager, trying to bypass Evangeline's disapproval or when I'd missed curfew, again. I knew of at least three different ways to get inside the house without a key, and without breaking a window. There was a loose window in the basement. I used to use the tree to climb up to my own bedroom window, and there was also the window to the study, which didn't have a lock.

The study. Where Bert slept.

And I hadn't seen Bert since I'd gotten up to go look and see what those footprints were.

"Have you seen Bert tonight? He wasn't in his bed before I came up here." I turned to head back through her apartment.

She grabbed my arm. *Is he missing?*

"Not officially. He tends to patrol the house a bit at night. I figured that was what he was doing when he wasn't in his normal bed. He's been pretty upset at things lately. I thought I wouldn't bother him, but at the same time, it would be nice to see that he was okay before I went back to bed. I'm just worried about him, I guess."

No; you're right to worry, with everything going on. Better to double check than to keep yourself awake worrying for no reason.

The two of us together tip-toed back out of the portal, and searched the house. No sign of Bert anywhere. I yawned as we got back to the portal.

"I'll look again first thing in the morning, when we can turn on all the lights and look better. Likely he just fell asleep somewhere while he was patrolling. Bob's got the study covered, and no one really knows about that window that I'm aware of."

She nodded.

"I think you'd do better to close up that portal behind you when you head that way tonight. I'm starting to think that someone is going to attempt to get in the house during the ceremony. Probably best if they can't even find the portal if they get in. We will have friends patrolling the house against unwanted guests during the wedding that have no idea about the portal."

Got it. Will be scarce, with portal locked up tight during the wedding. Too bad, would have liked to watch from the window. But understand.

It was too bad that someone who was interested in coming to the wedding wasn't going to be able to, and there was a part of me that wanted to have her be a lookout from the attic window, but how was she going to signal us as to a problem if she was hiding herself. And if she spoke and they saw raw diamonds and pearls dripping from her mouth, she would totally have been given away. I wasn't sure how I would explain that to Great Aunt Edna, who was getting a ride from her stepdaughter from the nursing home to watch the ceremony, as one of my few remaining relatives.

I yawned again, and warned her that she should lock up the portal tight before calling it a night herself, as I just had a bad feeling that someone had found a way into the house. Until I could talk to Bert, I'd have to wait and see what we could do to lock down the house even tighter. I wanted to know what he'd seen on his evening patrol.

Knowing he was likely walking (or rather hopping) the halls, I figured there wasn't much else I could do but go to bed. I walked around a bit longer, hoping I'd run into Bert, but I must be missing whatever pattern he was following around the house. I wasn't too worried; he was generally all over the house at night. At least he was on the nights he wasn't drunk, and I'd locked up whatever liquor was in the house. Or at least I thought I had.

I headed back to my room.

I didn't hear any more footsteps that night, and I didn't hear much of anything else. I felt secure that Bert had an eye and an ear out, and that if Gabriella had closed up the portal after herself, then no one but Bert could get in. If no one but Bert could get in, then we were fairly safe.

At least for the night.

I hung up my robe, slid into bed, and shut off the light, ready for a solid night's sleep.

It didn't seem like I'd been asleep too long when the alarm went off the next morning. I drug myself out of bed, my eyes feeling puffy and crusted shut with gunk. How much of a bride was I going to look like, with very little sleep, and bloodshot eyes? I stood in my bathroom with a cool cloth to my eyes, willing the puffiness to go down. When it started to look like I was a little more human, I decided that no matter what else was going on, I was going to have to obtain coffee in order to get through the day or the day was going to get the best of me before

I even got close to noon, much less getting dressed at three for the ceremony. Today was set to be a relaxing morning, with Mia and Allie and I getting our hair styled (by helping each other, not paying for a style), and doing whatever other small grooming that we felt we needed to do. Doris was coming over with breakfast. We'd just have to see how the morning went. I could always make a fresh pot of coffee. I might need it.

Mia and Allie weren't too far behind me, staggering their way to the coffee pot, but Doris had beat us to it; she was already in the kitchen, bustling around and making us breakfast.

"Doris, I hadn't meant for you to show up and cook! I'd have paid for us to go to breakfast," I exclaimed as she slid an omelet with ham, bacon, mushroom, and cheese in front of me. She'd made hash browns as well. How had she gotten in so early? I glanced at the clock. It wasn't that early. It was nine o'clock. I'd meant to get up and have coffee early and talk to Bert. I shrugged. A little late to talk to him, and I couldn't talk to Aiden until after the ceremony. My discovery of Gabriella could wait that long, I thought.

Doris had other things on her mind. "This was easier for me. And I've always thought of you as a daughter, but it's about to be official. So it's my way of telling you welcome to the family."

I smiled at her. I could definitely celebrate by eating her food any day, and I told her so. She smiled, and went a little pink at the cheeks. I'd have to tell her that kind of thing more often.

While we ate, I mentioned something to the others about the idea of hiding weapons in presents, and about my concerns about the spinning wheel spindle. Mia agreed to talk to Aiden and Jonah, and agreed to keep an eye out. Allie kept quiet. Normally she would be volunteering to talk to Bert about whatever we found, but they weren't exactly talking buddies these days. I had to do something; seeing her heartbroken face was harder and harder every day.

"I think Bert was patrolling last night," I said, casually, as I speared the last bite of omelet on my fork. "I heard footsteps and when I went to check it out, he wasn't in his bed."

Allie nodded, before she could catch herself. "He doesn't always sleep real well, so he ends up walking around the house, making sure everyone is secure and okay and in the house. He watches traffic out front, and he watches the backyard ever since we all came back from Wonderland, because he's concerned that someone is coming to get us." She took a breath. "And now it looks like it might actually happen." She sounded depressed.

"Don't give up just yet, Allie," I said. "I think I have an idea for you about Bert, and about his situation, but I don't have all the information yet, to be able to explain. Can you let me get through today and see what I come up with? I'm thinking that there might be another option."

"Really?" she asked. "Is it even possible?"

I saw the hope in her eyes. "Look, I just came up with something last night, and I haven't worked all the kinks out, but there is some hope. I don't want to falsely raise your expectations, but at the same time, I think it's possible."

She smiled, and this time I actually saw the smile reach her eyes.

"Okay, so let's get this wedding preparation started," I said. "When we've got the wedding done, there might be some figuring to do. So let's enjoy the day."

Easier said than done, I'd soon find out.

CHAPTER FORTY-FOUR

Mia insisted that I do more with my hair than just putting it up in a bun, so I let her spray and tease and curl it into something else. When I looked in the mirror, it did look more like me than a severe bun would have. I never wore my hair pulled back that tightly. I smiled at her. As much as I'd tried to save money by not having my hair professionally done, I was happy that Mia had insisted on taking over.

She helped me with my makeup as well, and produced a small bottle of White Diamonds perfume.

"Thank you," I said, smelling the familiar smell as she took the cap off. I dabbed it just behind my ears, and on the inside of my wrists, smelling what little I remembered of my mother.

We spent the day making sure that we had done whatever small beauty tasks we needed to do; filing a rough spot on a fingernail, touching up the polish on our toenails, plucking eyebrows, moisturizing, curling hair, and whatever else we decided needed to be done. Jonah and Aiden showed up at one point, just to tease us by threatening to come upstairs and check on us. Mia and Allie made a big deal about it, threatening all kinds of harm to them if they followed through, and I sat there smiling, knowing that they weren't going to follow through with it.

It was exactly what I thought the day would bring, normal wedding drama, with nothing magical about it. It was what I wanted. It was normal and expected and predictable. I even threw a little bit of a bridezilla moment, testing out what the reaction would be if I panicked a bit about a mundane detail; they reacted the way one would expect bridesmaids to react, and I calmed down immediately.

It was a normal day, for what it was.

Until, that is, Doris came running up the stairs about two hours prior to the wedding. "You're not going to believe this, but I think you've gotten another present. You have got to see this."

We all ran to the windows; none of us were heading outside in our bathrobes, worn over the undergarments we needed for our dresses. There were tiny lights floating in the air, giving the backyard a twinkly, fairy light kind of glow; but the lights weren't attached to anything. I recognized instantly where the lights were coming from; the tiny faerie beings that I'd met a couple of years earlier that had illuminated the path to the hut where the F.A.B.L.E.S. group had cured my Rapunzel Syndrome hair growth. But if they were working with F.A.B.L.E.S., how was this a gift? The tiny faerie beings involved in that location were supposedly free beings; they couldn't be a gift to me if they weren't property to be given. So what was going on?

To heck with the fact that I was wearing my bathrobe, and that my feet were in my fuzzy bunny slippers; I needed to go figure out what was going on.

I ran down the stairs, with Mia, Allie, and Doris at my heels, hurrying outside. When I hit the patio, one of the little lights came flickering up to me. I was right; it was one of the tiny faerie beings, in fact, it looked rather like the one I'd spoken to three years ago.

"Small being, why have you decided to visit my house for today? You've created a beautiful display, but I worry for your safety and wellbeing. Has anyone forced, coerced, or ordered your appearance here today?"

"No, Janie of the Grimm family," tinkled the voice of the one I assumed was their leader. "We have heard tales of your exploits, and your work in making sure that magical beings are treated fairly by their leaders. We are a free people, but we wished to thank you for your efforts by blessing and illuminating your nuptial ritual." I couldn't tell if the being was male or female, but I saw a tuft of blond hair, and a green and pink outfit covering the parts that would tell me what gender they were.

It was on the tip of my tongue to thank them, but I knew better. "The display is beautiful and will add much to our celebration, but I was informed that this was a gift, and did not know who was responsible. How did you learn of our ceremony?" I always felt a little weird talking to magical beings, being so careful not to overstep my bounds, to be careful enough not to thank them specifically, and to be properly grateful at the same time. I guess it wasn't any different than carefully choosing one's words at a trial, or in diplomatic negotiations with the monarch of another realm. I'd done both.

"We were told of your ceremony by some members of your F.A.B.L.E.S. organization. We organized the light display on our own, as you've done more to help our kind than you know, and this is a way to show our appreciation."

I drew a sigh of relief, and again caught myself and stopped before I thanked them. Too many years of Evangeline-drilled etiquette was making me crazy, trying to overcome an ingrained habit that could be a problem down the road. "We will enjoy your display, and be glad that it is freely given."

The tiny leader nodded at me and flew off.

Even though it was mid-afternoon, and the sun was high in the sky, the tiny lights were sparkling and twinkling in the sunlight. The wedding was set for a couple of hours from now, when the sun might be starting to make its way towards its descent, and the twinkle would be even better then. I could picture what it would look like with me coming down the aisle and the very air glittering. I smiled. It was all going to be perfect.

I turned and headed back into the house with a smile on my face. We were getting closer and closer to the ceremony. I was so looking forward to this.

We headed back inside, getting a light snack before heading back upstairs for a final hair and makeup check before starting to get into our dresses. Harold was going to take pictures of the three of us before everything started, both inside and outside, and that way we would have some of the formal pictures out of the way before the boys showed up. We'd wait inside while theirs were done, and then the ceremony would start, after everyone was seated and settled, and ready to go.

As we were getting ready, we played a bit of music; a bit of Pink, a bit of Aretha Franklin, and a bit of Evanescence. We were relaxed, we were ready. Mia snuck downstairs and opened a bottle of wine, "Not enough to get drunk, but enough to celebrate," she said. Even Allie, normally a nondrinker, joined in for a bit, and Doris did, as well.

We sipped our wine and laughed, waiting for Harold to show up with his camera. He did, and took serious and goofy shots of us, primping, and fixing my short train in different configurations, putting on my veil, and all the other standard pictures of brides and bridesmaids and friends. All day, I felt the need for my mother, though I knew she was gone. I almost wished that magic could bring her back, but as far as I knew, it couldn't. And I'd heard too many horror stories, as in horror movies, about how magic couldn't bring someone back from the dead without consequences, or coming back wrong. I might not have many memories of Mom, but I'd rather not have those kinds of memories of her to replace them. Ugh, no thank you.

It seemed like a normal day leading up to a wedding. The chairs were set. Allie went down to make sure that programs and birdseed were distributed to the few guests, and that all the ribbons and decorations were where they were supposed to be. Doris went down to call the hall and make sure that the catering details were taken care of. We were relaxed and happy.

I wasn't even a nervous bride. I was happy. I was having fun. And yet there was a part of me that was worried, waiting for the other shoe to drop, for some catastrophe to fall.

Alfred and a few of the other Wonderland crew showed up, taking positions at windows and doors throughout the house. We were covered.

But we sure weren't prepared for what happened next.

CHAPTER FORTY-FIVE

It was time.

We came downstairs, looking to get started, and Allie came in, upset.

"Have any of you seen Bert? I haven't seen him all day, and he wanted to hide out in my bag for the ceremony and reception, so that he didn't freak out anyone without magic. But I can't find him to put him in my bag." She seemed frantic.

"Allie, he might have decided to skip the wedding, with as upset as he's been." Mia, the voice of reason, had a valid point. I was kinda thinking the same thing.

"You've got to be kidding. He's been excited about your wedding for months. Yeah, he's been down with all of this going on, but there's no way he would miss all of this. Something has to be wrong."

Damn that frog, I thought. "How much do you want to bet he's decided to patrol with Alfred instead? I mean, he was up patrolling last night, right?"

Eventually, Allie decided that we were probably right. In fact, she was starting to get upset with him for making her worry. "Regardless of what is going on with us, he really can be inconsiderate with he gets an idea in his head, can't he? I mean, look how drunk he got the other night, and others had to clean up after him. I should know better."

"There's nothing wrong with caring, Allie," I said. "Or worrying, for that matter. You care about him. We all do. But this time, he's gotten a little obsessive, and he's done this to himself. You've got to show him what he's missing by going on with your life while we try to figure this out. I'm not saying date, but to start doing things without constantly worrying about him. Go say something to Alfred to keep an eye out and tell Bert you're pissed that he missed the whole thing, then go out there and enjoy the wedding, for yourself, instead of with him."

She nodded. "I know you're right, I just can't help worrying. I've done it so long, that it's a habit now."

"Not a bad habit. Just one that maybe he needs to realize isn't there for him if he continues down this path."

She went to talk to Alfred. Mia turned to me. "Are you sure he's okay?" she asked.

"No. I'm actually worried about him. But we've had no indication that he's left the house, and we're behind a threshold. How could anyone get to him? We've locked up the liquor, and Bob promised to keep him sober. If he was drunk, we'd find him singing, puking, or passed out, right in the way."

"Which makes me more worried," she said.

"Me too, but I think it's more likely that he's decided to take on the role of protector in chief than anything bad has happened inside the house."

Or was I trying to convince myself of it? Too late. The music had started. Aiden and Jonah were already at the front of the aisle, waiting for us. It was time to go. Harold and Stanley appeared; I'd asked them to jointly walk me down the aisle, and they'd been excited to say yes. Doris was already seated at the front row. I was running out of time without causing a major interruption, one that I couldn't explain to many of my non-magical relations.

I said a silent prayer to whatever deity watches over alcoholic stubborn princes turned frogs, that he not only be okay, but sober, safe, and ready for the tongue lashing we'd all give him for worrying us to death when it was all over. And then I stepped out into the sunshine.

Harold took one arm and Stanley took the other, and we started the walk across the backyard, up the aisle and towards the pastor. The ceremony started, and as we planned, it was brief, to the point, and personal all at the same time, the pastor telling an amusing anecdote about our jokes from when we were planning the wedding and coming in for marriage counseling sessions with him. The small crowd laughed appropriately, and we joined them. The pastor intoned something about us sticking together through thick and thin, and that our love for each other would increase our outward beauty as well as making us wiser on the inside. I thought it an odd sentiment, but it wasn't a bad one, just an unexpected one. And with that, we were pronounced married, and the pastor announced our first kiss.

Aiden leaned in, and his lips met mine.

How involved do you make that kiss? I will always wonder if we hit the right note between chaste kiss being witnessed by elderly aunts, my future mother-in-law, my stepmother and her sister, and the Snow Queen, and a kiss that has enough romantic feeling and caring that neither of us, nor the romantics in the not-crowd would be satisfied. I could only hope that our kiss, with a minimum of tongue and a definite hesitation, hit the appropriate mark. The audience cheered, and the music from Jonah's mp3 player sounded, to escort us back towards the house. I saw my stepmother in the back row, where we'd designated for her to sit outside of a circle, and she had an appropriate, but clearly fake, smile pasted on her face. And while it looked like she had a perfect makeup shell on her face, there was a faint shadow where I'd once thrown iron gall ink. As we passed her, I also noticed that she was wearing a sheer scarf tied around her neck, hiding where I'd once jabbed a metal screwdriver into her neck. Wounds made by metal didn't always heal on a magical being. I wondered how pissed off she was, but I wasn't picking up anything at the moment. I'd expected her to be glaring daggers at me through the ceremony, but I hadn't felt any such thing.

It had been as close to perfect as the ceremony could have been; no attacks, no mishaps, and Aiden hadn't fallen down once the whole afternoon. He did trip slightly as we stepped over the doorway in the newly fixed sliding glass door into the kitchen, but that was normal for him. He tripped over that specific doorway every time he went through that specific door.

We got inside, and both of us drew a breath of relief. We'd done it. We were husband and wife.

So why did I still feel uneasy at the whole thing?

"So, Aiden, do you feel different?" I asked.

He laughed. "Yes, and no. I feel like I'm supposed to feel different, now that we're married, but it's still you and it's still me, and we are still the same people that we were before we said 'I do'. That will never change. So why do I keep thinking that I'm supposed to have some different knowledge or feeling?"

"I don't know, but I feel the same way," I said. I was relieved that he'd said it. "And, not to change the subject, I know I'd like to sit here and talk about how I feel about you for a while, but I'm getting worried, the more this eats at the back of my mind."

"What's up?"

I told him about last night, hearing footsteps, and going looking, finding that Bert's bed was empty, and finding the portal, open, in the attic. I told him what I'd found, without describing the riches that I'd seen (no reason for any of my non-magical family to think that there was money that they might feel should be theirs, or to tell anyone that might be inclined to steal it). I didn't think my relatives would actually do anything truly sneaky, but at the same time, I just didn't feel like it was a good idea to trust anyone at the moment. I was too paranoid of protecting all of us to allow any exceptions.

Aiden's eyes got wider and wider and he finally stopped me. "Bert's missing, Gabriella is alive but my dad doesn't know, and you're saying that there are things up there that could be dangerous? But if it's in the house, then there's no danger, is there?"

"Well, as long as Gabriella is in the portal, or has it shut behind her, I would think that there's no danger. Obviously Bert had no idea she was alive, so he couldn't have known she'd walk through the house when he moved the portal here. So what can we do about it?"

He sighed. "What can we do? We are due to be at the wedding reception in forty-five minutes. We have hungry guests showing up, that won't get served until we get there. So what in the world are we supposed to do about it? Are we going to keep them waiting? You said that Gabriella was staying locked up in the portal during the wedding, so no one can get in."

"Yes, but she left the portal wide open last night. If she's done that before, then someone else, completely non-magical, could have gotten inside and could have done exactly as you did; step completely inside without any resistance whatsoever."

He was right. And even though we had people watching the house today, we hadn't been watching for anything like that for the last couple of weeks.

Shit. Shit. Double shit. With crapola sprinkles on top.

"What about Bert?" I asked. "Should we be worried? Despite what I told Allie, I am actually starting to get worried about him."

He thought a bit. "You know, I'd be worried as well, but you know him. He's probably nursing his own wounded pride off in a corner, convinced he's martyring himself for his cause."

"But if Gabriella is alive, he doesn't have to do that, does he? I mean, she's still around, so it's not like he is alone is protecting the Perrault stash. So why can't he be with Allie? Why can't he try to be human again, like he tried a couple of years ago? Why can't he have what normal he can have despite his previous life?"

Aiden shook his head. "I agree with you, but I don't know the answer. You'd have to ask him."

"And for that, I need to find him."

"And you don't have time for that. We have to get moving."

"Let me at least talk to Alfred. Allie had asked him to keep an eye out before the ceremony. Let me see if he's seen anything."

CHAPTER FORTY-SIX

Alfred hadn't seen Bert, even though he'd started to actively look for that slimy green frog. Of course, even though Bert was pretty big for a frog, he was actually not that big when it came to finding him in a house the size of mine. Alfred promised he and his friends would keep looking, and would start venturing out into the neighborhood to look for him if the house turned up empty.

Had he been frognapped? It wasn't out of the realm of possibility, but that frog could and would make one hell of a lot of noise if he was being grabbed or handled roughly or otherwise had something done to him that he didn't like. So why hadn't we heard anything from him all day?

I had a bad feeling about this.

"Janie, Aiden, look, I can't imagine he's gone far. You know him, he's probably drinking in a corner somewhere and pouting at the twists and turns his life has taken him. I heard he and Allie are having some problems. He'll turn up. I'm going to go looking for him. Mia has your cell phone, doesn't she? You have guests showing up at your reception. You can't stay here and search. I'll call when we find him. Go take care of your guests, and we'll take care of searching for him, and likely dry him out," Alfred said. It made me feel better that he was taking me seriously, and yet at the same time, he wasn't completely downplaying the dangers.

Eventually, they convinced me to go ahead and leave, but not until I'd heard multiple promises for phone calls and text messages with progress every half an hour.

Aiden and I looked outside, but our guests were gone. The tiny faerie lights were almost gone; as they had left when the ceremony ended. We were the last to leave to head to the hotel and the reception, and our guests wouldn't get dinner without us. We headed for our Escalade, still holding hands, and smiling, but my mind was still spinning, worrying about Bert. Damn that frog for making me worry about him so much!

We were at the reception within a few minutes, and I heard the music we'd picked out to walk into the reception hall with. I know that not everyone would have thought of Queen as the music to hear when we were announced and came inside the hall, but it sure felt like it had been a long, hard slog to get to this point over the last few years. We were definitely the champions, and felt like it when we were announced.

The crowd laughed and applauded, and the deejay shined a spotlight on us, segueing into our first dance as husband and wife, to Etta James' "At Last". It might have seemed a weird combination, but it fit us, and people seemed to be enjoying themselves. After that first song, the deejay announced the caterers would be serving dinner, in the buffet, and began releasing tables, starting with mine, to head to the line and get food. Doris was already at the cake, making sure that it was ready for cutting after dinner, and Harold and Stanley were helping the catering staff, by bringing in piles of plates and cups and silverware, ready for whatever we could throw at them, or rather, whatever the guests could throw at them. The favors were on the table, the gifts piled up by the door. The magical folks were milling around and not really mingling with the mortal guests, which I guess wasn't too bad of a thing.

Aiden and I sat down and ate while the guests were cycled through the buffet. It was hysterical to see Evangeline and her sister, the Queen of Hearts from Wonderland, several tables back in the line and not being able to bully their way to the front of the line. We'd laid down the law in that the catering staff was to start at one end of the room and end at the other, so that no one could say we were favoring one group over another. So far, it seemed to be working.

As I put the last bite of chicken into my mouth, and speared the last of the green beans on my plate, I caught a glimpse of my former stepmother's face. She seemed to be relaxed and enjoying herself. She kept checking a cell phone, which was out of character for her when she was in my life so much, but that had been three years ago. She would pull it out of a pocket, check for messages, and slide it back into her pocket. I watched for several minutes as this pattern repeated itself several times. What in the world was she doing, and who would be texting or messaging her? Finally, she pulled it out and checked the phone, and I saw a very large smile cross her face; something happened that had made her happy. I had no idea who or what was making her so happy, but it couldn't be good news for me.

The deejay was playing rather mild music during dinner, upbeat, but not dance party music. Everyone was having fun; no one seemed to be upset or insulted or put out in any way.

Mia was standing next to me when my cell phone went off. It was in her purse, though, so I had to wait for my friend to pull it out and check it herself first. When she did, she didn't even show it to me.

"We've got to go," she said.

"What, now?" I asked.

"Yes," she answered. "It looks like this is an emergency."

"For what?"

"For Bert. Apparently he's been found in the house, completely unconscious. They've been trying to wake him up for the last twenty minutes, but he's still out. In fact, they're not sure he's breathing on his own, but it's not like they can call the ambulance for him, can they?"

They certainly couldn't. No ambulance in the city was going to respond to a call about an unconscious frog, no matter the state of his breathing. They had to get him awake on their own. And we were on our way. I grabbed Aiden off the dance floor where he had been dancing with his mother. Doris took one look at my face, and nodded.

"It's Bert?" she asked.

"He's unconscious. Something's gotten to him," I said. "We've got to go."

Aiden and I took off at a dead run for the car. Mia and Jonah were right behind us, with Allie just a few steps behind that. Geoffrey insisted on coming, as well. We all piled into the Escalade and headed for the house, hoping that he's still be alive when we got there. Doris and the others were left behind to cover our absence. I hoped that we'd figure out what was going on with him and be able to get back with no one being the wiser. Of course, that would mean that Bert's condition wasn't an emergency, and I was desperately hoping that it wasn't.

The drive took way too long. I was imagining all kinds of bad situations all the way there. I noticed some crumbs on my dress from dinner, and busied myself in brushing them off while Jonah drove, trying to distract myself from my worries about Bert.

Maybe I'd been too hasty in dismissing concerns about his absence. How long had he been unconscious? How long had he been in trouble? How long . . .

I couldn't keep doing that to myself. I looked at Allie, as much as I was beating myself up, she had to be doing worse to herself as we sat in the car, wanting nothing more than for Jonah to go faster, to be there already, and for this all to be some giant joke.

I was pretty sure it wasn't.

Someone must have gotten into the house to get to Bert, unless he'd made arrangements to leave. I didn't think he'd do that, after what we'd been through in the past, but with his state of mind lately, who could tell what he might or might not do in pursuit of what he thought he had to do.

I didn't think he'd leave the house, not with the portal upstairs. Unless he had to leave to do something to protect the portal. Even if he'd been in his right mind, I wasn't sure he'd have left to go to the reception, because he'd been so worried about guarding the portal, and being there to make sure no one could open it.

He didn't know if could be opened from the inside, or that anyone was inside of it.

I'd assumed Gabriella was a good guy; that she wouldn't hurt anyone, and that she was on our side in preventing anyone from getting into it, or using those artifacts for evil. Was I wrong? How could I have gotten it that wrong?

I shook my head. I could sit here and second guess myself all the way home, or I could just wait to get home and deal with what we found when we got there.

That was probably the best thing to do.

CHAPTER FORTY-SEVEN

The minute the car hit the driveway, we jumped out of the car and ran to the house. I was through the door first, calling for Bert before I'd even gotten both feet inside the threshold. Alfred met us in the hallway.

"He seems to be stable, physically, but he's either in a coma or some kind of trance. I don't know what it is, but he's not asleep, that I can tell. There's no snoring, and no movement of any kind. In his case, it's my understanding that he's a restless sleeper," Alfred filled us in as we made our way to the living room.

"Where is he?" Allie asked, wide eyed. "I've got to see him."

"Just a minute," said Alfred. "As I said, he's stable, and I want you to know a few things before we go up to him. We found him in the attic, behind some trunks. I'm not even sure we'd have thought to look there right away, but one of the guys thought the trunks looked out of order from when we'd gone through the house last week getting ready for today. I don't know why he was in the attic, but it does look like he fought tooth and nail against whatever came up on him. He's got a black eye, and a bunch of scratches and bruises. Can't tell just yet if there's any internal damage, because we can't examine him for that without his response. Don't have medical equipment here that we could use, or even know how to use, so we have been very careful not to move him very far."

"I assume you at least made him comfortable," I said, heading for the stairs.

Alfred and the others all followed. "Yes, ma'am. We got his pillow out of the study and put him on it. He didn't stir when we lifted him, which of course either means that the injuries aren't that bad, or that the coma or whatever he's in is so deep that he wouldn't respond no matter how bad the pain was."

Not good options. I didn't like either one of them. Aiden squeezed my hand as we trudged up the stairs. I was thankful that we'd buttoned up the train of my dress to prevent it dragging on the floor at the reception; it made climbing the stairs a lot easier.

When we got to the attic, there was no portal open, as there had been the night before. There was no purple swirling air, no rune on the floor, no indication that it had ever been there at all. I felt bad that I hadn't shared that information with everyone, but right now, Bert was the bigger concern.

I walked over to where one of Alfred's friends was sitting on the floor, next to the large pillow that Bert used in Dad's old study as a bed. I was glad that they'd thought to do this, and I hoped that Bert realized their kindness. I'd make sure he knew if he ever woke up again.

Allie was standing stock still, tears streaming down her face, as she looked at Bert lying limp, helpless, and injured on the pillow. Several seconds ticked by as we all took in just how badly hurt he appeared to be. And then it was time to start asking questions.

"So what in the world is going on? How long has he been here? How can we get him some medical attention?"

Allie stepped in and started checking him for broken bones and other injuries, her tears shutting off and her aggravation with him showing through. "I've got some first aid training from working at the clinic. I don't see anything that time and patience won't heal, not that he ever takes the time, and he certainly doesn't have the patience. I'm more concerned about whether he's going to wake up. I need him to wake up."

We all tried various means of getting him to wake up; talking to him, pinching him, and Allie even tried slapping him. She was aggravated enough at him that we had to stop her from slapping him more than once; it looked like she enjoyed some part of it. "Allie, if he didn't wake up the first time, slapping him over and over isn't going to make it better. It'll just get him a sore cheek and jaw when he does wakeup."

"So what is this?" I asked. "He won't wake up. Glad you guys got him his pillow, but if there's very little wrong with him, why doesn't he open his eyes?"

Alfred shrugged. "We hoped you knew."

The sad part was that maybe I did know. "Does he have any marks or places he might have been pricked with something? Particularly his fingers, maybe his toes?"

Aiden leaned forward and began to search, but the light in the attic just wasn't that bright and it was hard to see anything. "I can't tell," he said. "We need to move him somewhere with better light, so we can take a closer look. Besides which, moving away from the attic might not be a bad thing, if what he's told us about is true."

Was Aiden saying that it was a good idea to move him away from the portal in case his coma or possibly his death would open it? Here was where I had information that he didn't; I hadn't yet had the opportunity to tell him about Gabriella. How was I going to do this, without letting everyone in on it? I mean, I trusted just about everyone, but at the same time, I didn't know all of Alfred's buddies. He'd vouched for them, but that was for staking out the house, not about keeping their mouths shut on something this big down the road. I couldn't ask him about their trustworthiness with a secret that much in demand, and that dangerous.

And were any of them on a payroll to my stepmother, to bring anything in, or take anything out of the house?

"Mia, why don't you and Allie and everyone take Bert down to the kitchen and get him comfortable on the island. There should be plenty of light there for you to start looking for those kinds of marks. Aiden, Geoffrey, and I will stay up here and look and see if there's anything up here that could have hurt him," I said. It was the best I could come up with on the fly.

They eventually started tromping their way down the steps, taking Bert with them. Alfred had to be convinced to go with them "because it was more likely that someone would try to come in the house from the ground floor, rather than through the attic window," I'd explained.

Alfred had seemed to see the wink I was trying to give him. "We can clear all the rooms in the house on the way down. You know, make sure we haven't missed someone."

I nodded. If Gabriella had come out of the portal, it would be closed again, wouldn't it? Maybe, maybe not, but it was definitely closed now. If she'd decided to and could close the portal and was hanging out in the house somewhere it would be some backup for what I was about to say. I waited until the others cleared the attic, before I said anything. Once they all left, other than Aiden and Geoffrey, it was time to spill the beans.

"Look, there was a development last night that you need to know about," I said. "I apologize that you didn't know earlier, but with the wedding and everything, I wasn't quite sure how to tell you."

"Suspense isn't necessary, Janie. Cut to the chase," Aiden said.

I could tell that he wasn't happy that I hadn't filled him in, but he wasn't angry. He sat down on one of my dad's trunks and crossed his arms.

"Well, I heard footsteps last night, and when I went to investigate, Bert was out of his bed. I never saw him last night. For all I know, he was already up here and behind the trunks where I couldn't see him when I was up here looking around. It is possible. Anyway, when I got up here, there was a portal up here that was wide open. I couldn't figure out where it came from or what it was, but I figured it was Bert's portal, and thought maybe he'd gone inside."

I described the tiny apartment I'd stepped into, with no sign of Bert, and a storage room in the back, but didn't go into a lot of detail about what I'd seen or not seen in the storage room. And then it was time to drop the bombshell on Geoffrey. "Gabriella was there. As of last night, she is still alive. She told me that she manipulated things so that Bert would move the portal when the owner of the apartment where it had been in Paris had died. Bert isn't the last guardian of the items that Perrault hid. Gabriella is. She didn't feel safe where she was, so she got things moved."

I don't think I could have shocked Geoffrey more if I'd whacked him upside the head with a cricket bat.

"She's alive," he croaked. "She's really alive?" He stumbled back and sat down heavily on one of the iron trunks, hissing and standing right back up again and sucking on the fingers he'd brushed against the metal. It appeared as though his clothes had protected the rest of him, but his fingers were red, as if they'd gotten a minor burn. Made sense, he was a member of faerie court royalty. If he'd been paying attention, he'd never have gone anywhere near the trunks.

Apparently he did still care for her, after all.

CHAPTER FORTY-EIGHT

"Anyway," I said, "I asked Gabriella to go back inside the portal and close it up until after the wedding, especially since we believed that someone was going to try to get in the house and it stood to reason that they wanted in the portal. She agreed, and I haven't seen her since. Oh, and the portal, as you see, is closed up."

A new voice sounded from the other side of the attic. It was Evangeline. "It's closed now, but it was definitely open earlier. And now I'm going to be able to get everything I ever wanted. That stupid frog was just in the way. I would have preferred to have targeted you with the spindle, but I'll take what I can get."

She was wearing the same clothing she had worn to the wedding, but she was wearing a pair of white cloth gloves and holding a gun. I had no idea what kind of gun. I was pretty ignorant about them, but I knew it was a kind that could put a big time hole in me that I might not recover from.

She'd never have been able to hold that gun in her bare hands. I hadn't noticed whether or not she had been wearing gloves at the wedding, but she had worn gloves so often, as an etiquette thing, that I likely wouldn't have noticed in the first place. The gun, I did notice. That was something I'd never seen in her hands before.

"Evangeline, we've all moved on from a couple of years ago. What do you hope to gain?" Aiden asked. "Your court is under new leadership. There's been a peace that hasn't been seen for years."

"And it's all your fault!" she cried, waving the gun in my direction. "If you'd just died with your father, or if you'd have just gone along with me and stayed in faerie then none of this would have happened, and I'd have been able to do what I wanted. I would have freed my sister, instead of you. I would have delivered the Andersen girl to the Seawitch. And I would have loved to have taken care of Tobias Andersen before that Bigfoot ever could have laid claw on him. Never mind how much I want my own powers BACK!" she ended on a yell.

I wondered how long she could hold that gun; even before she was waving it around, her hand was shaking. Was the metal touching skin between the fibers of her gloves? I had to keep her talking, and see what we could see. We had to see if she'd wear down and what would happen if she did. I realized that if Gabriella came out of the portal, she'd come out right behind Evangeline. But I had no way to signal her to come through the portal and save us, so it wasn't much of an option after I'd told her to stay in the portal until after the reception ended; there were still two hours to go on that.

"Evangeline, I have a question. How did you get past the circle in the yard around the house? And how did you get past the threshold?" I asked. It was a good question. Hopefully I'd make her calm down. And then again, maybe we could rush her if she put the gun down? Who knows? All I knew was that we were at her mercy, and we needed to know what else was going on. I wondered if she'd brought any reinforcements, like my stepbrother, Hansel, or any of her court allies.

She laughed, and it sounded hollow. How crazy had she become in the last three years?

"Well, first of all, your salt line was damaged by Maddie's snakes and toads, and that wasn't fixed when you fixed your yard. I made it past that by going through the backyard where they had been. Why do you think I made sure she had the opportunity to be there? It was my idea that she be released from her confinement. I knew exactly where she'd go. It didn't take much to suggest that her sister might be here. Didn't matter if she was or not, I'd still get what I was looking for, a way to damage your salt line."

Damn, she had me there. "But the threshold, Evangeline. How did you get past the threshold?" Keep her talking, I thought. I really didn't want to be shot in my wedding dress.

Geoffrey spoke up. "She can cross the threshold, but she leaves all her magic behind. She can't hurt you with magic if she came in without an invitation. And there's also the question that the house used to be hers. So she might have been able to come in without an invitation because she lived here. It's been hers before."

She smiled. "I'm not going to tell you whether the threshold worked or not."

"Of course it did," Aiden said. "Otherwise she wouldn't have needed the gun."

She stomped her feet, getting angrier, but didn't sling any magic, so he must have been right. Just as she lowered the gun, Aiden charged her, knocking her flat. He punched her in the mouth, and her head bounced off the wooden floor. She was unconscious on the floor when he was done.

"I'm calling the cops," I said. "I'm not sure a magical cell is what's called for here. A jail cell here, might well have metal bars. As it is, they will use handcuffs, and a metal cruiser to get her there."

Aiden nodded. "They'll get her out and take her back to the magical realm eventually, but we could probably get them to put off taking her back for a week or so. That way we'd have a fairly uneventful honeymoon. Won't even incur a debt for that, as she was supposed to be watched during the wedding and reception."

Geoffrey kicked the gun away from her, so that she couldn't open her eyes and reach for it with all of us standing so close to her. "Janie, you got any rope? Let's get her tied up for now, and go figure out what's going on with Bert, first, before you call the cops. I'm not sure how you'd explain an unconscious frog."

He had a good point. Aiden reached into a box sitting nearby and found an old jump rope of mine. He used that to tie Evangeline's hands together and Geoffrey and Aiden dragged her to her feet, still unconscious. Geoffrey threw my stepmother over his shoulder, and we started for the stairs, when the portal opened up and Gabriella stepped out.

Geoffrey almost dropped Evangeline. Of course I'd said that she was alive, but the chemistry between the two was incredible. How had they ever drifted apart? I motioned to Gabriella to follow us, and said, "Too much going on. Can you close the portal behind you and follow us downstairs? I promise, we'll explain more, but there may be others that come up to the attic that you don't want to see your portal." That would be too much to explain to the cops.

She nodded, silently, and I saw that she was wearing that dry erase board on a cord around her neck again. Smart, I thought. We'd have no issue with explaining the diamonds and pearls as long as she was careful.

We all trouped downstairs, with Geoffrey manhandling Evangeline to the living room sofa. He dumped her unceremoniously onto the couch, his hair getting slightly mussed in the process, the first I'd ever seen him other than perfectly groomed, before he turned to Gabriella, and kissed her full on the mouth. Once she got over her shock, she kissed him back.

The look on Aiden's face was priceless. I don't think he'd ever seen his father kissed like that, and it was pretty clear he hadn't expected it.

"Um, we'll leave you two to catch up," I said, starting to head to the kitchen.

Jonah stuck his head into the living room at that time, and said, "Whoa! Get a room!"

Geoffrey and Gabriella sprung apart, like guilty teenagers caught in a closet at the prom.

"Jeez," Jonah said. "I was kidding. We're all adults here. But can someone tell me who the tied up chick on the sofa is?"

I laughed. He hadn't been around to meet Evangeline; he'd come around about a year later. No wonder he didn't recognize her. And whoever thought I'd hear anyone refer to Evangeline as a 'chick'? I left Jonah with Gabriella and Geoffrey, for them to explain, while I went into the kitchen to see what was going on with Bert.

I really hoped his condition had improved enough that I could smile about him, too.

CHAPTER FORTY-NINE

It was a different story when I got into the kitchen. Allie was crying, softly, but she was holding Bert's hand (or was it a hand? Do frogs have hands?), and stroking the top of his head. The bruises were pretty brutal, but he wasn't moving. It didn't even look like he was breathing as I came in.

"Any change?" I asked.

She shook her head.

Mia was standing with her, and Doris, and they both shook their heads as well. The lights were on as bright as could be. Mia picked up Bert's left hand, and showed me a small mark on what would correspond to a finger.

So he had been pricked with the spinning wheel spindle. It had been a magical attack; it just hadn't been aimed at him. It had been aimed at me, but he had gotten in the way. And Evangeline had used the magic she could use to protect herself from him finding out about her; he'd just made her use the gun the next day.

That was a good thing. But wait . . .

There had been something about how to break that spell. I remembered talking about it with Gabriella the night before. What had it been? Where was the spindle? I ran back into the living room, and asked both questions.

Gabriella took out her neck sign and marker and wrote, *Didn't realize the spindle was gone. Need to get it back before someone else can get hurt.*

Jonah had it in his back pocket. "It looked like a weapon, and it looked like something that shouldn't be lying around, so I grabbed it when we were upstairs."

"Evangeline must have dropped it after she used it. She knew it could only be used on one person at a time, so it couldn't be used until Bert woke up, and I think she was hoping that if she had to use it on him, that he wouldn't actually wake up in time to help Janie. I don't think it was her plan, but it wasn't of use to her anymore, so she discarded it. Just like she discards loyal servants." Geoffrey sounded bitter. I wondered what she'd done to him, other than how she'd treated him and Aiden three years ago, when she'd lost against me in front of her whole court.

Makes sense, Gabriella wrote. *Is there anyone he loves?*

"That's right!" I said. "Didn't you say that true love's kiss could break the spell?"

She nodded, and wrote, *but only if he loves her too.*

He did. I knew he did. I ran back into the kitchen. "It's a spell. There's a way to break the spell."

Allie looked up, hope written all over her face. "What do I have to do?"

"Kiss him."

She looked doubtful.

"I'm not kidding. If you love him, and he loves you back, he will wake up." I was excited. I knew she qualified for it. She just had to have faith and believe.

"I'm not sure he loves me back," she said. "What happens if he doesn't love me?"

I sighed. "Allie, I'm probably ninety-nine percent sure that he does. If he doesn't, then he doesn't wake up. And if you don't qualify, then probably no one can wake him up. He'll be like this forever. I don't know of anyone else that qualifies. You've got to try. You have nothing to lose."

She looked doubtful.

Doris spoke up. "Allie, child, you cannot live in doubt forever. I know you and Bert have built a strong friendship, and it was what you needed at the time to recover from your own past. But now he needs you, to recover from his present. If this does work, then the two of you can work out your own future together. But you have no future unless you can find it within yourself to believe in him, and to believe in his heart. It's strong, and it's true. He never would have been so hurt, or so drunk at the idea of walking away from you if he wasn't completely head over heels in love with you."

Mia smiled. "What she said."

Allie took a deep breath. "I'll do it." She leaned over him, and brushed her lips against his, very lightly and very gently. Nothing happened at first.

"I'm not sure it's enough yet, Allie. Lean in. You look hesitant. I know he's a frog, but it's *Bert*. You can do this." I was being a cheerleader, and I knew it, but she needed to hear encouragement, rather than any of us being weirded out that she was actually kissing a frog.

She did what I said, leaning in and kissing him harder. I felt a wave of something warm pushing up against me, but there was nothing there. I smelled stale peppermints and old books, and I knew something was happening. Slowly, ever so slowly, magic rolled over Bert, and was affecting every part of his body, which seemed to be getting bigger, and bigger, and turning pale.

Holy crap, Bert was turning human.

Wait a minute. What was the story about the frog prince that I'd read? That love's kiss would break the spell and turn him human! That meant that Allie's kiss did work. It was just healing the oldest curse first, or at least I hoped so. If nothing else, I'd make her kiss him again.

It took a few minutes, but sooner or later, I saw that young man we'd met two years ago, when he'd taken a potion to become human. He had scraggly dark hair, long enough for a ponytail, and a giant scar across his back like a burn scar over his shoulders. He had another scar, as if he'd been slashed with a sword, over his ribs. I'd seen those scars when he'd turned human before.

Slowly, very slowly, his eyes opened. They were the same pale green I remembered from before.

"Allie," he coughed. "It's me, Bert."

She broke into tears, and collapsed in his arms. He wrapped his arms around her, and held her as if he planned never to let go.

I ran into the living room to grab the quilt off of the back of the sofa. He might not plan to let go, but I didn't plan on seeing more of Bert than his shoulders and ribs, and if Allie twitched in just the right way, I would; he was naked.

It seemed like things were falling into place. Jonah ran upstairs to grab some clothing for Bert, who seemed to be recovering okay, other than some bumps and bruises. Apparently he'd fallen hard off of a pile of boxes in the attic when Evangeline had gotten him with the spindle, but nothing was broken.

By the time the police were called, and their report taken, we'd missed a good portion of the wedding reception. If Aiden and I didn't get back soon, there was no doubt we'd be missed. We probably already had been. We left Jonah, Geoffrey, Gabriella, Doris, Bert, and Allie at the house, while Mia drove Aiden and I back to the Marriott to cut the cake.

Our guests had noticed we were gone. There was a significant amount of pointing and whispering, as if they were accusing us of having run off to rent a room during our reception. I didn't correct anyone. Better that they believe us to be so infatuated that we couldn't keep our hands off each other than to believe that magic had attacked and that my stepmother was on her way to jail.

We spoke briefly to the Snow Queen, who appeared angry at Evangeline for her actions. "She's gone too far this time. We will take care of her, but as you say, your human jail may be the best place for the next week. I'll come up with a better solution down the road." I nodded to her, but did not thank her, although I desperately wanted to.

Aiden and I smashed cake in each other's faces, careful not to get any of the raspberry filling when we did so, and we were laughing as the evening wound down.

I figured at this point that life would just be like this. No matter what we tried to do, there would be some magical interference, but if I could manage to pull off a wedding, and take the bar exam, in the midst of a magical emergency, I couldn't imagine anything that I couldn't do.

The last song for the last dance ended, and I was in Aiden's arms. "I love you," he said, simply.

"I love you, too. Let's go figure out our honeymoon, and start our lives together," I replied, taking his hand as we walked off to do exactly that.

EPILOGUE

Aiden and Janie did get magical wedding gifts, but mostly they were household items, nothing lethal or dangerous. They received the Tinderbox from the Snow Queen, who admonished them only to use it in times of true need, but she figured there would be need at some point in their lives. They also received a very interesting mirror, but that's another story for another time. They did end up taking a very nice honeymoon, camping in Put-In-Bay, on South Bass Island in Lake Erie.

Janie and Mia both passed the bar exam on the first try. They established their law office, Grimm & Andersen LLC, and took both magical and non-magical clients. Aiden ended up joining their law office as a paralegal part time while he went back to school to finish his studies in folklore and linguistics.

Janie and Aiden had two children, Jessica Doris Ferguson and Robert Jonathan Grimm, Jr., fraternal twins. Jessica grew up to study the law; Bobby decided to learn to be a tailor, like his paternal grandfather, although he stayed in the mortal realm.

Doris and Harold married shortly after Janie and Mia got their bar results, in Janie and Mia's backyard. The two of them lived for another twenty years as husband and wife, enjoying each other's grandchildren and helping with the occasional magical emergency or wedding, whichever was more pressing at the time.

Mia and Jonah never married, but lived together for the rest of their lives. Together, they had one child, a son, named Henry Tobias, who grew up to take on his grandfather's legacy, becoming a warrior protecting the humans from magical threats. He moonlighted at his mother's law firm, doing security for both magical and non-magical clients. Henry and Jessica became a couple when they grew up, and Janie and Mia eventually shared grandchildren.

Bert and Allie went to Vegas and got married by Elvis. Bert worked for Janie and Mia as an office manager, and Allie kept working at the women's shelter, helping abused and abandoned children.

All of them worked to establish and maintain the Abigail Grimm Home for Abandoned People. It became a refugee home for those displaced by magic, including the Wonderland refugees, who also returned on a regular basis to help out with new residents. The facility was first at the buildings on Stanley and his wife's land, but soon grew, and they opened two locations, one in New York City and one in Salt Lake City, Utah. As of this writing, there are plans to open another in Paris.

Five years after opening their law firm, Janie and Mia moved their offices to the Oregon District, in downtown Dayton. Allie and Bert lived in the upstairs apartment, and the portal to the Perrault treasure leading to Oak Island was moved to their basement, in the laundry sink. Bert wanted it moved to the toilet, so that no one would actually try to get inside the portal because they'd have to step into a toilet. Allie put her foot down on that one because she didn't want to clean up toilet water every time someone decided to try to break into the treasure chamber. Bert used the chamber to host twice weekly poker games with Aiden and Jonah, where they could smoke cigars and drink beer and use magic without worrying about causing a problem for their wives.

Geoffrey and Gabriella decided to try again to rekindle their romance, and traveled to Paris together to see what remained of what they remembered. They visited the palace at Versailles and some of their former haunts, but Geoffrey was depressed at seeing one of his favorite restaurants had been turned into a McDonalds. Gabriella bought him a cheeseburger and told him to get over it, and they traveled through Europe for several years before finally deciding to split their time between the magical realm and the mortal realm. They wintered in the magical realm and summered in the mortal realm, and Geoffrey made a point to make it to all of his grandchildren's baseball games and dance recitals.

Magical emergencies continued to pop up from time to time, but the group learned how to handle it. They took over the running of the F.A.B.L.E.S. organization, and ran it out of the same offices as Janie and Mia's law firm.

Evangeline was never seen or heard from again. The faerie courts ruled that she was dead, and no longer eligible for her throne due to death, so even if she was resurrected by magic somehow, she would not be eligible to regain her throne, or her powers.

The Snow Queen remained in charge of Evangeline's court, and maintained a good relationship with Janie and her friends for the rest of their lives. The Queen of Hearts had to agree that Evangeline had violated her rights as a guest, and reluctantly agreed that her sister did not deserve to take the throne again, ever.

ACKNOWLEDGEMENTS

Many special thanks to . . .

~Ray Westcott, my husband, my best friend, and my partner-in-crime. My life would be so much less everything without you.

~Daniel and Olivia Westcott, aka The Boy and The Girl, for keeping life interesting while this book was written.

~Alvin King, Karen King, Gene Westcott, and Sandy Westcott, for being the best PawPaw, Grammy, Grandpa, and Grandma ever, helping with child care and child transportation while I chase this writing thing, as well as being enthusiastic supporters and the best cheerleaders ever. Also to Mary Jane Woodruff for being the best Grandma Mary in the world . . .

~Blake and Kenley Ballard, for reminding me of the fun of all the details we take for granted, because it might have been the first time they've seen them.

~The Springfield and Urbana writers groups I've belonged to; your insight and support are irreplaceable.

~James O. Barnes, Kathy Watness, and all the others at Loconeal Publishing, for helping me see this all the way to the end.

~And to the readers who have gone on this journey with me. It's been a pleasure to write this series, and it wouldn't have been possible without you!

AUTHOR INFORMATION

Addie J. King

Addie J. King is an attorney by day and author by nights, evenings, weekends, and whenever else she can find a spare moment. Her short story "Poltergeist on Aisle Fourteen" was published in MYSTERY TIMES TEN by Buddhapuss Ink, and an essay entitled, "Building Believable Legal Systems in Science Fiction and Fantasy" was published in EIGHTH DAY GENESIS; A WORLDBUILDING CODEX FOR WRITERS AND CREATIVES by Alliteration Ink. Her novels, THE GRIMM LEGACY, THE ANDERSEN ANCESTRY and THE WONDERLAND WOES, THE BUNYAN BARTER, and THE PERRAULT VOW are available from Loconeal Publishing. Her website is www.addiejking.com

Made in the USA
Middletown, DE
20 June 2019